16

PRAISE FOR
Redemption, Kansas

"*Redemption, Kansas,* James Reasoner's newest tale, has everything a truly good Western novel should have—a gritty, likabl... ...ng plot ...t's no ...rs. A c... ...eason... —... *...ger*

"A ... ...ck-erja... ...eri-tage ...ur and ... —... *Air*

"*Re*... ...nd-read... —... *All*

"Ja... ...ced a su... ...ero wh... ...me, onc... —... ...ning ...*oon*

"*Re*... ...old. Jan... ...ced story that reaches into the hearts of his ... ...n his readers."
——Frank Roderus, author of *Paroled*

"*Redemption, Kansas* is a fast-paced cowboy tale written with the flair of a master. If you've never read a Western by James Reasoner, pick this one up. You won't put this novel down until you've f... ...re."
——... ...ard–winning ...*orpion Trail*

REDEMPTION, Kansas

James Reasoner

BERKLEY BOOKS, NEW YORK

THE BERKLEY PUBLISHING GROUP
Published by the Penguin Group
Penguin Group (USA) Inc.
375 Hudson Street, New York, New York 10014, USA

Penguin Group (Canada), 90 Eglinton Avenue East, Suite 700, Toronto, Ontario M4P 2Y3, Canada
(a division of Pearson Penguin Canada Inc.)
Penguin Books Ltd., 80 Strand, London WC2R 0RL, England
Penguin Group Ireland, 25 St. Stephen's Green, Dublin 2, Ireland (a division of Penguin Books Ltd.)
Penguin Group (Australia), 250 Camberwell Road, Camberwell, Victoria 3124, Australia
(a division of Pearson Australia Group Pty. Ltd.)
Penguin Books India Pvt. Ltd., 11 Community Centre, Panchsheel Park, New Delhi—110 017, India
Penguin Group (NZ), 67 Apollo Drive, Rosedale, North Shore 0632, New Zealand
(a division of Pearson New Zealand Ltd.)
Penguin Books (South Africa) (Pty.) Ltd., 24 Sturdee Avenue, Rosebank, Johannesburg 2196,
South Africa

Penguin Books Ltd., Registered Offices: 80 Strand, London WC2R 0RL, England

This is a work of fiction. Names, characters, places, and incidents either are the product of the author's imagination or are used fictitiously, and any resemblance to actual persons, living or dead, business establishments, events, or locales is entirely coincidental. The publisher does not have any control over and does not assume any responsibility for author or third-party websites or their content.

REDEMPTION, KANSAS

A Berkley Book / published by arrangement with the author

PRINTING HISTORY
Berkley edition / March 2011

Copyright © 2011 by James Reasoner.
Cover illustration by Dennis Lyall.
Cover design by Diana Kolsky.
Interior text design by Kristin del Rosario.

ISBN: 978-0-425-24010-6

BERKLEY®
Berkley Books are published by The Berkley Publishing Group,
a division of Penguin Group (USA) Inc.,
375 Hudson Street, New York, New York 10014.
BERKLEY® is a registered trademark of Penguin Group (USA) Inc.
The "B" design is a trademark of Penguin Group (USA) Inc.

PRINTED IN THE UNITED STATES OF AMERICA

10 9 8 7 6 5 4 3 2 1

For Livia, Shayna, and Joanna

*This is the first book I've been able
to dedicate to them for a while,
but really, everything I write is for them.*

Prologue

Redemption, Kansas
1876

The sound of hurrying footsteps on the boardwalk outside his office made Marshal Frank Porter look up from the cup of coffee he had just poured for himself. He hoped the footsteps would keep going, since he was in no mood for trouble tonight, but even before they came to a stop just outside the door, he knew he was going to be disappointed.

The door opened, and Hendrickson, the burly, white-haired Dutchman who owned the bakery, hurried into the office.

"Marshal!" he exclaimed when he saw Porter standing beside the stove. "This cannot go on! That . . . that man Norris—" The baker broke into a torrent of angry German.

Porter sighed and put his cup back on top of the stove where the coffee would stay warm. He held up a hand and said mildly, "Hold on, hold on. You know I don't understand that Dutchy talk, Hendrickson."

Through gritted teeth, Hendrickson said, "*Yah, yah.* In English I tell you, Marshal, that man must be stopped! He comes to my bakery tonight and demands money. He says I must pay him, or bad things will happen!" Hendrickson threw up his flour-covered hands. "We finally get rid of those *verdammt* Texans, and now this!"

"All right, settle down, settle down," said Porter. "What did you do when Zach asked you for money?"

"I tell him I come over here and see you, tell you what he is doing!"

Porter nodded solemnly. "And what did he say?"

"He told me to go ahead, but he said he could not be responsible for what might happen while I was gone." A shudder went through Hendrickson. "He is an evil man, Marshal. Surely you can see that."

Porter reached for his hat, which was hanging on a nail just inside the office door. "Let's go back over to your place," he said to the baker. "I'll get this all straightened out."

Hendrickson sighed and nodded, relief etched on his florid face. "I knew you would put a stop to this, Marshal, just as you stopped the Texans and their cattle from ruining our town."

Porter put his hat on and stepped out onto the boardwalk, followed by Hendrickson. There was no need for the marshal to strap on his gun belt. He was already wearing it, the walnut-handled Colt Single-Action Army revolver riding easily in the holster. Porter strode easily across the street at an angle, a man on the edge of middle age with blond hair that was turning gray and pale blue eyes that seemed to say they had seen everything, good and bad, that the world had to offer. Hendrickson walked alongside him, hurrying to keep up with the marshal's longer strides.

Main Street was dark and quiet. Porter had made his rounds hours earlier, checking to see that the doors of all the businesses were locked. By this time, even the town's lone saloon was closed, and no one moved on the street except the two men. All the windows of the buildings were dark except in Hendrickson's bakery. The Dutchman rose very early every morning to get started on the day's baking.

As the two men approached the bakery, another man stepped out through the open door. He was young, lean, dark-haired, with a scar on his left cheek that gave his face a grim cast. As he turned toward Porter and Hendrickson, the light from inside the bakery glinted for a second on the badge pinned to his vest.

"Hello, Zach," Porter said to his deputy as he stepped up onto the boardwalk. "Hendrickson here has lodged a serious complaint against you."

Zach Norris's thick eyebrows lifted in surprise. "What did I do?" he asked.

Hendrickson sputtered in outrage. "You . . . you tell me I have to pay—"

"You misunderstood me, old-timer," Norris said with an easy smile. "I said that good law enforcement doesn't come cheap. And you can't deny that the marshal and I have made this town a safe place to live again since we stopped those trail herds from passing through."

"But I am not a rich man!" protested Hendrickson. "All the money I make goes back into the bakery, so that I can improve it—"

"Place looks fine to me," Norris said with a glance over his shoulder into the building.

Marshal Porter held his hands up to silence both men. "Like Zach said, I'm sure this is just a misunderstanding," he told Hendrickson. "Why don't we go inside and talk about it? I'm sure we can straighten out the whole thing."

"We can talk all you want," said Hendrickson, "but I will not pay. This is not right."

"I said we'd talk about it," Porter went on as he steered Hendrickson and Norris into the bakery. He paused just inside the door and took a deep breath, inhaling the delicious aroma of baking bread. A smile touched his face as he said, "That's one of the best smells on earth. I do love fresh-baked bread."

"I give you a loaf," said Hendrickson with little grace. "But nothing else! I will not be bullied, even by a man with a badge!"

Angrily, Norris began, "I never bullied nobody—"

Porter held up his left hand again as he used his foot to push the door shut behind them. "Now hold on, Zach," he said. "There's no need to argue. Mr. Hendrickson has made his position very clear."

Hendrickson was shuffling toward the counter that separated the front part of the bakery from the area in the back where his ovens were. *"Yah, yah,"* he said without looking around. "I will not pay. Now I must check on my bread—"

Porter slid his Colt from its holster, thumbed back the knurled hammer as he raised the gun, and squeezed the trigger.

The bullet slammed into Hendrickson's broad back at almost point-blank range, knocking him forward so that he crashed into the counter and fell over it. Porter knew the baker was dead, shot through the heart. He holstered the Colt and said to his deputy, "Give me a hand, Zach. The Dutchman was so worried about his bread, we'll just put him in the oven with it so he can keep an eye on it."

Chapter 1

The night was quiet, quiet as the grave. That thought made a shudder run through Bill Harvey as the young cowboy stood up in his stirrups to ease muscles that ached from long hours in the saddle.

Hours, days, weeks . . . it had been so long since he had left South Texas with the cattle drive that time had ceased to have much meaning for Bill. He went from horseback to bedroll, where oblivion claimed him, and back to the saddle after only a few hours of exhausted sleep.

But that's the life of a cowboy, Bill told himself. *You knew what the job was when you took it, you dang fool.*

That was when he saw the woman.

The herd was bedded down in a broad, shallow valley. There wasn't any other kind here in southern Kansas, just a short distance north of the border with Indian Territory. The sleeping cattle stretched out in a dark, unmoving mass across prairie that was deeply rutted from the hooves of countless other drives. The figure Bill saw was walking along the edge of the herd, long pale hair streaming down her back and shining in the faint light from the moon and stars.

What in blazes was a woman doing out here? Bill asked

himself. This was his first drive north, but he had heard from some of the other men how soiled doves sometimes came down from the railhead at Dodge City to meet the herds. But they were still a long way from Dodge, and besides, a woman like that wouldn't show up in the middle of the night. She would meet the chuck wagon as it drove on ahead of the herd, so that she could be waiting when the boys made camp for the night.

Then the woman turned and from a distance of fifty yards or so, Bill saw the jut of a beard and knew that the woman wasn't a woman at all. She was a man. Bill shook his head. A stranger wandering around the herd in the middle of the night could mean only one thing.

Bill opened his mouth to shout a warning, then stopped short before he uttered a sound. If he yelled out and broke the silence of the night, that would probably be enough to send the cattle surging to their feet and lunging forward wildly.

It didn't really matter, because the next moment, the long-haired figure jerked up his hand and moonlight shone on what he was holding. Orange flame lanced from the object along with the boom of exploding gunpowder. Bill heard the sound of the shot, but he never heard its echoes roll away across the plains. They were drowned out in the clash of horns and the roar of hooves as the herd sprang up from the bedground and started to move.

Bill threw back his head and bellowed, *"Stampede!"*

That was the thing feared most by the cowboys who brought the herds up the trail from Texas. Nothing was more dangerous. That was why the drovers rode night herd, endlessly circling the sleeping mass of longhorns, crooning soft-pitched songs that soothed the animals' nerves and kept them from spooking. Anything could set off a stampede, anything . . . A crackle of lightning, the rattle of a sidewinder's tail, the snap of a branch under a horse's hoof.

A gunshot did the job just fine.

Bill jabbed the rowels of his spurs in his cow pony's flanks and leaned forward in the saddle as the animal broke into a gallop. The only hope of stopping the stampede quickly was to reach the head of it and turn the leaders so that the herd would begin to run in a great circle. If he could do that, the cows would eventually mill to a halt.

Of course, that also put him in front of the herd, so if his horse tripped and fell, or threw him, the pounding hooves of the cattle would chew him into something that wouldn't even be recognizable as human. Bill hoped the buckskin pony under his saddle was sure-footed. He had drawn the horse from the remuda a few times during the drive, but it wasn't one of his regular mounts.

Lashing the reins from side to side, he urged greater speed from the buckskin. It was running smoothly and easily, seemingly unbothered by the stampeding longhorns a few yards away. Bill wondered fleetingly what had happened to the bearded, long-haired man who had fired the shot. The man he had mistaken in the moonlight for a woman. Had the stranger already been trampled, or had he been able to get out of the way of the stampede?

The wind of his passage whipped the hat from Bill's head, but it caught on its chin strap and dangled on the back of his neck. For a second his long brown hair hung in front of his eyes, but then it was blown back behind him as well as he cleared his vision with a shake of his head.

Galloping along in the darkness with the herd like a single massive entity beside him, he felt alone, as if he were the only human in a thousand miles. But gradually, over the thunder of hooves, he became aware of men's shouts and the popping of gunfire. The other night herders would be trying to turn the longhorns, too, and the men who had been rolled in their soogans at the camp would be mounted up and joining in the pursuit by now. Somewhere out here in the swirling melee of the stampede were Hob Sanders, the trail boss, and Dorsey McClellan, Hob's *segundo,* and all the other fellas—Pete and Santo and Wiley and Red and—

That thought vanished abruptly from Bill's mind as the pony stumbled beneath him. Bill tightened one hand on the reins while with the other he sought the saddle horn and steadied himself. The buckskin's racing gait smoothed out again, and the sheer terror that had filled Bill for an instant faded. He looked back over his shoulder and saw the sweeping curve of the herd. He was close to the leaders now. "Run!" he pleaded to the horse. "Come on, come on . . ."

In the inconstant light he saw the brindle steer that was always at or near the head of the herd. He veered the buckskin toward the lumbering steer and freed the coil of rope attached to his saddle. Guiding the pony with his knees, he transferred the rope to his left hand and the reins to his right, then came even closer to the steer. With a shout, he leaned over and slashed at the steer's flank with the coiled rope. "Hyyaaahh! Get over! Turn, you son of a buck, turn!"

The brindle steer moved away from him, and Bill felt a surge of exhilaration. It was working. He edged the pony toward the steer and swiped at it again with the rope, still yelling. The rangy old longhorn moved once more, turning to its left. The cattle pounding along in its wake followed.

After a moment Bill realized he was riding back almost in the direction from which he had come. The cattle were circling and slowing, just as Hob had said they would if the leaders were turned.

Bill felt a flush of pride. This was his first stampede— shoot, it was his first real cattle drive—and he felt like he had met the challenge and come through with flying colors. He pulled back on the buckskin's reins, slowing the pony, and angled away from the herd. Some of the other drovers were waiting up ahead, he saw. They would keep the cattle moving in the right direction.

Some of the longhorns were bound to have scattered during the confusion, and it might take a day or two to round them all up, but it could have been a lot worse, Bill reflected as he jogged along easily on the buckskin. He reached behind him and got hold of his hat. As he settled it on his head, though, he felt something strange about it. Frowning, he took off the hat and held it in front of him, peering at it in the moonlight.

There was a hole in the crown that hadn't been there before. Bill stuck his finger through the ragged opening and wiggled it.

The blood in his veins seemed to turn to ice water. That was a *bullet hole.*

He remembered the long-haired man firing the shot that had started the cattle running. Bill had seen the muzzle flash from that shot, had seen it quite plainly.

That was because the gun had been pointed at him, he realized now.

The stranger had tried to kill him—and judging by the hole in his hat, the slug had come mighty close to doing just that.

"Watch out, Bill!"

That was Hob's voice, Bill thought as he jerked his head up. He caught a glimpse of the trail boss galloping toward him, then saw more movement out of the corner of his eye. Lunging toward him was that brindle steer, which had broken away from the milling mass of the rest of the herd. The steer had its head down and was charging him, and Bill tried desperately to yank the cow pony out of the way.

He was too late. The steer tossed its head, sweeping its long, wicked length of horn at him, and Bill heard the buckskin scream as the horn ripped into its flank. The next instant, the horn struck Bill's left leg about midway up his thigh. It was like having a sledgehammer and an ax slam into his flesh at the same time. He screamed as pain shot through him.

Bill felt the buckskin falling but could do nothing to stop it. Horse and rider both toppled, and the dusty ground turned into a sea of agony that pulled Bill down and swallowed him without a trace.

Chapter 2

Eden Monroe heard the shouting from Redemption's main street and wondered what was going on. *Not another killing,* she prayed silently. Moving out from behind the counter, she started up the aisle between the shelves of merchandise toward the front of the store.

Her father emerged from the back room and said sharply, "Eden." She looked over at him, and he shook his head. "Whatever's going on out yonder, it's none of our business," he said.

Eden sighed. With his long white beard and barrel chest, Perry Monroe looked like an Old Testament prophet. Maybe at one time in his life, he had been a religious man. After all, someone had been responsible for naming her after the garden where Adam and Eve had lived, and Eden had never known if that had been her father or the mother who had died when Eden was only a child. But no one would mistake the storekeeper for devout now. He cussed like a mule skinner and retreated most nights into a bottle of whiskey.

"I heard someone yell for the doctor," said Eden as she pushed her honey-colored hair back from her face. "Somebody's hurt."

"Somebody's always hurting in this world. It's still none of our business. You get back behind the counter where you belong."

Eden wasn't sure why she had to stay behind the counter. It wasn't like there were any customers in the store. Monroe Mercantile's trade was drying up, just like all the other businesses in Redemption. Folks didn't buy as much when they were scared all the time, never knowing when someone else was going to be murdered.

But her father was glaring at her, and Eden turned back toward the rear of the store as he had told her. Then, abruptly, she stopped, her back stiffening. With a defiant glance at him, she turned around again and walked swiftly to the front door. As she stepped out onto the porch, she heard her father's muttered, angry curses behind her.

A few doors down the street, half a dozen men on horseback sat in front of the marshal's office. Eden caught her breath. The strangers' clothes marked them as cowboys from Texas, and Marshal Frank Porter didn't allow cowboys inside the town limits. Porter stood on the boardwalk in front of his office, thumbs hooked in his gun belt, looking up at the horsebackers with a curious expression on his weathered face.

"There a sawbones in this town?" asked one of the Texans. "We got a hurt man here, needs some medical attention."

For the first time, Eden noticed that one of the cowboys was tied onto his saddle. He was hunched forward, his young face gray and haggard so that he looked older than his years. A bloody bandage was wrapped tightly around his thigh.

"Guess you didn't see the sign at the edge of town," Marshal Porter said, his voice calm and unruffled as usual.

"We saw it, but like I said, we got a hurt man who needs help. And the herd ain't anywhere near the town. We've got 'em bedded down a good two miles east of here. Now, you got a doctor or not?"

"Closest pillroller's in Dodge City," said the marshal. "Reckon you'll have to take this fella on there."

The spokesman for the cowboys shook his head. "Can't

do it. Bill needs help now, not in the three or four days it'd take to get to Dodge."

Porter shrugged and said, "You can get there faster'n that if you ride hard."

"Bill can't ride hard with a leg hurt this bad," grated the Texan, who was clearly on the brink of losing his temper.

Eden glanced down the street and saw Zach Norris coming along the boardwalk toward the marshal's office. Norris was Marshal Porter's deputy, a young man who might have been handsome had it not been for the hard cast to his features and the pale scar that ran from his left eye down past the corner of his mouth. The townspeople who had gathered on the boardwalk to watch the commotion in front of the marshal's office didn't waste any time getting out of the way to let Norris by.

"You can bring him over here."

The words were out of Eden's mouth before she even knew she was going to say something. From the door of the mercantile behind her where her father stood, she heard a startled curse rip out. "No, you can't," Perry Monroe declared stubbornly.

"Bring him over here," Eden repeated as the Texans turned to look at her, surprise etched on their darkly tanned faces.

Zach Norris had reached the marshal's office. He propped one hip against the railing that ran along the edge of the boardwalk and watched with seemingly casual interest as Marshal Porter walked toward Eden, a frown on his face. "Are you sure you want to do that, Miss Monroe?" asked the lawman.

Eden felt herself nod. "I can take care of that injured leg."

"I know you've patched up some folks before, but this man—" Porter leaned his head toward the strangers as he went on in a low voice, "This man is a Texan."

"He's still a human being."

Porter grunted as if he had a difficult time wrapping his mind around the concept of a Texan being human. Then he shrugged and said, "If that's what you want." His tone of voice made it plain that he was washing his hands of the whole matter.

"Blast it, nobody asked me what I think!" Eden's father protested. "I won't have it—"

Eden turned to look at him. "I can take him somewhere else," she said. She didn't have to add that in that case, she would leave, too.

Monroe blanched. She was all he had left, and they both knew it. For all his bluster, he didn't want to force the showdown that had been brewing between them. "All right, all right," he said with a grudging nod. "Bring the fella over here. We'll do what we can to make him comfortable."

The Texan who had done the talking reached over to grasp the reins of the injured man's horse. He was middle-aged, his face lined and cured from years of exposure to sun and wind, and a thick, graying mustache hung over his mouth. As he led the little group over to the mercantile, he nodded to Eden and said, "We're much obliged for the help, ma'am."

Eden returned the nod and didn't look at Porter and Norris. She knew the marshal was watching the proceedings with a frown of disapproval, and the deputy more than likely had the same cynical amusement dancing in his dark eyes that was nearly always there.

"There's a cot in our storeroom," Eden told the Texans as they began to swing down from their saddles. "You can put him there."

Several of the cowboys untied the injured man and eased him down from the saddle. He was only half conscious, Eden saw, but he was awake enough to feel the pain that must have shot through him every time his friends jostled him. She stepped aside to let them carry him through the door.

The spokesman moved up alongside her and asked, "How come this town hates cowboys so much?"

Eden thought about the crudely painted sign displayed so prominently beside the trail leading into Redemption from the south. NO COWBOYS OR TEXANS OF ANY SORT ALLOWED

INSIDE TOWN LIMITS UNDER PENALTY OF LAW! it read, and most of the time Marshal Porter and Zach Norris enforced it stringently.

"We have our reasons," Eden said. "When the railhead first moved to Dodge and the cattle trails shifted to the west, herds came through here all the time. They tore up the gardens people had planted, and the drovers caused a lot of trouble in town. We just decided we didn't want them here anymore."

The Texan looked at her through eyes slitted by sun and suspicion. "Some places tried to charge a toll on every herd that came through," he said. "Sometimes the price was so high it was out-and-out robbery. Fellas who'd been on the trail for weeks comin' up from Texas would get a mite upset when you Kansans tried to pull such high-handed tactics. Maybe Redemption was one of those towns."

Eden didn't confirm or deny the accusation. She just turned toward the door and said, "I'll see what I can do for your friend."

She went to the storeroom, and behind her she heard the Texan say to her father, "Rustlers tried to hit us last night. Started a stampede, thinkin' they could cut out a good bunch of our cattle after they'd scattered. Only they didn't scatter, thanks to that boy in there. He turned the herd before the stampede could get started good." The man's voice was full of pride.

"What happened to the rustlers?" asked Monroe, curious in spite of his hostility.

"They got away in the confusion. We pegged a few shots after 'em, but I don't reckon any of the slugs hit anything."

"Rustling's a bad business."

That was the last thing Eden heard as she stepped into the storeroom. The cowboys who had carried the injured man in moved back from the cot where they had placed him and hurriedly jerked their hats off. They all nodded politely to her.

"I'll take a look at him," she said as she moved to the side of the cot.

"Beggin' your pardon, ma'am," said one of the men, "but are you a doctor?"

Eden shook her head. "No. Like the marshal said, the closest real doctor is in Dodge. But I've done some midwifery."

One of the other cowboys said dryly, "I don't reckon that's ol' Bill's problem, ma'am."

"What happened to him?"

"He got gored by a contrary ol' steer," said the first cowboy who had spoken to her. "That longhorn ripped his leg open real good, too."

Eden could see that for herself as soon as she got the bloody bandage unwrapped. The cowboy's pants leg had been cut away, leaving his thigh bare. The wound was an ugly one, long and ragged. It should have been sewn up by a real doctor, so that the scar wouldn't be so prominent when it healed, but she would do the best she could. She could keep the injury clean and stitch it so it would heal. It wouldn't be pretty, though.

"Is the bone broken?" she asked.

"Don't seem to be."

The leg looked straight enough. Eden nodded. "All this man needs now is some stitches and to stay off his feet for a while so that wound can heal up. I shouldn't have any trouble tending him."

"Well, I sure hope you take good care of him, ma'am. We set quite a store by Billy since he stopped that stampede last night. Probably kept some good men from gettin' trampled."

"Billy . . ." she repeated. "What's the rest of his name?"

"Harvey," replied the cowboy. "Bill Harvey. He don't really like it when you call him Billy."

Eden nodded. "I'll try to remember that."

The older Texan who had been talking to her father opened the door and came into the storeroom. "How's he doin'?"

Eden glanced at the young man on the cot. His eyes were closed, and he was breathing fairly regularly. She didn't know if he had fallen asleep or passed out, but she said, "He's resting easily, and that's the best thing for him right now."

The Texan nodded. "Like I was tellin' your daddy, ma'am, my name's Hob Sanders. I'm the trail boss of our outfit, and I surely do appreciate you takin' care of Bill this way. When we come back through from Dodge, I'll be glad to pay you whatever you think's fair for your time and trouble."

"You're going to leave him here until after you've taken your herd to the railhead?" asked Eden, surprised.

"Don't see as we've got much choice," replied Sanders. "Figured you knew that's what we meant to do. Bill ain't in no shape to travel and likely won't be for several weeks."

"No, that's true," Eden admitted. What the trail boss said made sense; she just hadn't thought it through until now. The offer to help had been made impulsively.

Hob Sanders had his hat in his hand, like the other Texans. Now he put it back on, tugging it down hard on his graying hair. "We'd best get back to the herd," he said. "Take good care of that boy, Miss Monroe."

Obviously her father had told the Texan their name, Eden thought. "I intend to," she said.

The drovers filed out of the storeroom. Eden followed them and found that Marshal Porter and Zach Norris had come into the store. The two lawmen were waiting for the Texans. Porter said to Hob Sanders, "All right, you've taken care of what brought you here, mister. I'll thank you if you and your friends get on out of town now."

"We're goin'," said Sanders. "I don't reckon we got any reason to stay where we ain't wanted. But I'll tell you right now, Marshal, we'll be comin' back to get our pard back there."

Porter nodded. "That's fine. But no more than two of you will have to come back into town to pick up your man."

Sanders shrugged, neither agreeing nor disagreeing with the condition the marshal had set. The Texans trooped out of the mercantile, followed by the marshal and Norris, who watched the men mount up and ride out of Redemption.

Perry Monroe heaved a sigh of relief, then turned to glower at his daughter. "What in blue blazes have you got us into this time, girl?" he demanded.

Eden thought about the man lying asleep—or unconscious—in the back room and shook her head. She didn't know how to answer her father's question.

She just didn't know.

Chapter 3

Bill didn't remember anything clearly after he'd passed out the night before. In fact, as awareness seeped back into his brain and he realized he was lying on a cot, he wasn't even sure it had been the night before when that brindle steer had gored him. For all he knew, he could've been unconscious for days or even weeks.

He managed to open his eyes, even though his eyelids each seemed to weigh a hundred pounds. He saw crates stacked on the floor and burlap bags leaning against the wall and some rolls of cloth angled in a corner.

On the other side of the small room was an open door. It let enough bright light into the room to make Bill's eyes narrow and he winced a little as he tried to get used to the glare. As his vision began to adjust, he was able to make out some sets of shelves holding store goods. His brain was pretty foggy, but he figured out he was in the back room of some sort of mercantile.

That meant he was in a town. Hob and the boys must have brought him here in search of a sawbones to take care of him.

That was good. Hob was loyal to the men who rode for him, and that made them loyal to him. Bill hoped the doc would be through with him soon so he could get back to the herd.

He pushed himself up on an elbow so he could look down at himself. Somebody had draped a sheet over the lower half of his body. For a second he was struck with a feeling of utter horror as he wondered if his leg had been hurt so bad the doctor had been forced to cut it off. He had heard men who'd fought in the war talking about how army surgeons had hacked off thousands of wounded limbs, so many sometimes that the amputated arms and legs stacked up like cordwood outside the hospital tents.

The pain he felt convinced him his leg was still there, but not completely. He had also heard veterans talk about how a missing limb could hurt just as bad or worse than one that was still attached. He had to reach down with a trembling hand and touch his left leg through the sheet before the wild pounding of his heart began to slow to a normal rate.

He pushed the sheet down and saw to his surprise that he was naked from the waist down except for what appeared to be several layers of fresh bandages wrapped around his injured leg. The sound of a footstep somewhere nearby reminded him the door was open and anybody walking by in the store could look in at him. He grabbed the sheet and jerked it back up so he was covered.

Just in time, too, because a figure moved into the doorway, blocking some of the light, and a woman's voice said, "You're awake. Good."

As the woman came into the room, Bill's strength gave out. He sagged back onto the pillow somebody had placed under his head. He made sure he kept hold of the sheet, though, so it didn't slip.

The woman smiled at him. Bill's heart thumped hard again. She was *that* pretty, with dark blond hair framing a face faintly dotted with freckles. She had a tiny dimple in her chin, so small you could almost miss seeing it if you didn't look close. And her eyes were as blue as a mountain lake, he noted as she came closer.

"How do you feel?" she asked. "Would you like something to drink?"

His lips and tongue felt thick. He had a little trouble getting the words out as he said, "Uh, I . . . uh, where . . . where am I, ma'am?"

"This is Redemption, Mr. Harvey."

Bill's eyes widened. "You mean I've died and gone to heaven?" He could almost believe it, as pretty as she was.

But she laughed and shook her head. "Hardly. Redemption, Kansas. It's a town."

"Oh." Now that he thought about it, he seemed to recall Hob mentioning the place a few days back. It had a bad reputation among the drovers, and the plan was to swing the herd around it.

Something else occurred to him. He went on, "You know my name."

"Yes, Mr. Sanders told us who you are. He said you were injured stopping a stampede last night."

So it was just the night before, Bill thought. He was relieved he hadn't lost any more time than that. He could probably catch up to the herd without much trouble.

"Hob brought me into town, did he?"

"That's right."

Bill nodded. "Yeah, Hob's a good trail boss. Best there is. I'll be sure to thank him when I get back to the herd."

The woman frowned. "What do you mean, when you get back to the herd? You're not going anywhere, Mr. Harvey."

Bill summoned the strength to push himself up on an elbow again. "I got to," he said. "I signed on to help take those cows to Dodge."

"Well, you're not going to be able to," she said with a shake of her head. "You're hurt too badly."

"Yeah, but the doc's already patched me up—"

"A doctor didn't bandage your leg. We don't have a doctor in Redemption. I cleaned the wound and put fresh bandages on it."

His first impulse was to argue with her and insist he was

fine, but now that she mentioned it, his leg was bound up so tight he couldn't move it. Then he realized the full import of what she had just said and suddenly felt as warm as if he'd been out in the sun all day.

"You mean you, uh, saw my . . . oh, Lord . . . I never . . ."

"Really?" Mischief glinted in those dark blue eyes. "Never? I'm surprised."

That made him feel even warmer. Downright uncomfortable, in fact.

She laughed and gave a little shake of her head. "I'm sorry. I shouldn't tease you that way. You've been through an ordeal. Please don't worry about it. I've done some midwifery and doctoring before. It was just easier to clean the wound properly without any clothing in the way."

Bill turned his head to look at the wall. Where he came from, there were decent women, and there were gals who worked in the saloons and dance halls, and the gulf between them was as wide as the ocean. He swallowed hard and said, "I'm sorry you had to subject yourself to that, ma'am."

"You can stop calling me ma'am. I'm not married. My name is Eden Monroe."

If she was trying to make him feel better about her seeing everything she had seen, telling him that she wasn't a married lady wasn't a very good way to go about it. He said, "I'm really obliged to you for your help, Miss Monroe. But I reckon I'd better try to get back to the herd somehow—"

"That's impossible. Mr. Sanders said they were moving on to Dodge City and would come by here on their way back to Texas to pick you up. I'm not sure you'll be able to travel even then. You'll have to stay completely off that leg for at least a week, maybe longer. I suppose if they bring a wagon, you might be able to ride in it, but it would still be a grueling journey. The wound might not heal properly. It might even get worse."

Bill struggled to wrap his mind around what she was telling him. This was a disaster. He couldn't afford to be stuck here in some backwater Kansas settlement. The wages he was supposed to receive for coming along on the cattle drive were going to give him a start on saving up for a spread of his own. Now he was going to wind up beholden instead of making money.

"Don't worry, you can stay here as long as you need to," said Eden.

"I'll pay you," he choked out. "I reckon Hob'll have to dock my wages some since I didn't finish out the drive, but whatever you're out on me, I'll see that you get it back somehow."

"Didn't I just tell you not to worry?"

"Yes, ma'am . . . I mean Miss Monroe . . . but I was raised not to take charity."

Actually, charity of any sort was pretty much an unknown commodity in the house of the relatives who had taken him in after his folks died, when he was just a shirttail kid. He'd been another mouth to feed, and his aunt and uncle had made sure he earned every bite.

"We'll talk about that later. I'm sure we can work out something that's agreeable to my father."

"Your father?"

"Perry Monroe. He owns the store. I'm sorry we don't have a better place for you to stay than this old storeroom, but—"

"No, this is fine. Mighty fine. I'm sure I'll be comfortable here. I just don't want to be a burden to you folks, that's all."

"We have bigger burdens than taking care of you, Mr. Harvey, I assure you."

When she said that, Eden's voice sounded like she was carrying the weight of the world. Bill wanted to ask her what was wrong, but at the same time he knew there was no point in it. After all, as long as he was laid up like this, there wasn't a blasted thing he could do to help her.

After a moment of awkward silence, Eden took a step toward the cot and said, "Maybe I ought to check those bandages again—"

Bill tightened his grip on the sheet and tugged it higher. "They're fine," he said. "The leg feels fine."

"Really? After seeing what that longhorn did to you, I'd imagine that it hurts like hell."

Her plainspokenness surprised him, but at the same time it made him want to grin. He said, "Well, to be honest, it does. I've got a pretty bad headache, too. And my mouth's mighty dry."

"Of course it is. You've got a hangover."

Bill frowned. "A hangover? I don't remember doing any drinking. Hob doesn't allow any of that on a drive."

"But I'll bet he carries a bottle of whiskey in his saddle-bags for medicinal purposes, doesn't he?"

"Yeah, he does," said Bill. "They must've poured some of that who-hit-John down my throat to keep me quiet last night while they were working on my leg."

"That's exactly what I was thinking."

Knowing it would probably hurt, Bill tried not to shudder as he thought about old Samuel Haddon roughly cleaning his ripped leg. Uncle Sam, as all the cowboys called him, had never been gentle with anything in his life, as far as Bill could tell. He was glad he'd been drunk, passed out, or both while that was going on.

"You really need to drink something," Eden went on. "Between the hangover and the blood you lost from the wound, I'm not surprised you're thirsty."

Bill licked sun-cracked lips. "Yes'm, I surely am."

"I'll bring you some tea. Stay right there." She started to turn away but stopped to laugh. "Of course you're going to stay right there. Where could you go, in the shape you're in?"

That was a good question, thought Bill, and the answer was, nowhere. He couldn't budge from the cot.

Eden went out into the store. Bill lay there with his eyes closed, resting and trying to come to grips with what had happened to him.

When he heard a footstep about a minute later, he thought Eden was back already and opened his eyes. The pretty blonde wasn't the one who stood in the doorway, though, with a shoulder propped casually against the jamb.

The newcomer was a lean, dark-haired man with a scar

down his left cheek. Something about him struck Bill as being vaguely familiar. Maybe he had seen the man earlier when Hob and the boys had brought him into Redemption.

Whoever he was, he didn't look the least bit friendly. In fact, as he sneered down at Bill, he looked like it would suit him just fine to draw the revolver from the holster on his hip and fill the Texan with lead.

Chapter 4

Bill's skin crawled under the scar-faced hombre's hostile gaze. He'd been wearing a pistol when the stampede had started the night before, but he didn't know what had happened to it. His eyes flicked around the room, searching to see if Hob had left it with him, even though he knew that, short of throwing himself off the cot, he probably couldn't reach it.

And he damned sure couldn't reach it and get a shot off before this fella ventilated him.

"Is he awake, Zach?" asked another man's voice from behind the one in the doorway.

"Yeah, he's awake. Looks kind of spooked, too."

"I want to talk to him. You go on back to the office."

"You sure you won't need my help, Marshal?" drawled the first man.

"I think I can handle one Texan. Especially one who's laid up."

Zach moved out of the doorway. "Whatever you say."

An older man took his place. This one took off his hat to reveal graying sandy hair and gave Bill a pleasant enough nod. "Hello," he said.

"Howdy."

The lawman, who wore a tin star of office pinned to his vest, moved into the room and asked, "Your name's Harvey, right?"

"Yes, sir. Bill Harvey. From Texas."

The marshal grunted. "You don't need to tell me that, son. I was there when those other cowboys brought you into town." He hooked a three-legged stool with his boot toe, dragged it closer to the cot, and sat down. "Normally, we don't allow Texans inside the town limits of Redemption, especially cowboys."

"Well, sir, I'm, uh, mighty glad you made an exception for me."

"Miss Monroe insisted on it." The marshal shrugged. "I've made it a rule never to argue with a pretty girl unless I absolutely have to." He held out a hand. "I'm Frank Porter, by the way."

Bill was still weak, but he lifted his arm and gripped Porter's hand. "Pleased to meet you, Marshal."

"I expect you've heard talk about Redemption among the trail herds, haven't you?"

"Some," admitted Bill. "But just that the herds all go around it. I reckon it has something to do with that rule against Texans."

"It's a rule the town council put into effect for a reason. This is a quiet town. Only one saloon. We can't handle a bunch of rowdy cowhands coming in here to blow off steam, and folks don't want their gardens ruined by a bunch of cows trampling through them, either."

Bill understood that, but Marshal Porter's words indicated there had been trouble with trail herds in the past, and that surprised him a little. Redemption was south of the railhead, so when the herds came through this area the cowboys wouldn't have been paid off yet. That didn't happen until the cows were sold. So they wouldn't have had much money for celebrating, or any real reason to celebrate since the drive wasn't over.

However, some trail bosses had been known to give their

hands a small advance on their wages and let them visit towns the herd bypassed. Hob wouldn't do that, but some did. That might have happened here in the past. Just like some trail bosses wouldn't take the herd around but would drive straight through a settlement if it lay on the shortest route to the railroad. Bill was a Texan through and through, but he was also smart enough to know that some fellas were jackasses, no matter where they came from.

"You don't have to worry about me causing any trouble, Marshal," he said. "With this leg of mine, I couldn't even if I wanted to, which I don't. I just want to heal up so I can go on about my business."

Porter nodded. "That's good to hear. But for the record, Harvey . . . I wasn't worried about you causing trouble."

Bill might have asked him what he meant by that, but just then Eden stepped into the storeroom again, carrying a cup and saucer and saying, "I've got that tea for you—" She stopped short at the sight of Porter sitting there on the stool. "Oh. You're here, Marshal."

He smiled at her as he stood up. "I sure am. I was just having a talk with Mr. Harvey, making sure he understands how things go here in Redemption."

"Would you like some tea?"

"Oh, no, I've got to be movin' on. A lawman's always busy, you know. But thank you mighty kindly for the offer." Porter put his hat on and leaned over to pat Bill on the shoulder. "I hope you get to feelin' better real soon there, Mr. Harvey."

The marshal gave Eden a pleasant nod as he left the storeroom. Bill heard Porter's feet on the floorboards as he walked out through the mercantile.

Eden set the cup and saucer on a crate and said, "Let me help you sit up a little."

This was going to be awkward, thought Bill, and sure enough it was, as Eden came over to the cot and bent down to slip an arm around his shoulders. That put her face right next to his, close enough he could feel the warmth of her breath against his cheek and smell the fragrance of her hair.

He was all too aware, as well, of the soft thrust of her left breast against his arm as she lifted him.

Throw in the way he had to keep a tight grip on the sheet, lest it slip down, and those few seconds were mighty tense and uncomfortable. He was glad when she propped the pillow behind him and stepped back so he could lean against the wall.

"I'm obliged," he told her. "If you'll just hand me that cup and saucer . . ."

"And have you dump hot tea in your lap because you're too weak to hold them?" She shook her head. "I don't think that would be a very good idea, especially under the circumstances. Do you?"

"Well . . . no."

She sat down on the stool the marshal had been using and lifted the cup to his lips. He took a sip of the tea. It was hot, but not so hot he burned his mouth, and it tasted good. The overwhelming thirst he felt made him want to empty the cup in one gulp. But with Eden giving it to him, he had to be content with sips. That was probably better for him anyway.

"What did the marshal have to say?" she asked.

"Oh, he was just explaining about how folks here in Redemption don't usually let Texans come into town."

Eden nodded. "There's an ordinance against them being here."

"Seems like that would be sort of hard to enforce. I mean, you can't always tell where a fella's from just by looking at him."

"Well, to tell you the truth, if a lone Texan were to ride in here and stop for a while but didn't cause any problems, Marshal Porter might not run him out of town. The purpose of the ordinance is really just to keep the trail herds and their drovers from causing trouble."

"That's happened in the past?"

Eden gave him another sip of tea and said, "Last year several herds drove straight through town. Right up Main Street, in fact. We didn't have any law here then, so there was no one to stop them. The first time it wasn't so bad, but when it happened again and people complained to the cowboys about the damage, they went on a rampage and caused even more. They shot out windows and pulled down false fronts and injured several of the townspeople."

"Lord," Bill said as he shook his head. "I'm sorry. I got to tell you, though, Hob would never let a crew of his get away with something like that. Every trail boss is different and does things in different ways."

"I'm sure that's true," said Eden, "but after that happened, the town council decided they didn't want to take a chance. They passed the ordinance, and the next time we saw the dust of a trail herd approaching from the south, the mayor and a couple of councilmen rode out to tell the Texans they'd have to go around Redemption."

"What happened?"

"The mayor and the other men came back into town on foot. They'd been attacked and beaten by the cowboys. And then the herd came through anyway, and I think the Texans made sure the cattle wreaked as much havoc as possible."

Bill frowned. "No offense, Miss Monroe, but that doesn't sound like something anybody I know would do. Most of the boys on these trail drives are just simple, hardworkin' fellas who only want to get the cows to the railhead and collect their wages. They're not interested in causing trouble."

"I saw it with my own eyes," said Eden.

"I don't doubt that," Bill said quickly. He'd meant it when he said he didn't want to offend her. "It just strikes me as a mite odd, that's all."

She shrugged. "After that incident, the town council advertised for a marshal, and Frank Porter showed up and took the job."

"That fella with the scar." Bill touched his left cheek. "He's Porter's deputy?"

"That's right. Zach Norris."

The dislike in Eden's voice when she mentioned the deputy's name was plain to hear.

"Looks like a pretty tough hombre."

"He thinks he is, anyway. And I suppose he really is. He's fast with a gun, there's no doubt about that."

"A pistoleer, is he?"

"I don't know exactly what that means. But he's killed two men in gunfights since he's been wearing a badge here."

Bill wasn't surprised. He'd seen the killing urge in Zach Norris's eyes for himself. Down in Texas, there were men like that, men who had been so embittered by the war and the oppressive reconstruction following it that human life, their own or someone else's, no longer meant much to them. If they were crossed, even if it was just a minor confrontation, they instinctively reached for a gun.

"What about Porter?"

"What about him? He's not like Deputy Norris, if that's what you mean. He's tough enough that no one wants to argue with him—he's been a lawman in several other towns, I've heard—but he's not the same sort of cold-blooded killer Norris is. In fact, he keeps Norris under control. Between the two of them, they see to it the trail herds don't cause us any more trouble."

"Was there any gunplay, the first time a herd tried to come through after they were hired?"

Eden shook her head. "No. I've heard it was rather tense when they rode out to talk to the trail boss, but nothing happened. The herd went around the town."

Bill wondered if something really had happened, and Eden just didn't know about it. Any man with enough backbone and grit to ramrod hundreds of cattle and a dozen cowboys all the way from Texas wouldn't be the sort of fella who backed down easily. But maybe she was right; he didn't know.

"With the trail herds all going around the settlement, I wouldn't think there'd be much for a pair of lawmen to do in a town like Redemption."

A worried look appeared in Eden's eyes. "There are other troublemakers in the world besides Texas cowboys, Mr. Harvey."

He wanted to suggest that she call him Bill. Mr. Harvey sounded too much like his pa. But that struck him as being a mite too forward, so he didn't say anything about it.

Instead he asked, "What sort of troublemakers?"

"We do have a saloon, which means men get drunk and fight from time to time. A lot of buffalo hunters and freighters pass through, and they can be rough sorts. Also there's a bank, and some men tried to hold it up once. Deputy Norris had to shoot one of them."

"What about the other man he killed?"

"That was a man who drove a freight wagon. He treated one of the, ah, women who work for Miss Stanley too roughly, and when Deputy Norris showed up to handle the complaint, the man pulled a gun on him."

So Redemption had a whorehouse as well as a saloon, thought Bill, and the Miss Stanley Eden mentioned would be the madam. That didn't really mean much to Bill. He had been with a few soiled doves in his life, but something about them always made him sad, and he didn't seek out whorehouses with the same eagerness his friends usually displayed. He'd always had a curious mind, though, and liked to learn as much about a place as he could.

Despite that, he wasn't going to ask Eden for more details. Anyway, he wasn't in any shape for any sort of cavorting. Sipping tea was about as wild as he could handle right now.

"You think I could, uh, have a little more of that tea?"

"Oh! We've been sitting here talking, and I forgot all about it. I'm afraid I've let it get cold."

"Doesn't matter," he told her. "Cold's fine."

She helped him drink the rest of it, then said, "You should get some rest now."

His eyelids had started out heavy and gotten heavier as they talked. He nodded and said, "Yes'm."

"I'll help you lie down again . . ."

That was easier than it had been for her to get him sitting up. She still had to get close to him again, though, and he wasn't so tired that he didn't enjoy it.

"I'll pull the door up almost closed so it'll be darker in here and you can sleep better," she said. "But if you need anything, call out. I'll hear you, or my father will."

"Much obliged, Miss Monroe," he said, his voice thick with weariness.

"Eden," she said. "Call me Eden."

He started to smile, but he dozed off before he could tell her how pleased he'd be to do that and how she should call him Bill.

Chapter 5

When he awoke, he felt a pressing need to relieve himself. He hesitated to call out, worried Eden would answer the summons, but some things couldn't be ignored.

Luckily, her father pulled the door back in response to the call, and he fetched a bucket and helped Bill do what had to be done. When that was taken care of, Bill said, "I sure am much obliged, Mr. Monroe. Not just for this, but for taking me in to start with."

Monroe grunted. "You can thank my daughter for that," he said with a sour look on his bearded face. "It was her idea, not mine. After all the hell you Texas boys have raised around here, I wouldn't walk across the street to spit on you if you were on fire."

Bill felt a surge of anger inside him. "I'm sorry you've had problems, but I didn't have any part in them."

"It was your kind." Monroe slashed at the air. "Never mind. You're here, and with that bad leg I don't imagine you'll be going anywhere for a while. Eden's always been too softhearted for her own good. I've tried to tell her you can't trust just anybody, and the place would've gone bankrupt from extending credit to every miserable sodbuster in these parts if it was up to her!"

From the sound of it, father and daughter didn't get along too well, and while Bill was sorry to hear that, it wasn't any of his business. He said, "Well, I sure appreciate what you and Miss Eden have done for me, and I intend to see to it that you get repaid for your trouble, even if it takes a while."

Monroe snorted as if to say he'd believe that when he saw it with his own eyes. Then he said, "One more thing while I'm talking to you . . . While you're here, you'll treat my daughter with respect. I know you Texans think every woman in Kansas is fair game for your lewd advances, but if I catch you doing or saying anything improper to her, I'll thrash you within an inch of your life, hurt leg or no hurt leg!"

Bill couldn't hold his anger in this time. He pushed himself up on an elbow and said, "Listen here, sir. You got no call to accuse me of such a thing. I plan on treating Miss Eden like the lady she obviously is. Anyway, it's not like I can get up and waltz her around the damn room!"

Monroe glared at him. "It's not waltzing I'm worried about." He pointed a finger at Bill and went on, "You just remember what I told you."

With that, he left the storeroom, and Bill was glad to see him go. He'd felt an instinctive liking for Eden, but the same couldn't be said of Perry Monroe.

When Eden brought Bill some supper that evening, she wore a worried expression. "I hear you had a run-in with my father."

"Oh, it didn't amount to anything," he said with a shrug. "Nothing for you to concern yourself with, Miss Eden."

"Father can be pretty gruff and outspoken," she said as she set the tray of food on a crate. "We don't always get along very well. It hasn't been easy on him, raising a daughter by himself."

"Your ma . . . ?"

"Passed away when I was young," said Eden. "I remember her, but just barely."

"That's a shame. I was just a kid when both my folks died, so I know what you're talking about."

"I'm sorry to hear that. Here, let me help you sit up again, and you can eat."

Bill held up a hand to stop her. "I'm feeling a lot stronger now since I rested some more. I reckon I can sit up by myself."

"Are you sure?"

"I'd like to give it a try, anyway."

She smiled. "All right, suit yourself. But whatever you do, don't fall off that cot. You don't want to undo all the hard work your chuckwagon cook and I put into patching up that leg."

Carefully, Bill worked himself into a sitting position. He'd been telling the truth. He really did feel stronger now. But he was famished, and the smell of the roast beef and potatoes and greens on the plate was making his mouth water.

"Should I feed you?" asked Eden.

"No, ma'am. I can manage."

He did, although Eden stayed close by, sitting on the stool where she could reach him easily if he had any trouble. Bill forced himself to eat slowly instead of wolfing down the food. He didn't want to make himself sick.

The meal made him feel even better. He had spent a lot of his life outside, doing the work of a ranch hand for his uncle since the time he was twelve years old, and that had toughened him up considerably. Anytime he came down with some sort of illness, he got over it quickly, and he figured he could shake the effects of this injury sooner than anybody expected, too.

Eden had brought him a cup of cool buttermilk to go with his supper. He washed down the last of the food with it and licked the buttermilk off his lips. With a smile, he said, "That was mighty good. I feel like I could whip my weight in wildcats."

Eden laughed. "I don't think you'll get a chance to try. We don't have any wildcats around here." Her face suddenly grew serious. "Some other predators, maybe, but not wild-cats."

"What do you mean by that?" asked Bill.

She waved off the question. "Oh, nothing. Don't worry about it. Can I get you anything else?"

Bill thought about it. "Something to read, maybe. That'd help pass the time."

She smiled again. "Of course. I'll bring a lamp in here and put it on that crate right beside the cot where you can reach it to blow it out when you get tired and want to go to sleep. And I have several books you might like. Have you ever read anything by Jane Austen or the Brontë sisters?"

Bill shook his head. "No, I, uh, don't reckon I have. I like the books by that Fenimore Cooper fella, though. The ones with Indian fights and such."

"Well, I'll see what I can find." She lowered her voice. "If nothing else, my father has a stack of those penny dreadfuls that he doesn't know I know about."

"Whatever you think best, Miss Eden."

She took the tray with its empty plate and cup and left the storeroom. Bill leaned back against the wall. The cot was set up in a corner, so he had a wall behind him and on his left. With the pillow propped up to lean on, he was comfortable.

Comfortable enough, in fact, that he went to sleep with-out meaning to.

Sometime during the night he woke with his heart slugging hard in his chest. He knew he'd been dreaming, but other than a few fuzzy images lingering in his brain, he couldn't recall what the dreams were about. There had been a loud noise and a bright light, and as he lay there on the cot with his hammering pulse gradually slowing, he figured he must have had a nightmare about the rustlers' raid on the herd the night before. That noise he recalled was the long-haired rus-tler shooting at him.

After a while he calmed down enough to realize he was lying down with the sheet pulled all the way up. The last thing he remembered was leaning against the wall after supper, while Eden went to fetch a lamp and a book.

She must have come back in, found him sound asleep, and gotten him lying down again without waking him. Or maybe her father had done it. Bill didn't know which to hope for.

All he knew for sure was that he was a damned lucky cowboy. That brindle steer could have killed him, and when it hadn't, he'd had the good fortune for the herd to be near a town where folks could help him. He couldn't ask for anybody better to be taking care of him than Eden Monroe.

He sure wasn't likely to find a prettier nursemaid, either.

With that thought putting a smile on his lips, Bill went back to sleep.

He knew something was wrong as soon as he looked at Eden the next morning. When she came into the storeroom to see if he was awake, her face was pale and drawn, as if she hadn't gotten enough sleep.

"What happened?" asked Bill.

Her eyes widened in surprise. "What do you mean? How do you know anything happened?"

"I can tell by looking at you." Her eyes were slightly red-rimmed, he noted, and a hunch told him it was from more than a lack of sleep. "You've been crying."

She sighed. "You're right. A friend of the family . . . died last night."

"I'm sorry. Who was it, if you don't mind me askin'?"

"Abner Williams. He was one of the partners in the Williams and Hartnett Livery Stable. A good friend of my father, and one of the founders of the town."

Bill shook his head. "That's a real shame. Had he been sick for a while, or was it sudden?"

"Oh, it was sudden, all right." Unexpectedly, Eden laughed, but the sound was hollow and brittle and there was nothing real about it. "Very sudden."

"What do you mean by that?"

She shook her head. "Never mind. I was just seeing if you were awake. I'll bring you some breakfast in a little while."

"Thanks. I'm obliged."

"You know, you don't have to keep saying that every time I do something for you. Otherwise we'll never get around to any other conversation."

"Fine." She was annoyed with him, he thought, and if that's the way she wanted to be, he wasn't going to argue with her. "I didn't mean to fall asleep on you last night."

"I wasn't aware that you were on me last night."

"That's not what I—" He stopped. "You know that's not what I meant, don't you?"

She didn't answer. Instead she said, "I'll be back with that breakfast."

Perry Monroe came into the storeroom a few minutes later. "Eden said you probably needed some help with your, ah . . ."

"Yeah," Bill said. "I do."

He sure hoped Eden was wrong about how long his injured leg would keep him from being up and around. This was no fit way for a man to live.

When those personal chores were finished, Bill said, "I heard about your friend Mr. Williams passing away. I'm sorry about that."

"Why should you be sorry? You didn't even know him."

Monroe was bound and determined not to be friendly. If that was the way he wanted it, thought Bill, that was the way it would be. He shrugged and said, "I just know what it's like to lose a friend."

"You don't know a damned thing about it," Monroe snapped. He stomped out of the storeroom, leaving Bill staring after him.

Eden returned about a quarter of an hour later with a tray of food. This time the plate held eggs, flapjacks, and bacon, and steam rose from the cup of coffee beside it.

"I assume you take your coffee black?" she asked.

Bill grinned. "Black as sin. Uncle Sam, our cook, he

brews it up strong enough so he has to be careful the pot doesn't get up and walk off on its own hind legs. The only sweetening he uses is the little peppermint stick that comes in the Arbuckles bag."

"Well, I don't think your cup is going anywhere under its own power, but maybe it'll be strong enough to suit you."

"I'm sure it'll be fine." Bill was already sitting up, so when she placed the tray on his lap, he dug right in. After a few bites, he added, "Say, I didn't mean to rile your pa earlier."

"My father riles easily," said Eden. "What happened?"

"I just told him I was sorry about what happened to his friend Mr. Williams, and he got upset. Said I didn't know a thing about it." Bill left out the curse Monroe had added.

"It's not just him. The whole town is upset . . . and scared."

"Scared?" Bill repeated. "Why would folks be scared? Did that liveryman die of some sickness that's contagious?"

Eden didn't answer, but the man who stepped into the doorway in time to hear Bill's question said, "No, the thing that killed Abner Williams isn't catching. But it seems to be going around anyway."

Bill looked up and saw Marshal Frank Porter standing there. The lawman wore the same sort of weary expression Bill had seen on the faces of the Monroes.

"What do you mean by that, Marshal? What happened to Mr. Williams?"

"He was killed," said Porter. "Murdered. Shot down from behind like a dog." A thin, humorless smile curved his lips. "You might've been better off getting gored by that bull while you were closer to some other settlement, Harvey. We've got ourselves a backshooter in Redemption."

Chapter 6

Porter came on into the room and took his hat off as he gave Eden a polite nod. "Morning, Miss Monroe," he said.

"But not a good one," said Eden.

Porter pursed his lips. "No, not particularly. You mind if I ask you a few questions?"

"What sort of questions?"

"Well, the livery stable's not far from here. I thought maybe you might've heard some sort of disturbance coming from that direction during the night."

"You mean like a gunshot?"

Porter shrugged. "Yes, ma'am. That's sort of what I was gettin' at."

"No, I'm sorry," Eden replied with a shake of her head. "I didn't hear anything unusual. I must have slept through the shot."

Bill spoke up, saying, "This fella Mr. Williams, he was killed at the livery stable?"

Porter looked at him. "That's right. Abner was an old bachelor, so he had a cot in the tack room where he slept nights, in case somebody needed to bring in a horse or take one out. Josiah Hartnett, his partner, has a family and lives a few blocks away."

"And the stable's close by?"

"In the next block, same side of the street." Porter frowned at him, and Bill noticed that Eden was watching him curiously, too. "Why all the questions, Harvey?"

"Well . . ." Bill rubbed at his jaw as he thought about what he was going to say. "Sometime during the night I woke up and thought I'd heard a shot. I figured I was just dreaming, though, probably about those rustlers who raided the herd night before last. But I reckon it could've been an actual shot."

"You know what time that was?"

Bill had to shake his head. "No, sir, I'm afraid not. It was mighty dark, though, so it had to be the middle of the night."

"If you can't pin it down any closer than that, I don't see how it helps me. Abner was alive last evening and dead this morning when Hartnett got to the stable early, so we already know somebody shot him during the night."

"Shot him in the back, you said?"

Porter nodded. "That's right. He was in his office, next to the tack room."

"Just like Mr. Hendrickson was in his bakery," said Eden. "And John Lightner was at the saddle shop and Mr. Tompkins was behind the counter in his apothecary shop. All of them shot from behind in their own businesses at night. Four murders in the past two months, Marshal."

"You're not telling me anything I don't already know, Miss Monroe," Porter said with a grim heaviness in his voice. "I've trying to find out who's responsible for those killin's. Give me time, and I will; you can count on that."

"But how many more men will die first?"

Porter grunted angrily and clapped his hat on his head. "I'm gonna pretend I didn't hear you say that, miss."

He turned and walked out of the storeroom.

Bill cocked an eyebrow. "Sounds like the marshal's a mite touchy."

"I suppose I shouldn't have said what I did," Eden replied with a shake of her head. "I'm sure Marshal Porter's trying to find the killer. I'm just not certain he's looking in the right places."

"What do you mean by that?"

"Nothing," she said. "Are you finished with breakfast?"

Bill looked at his plate, which still had food on it. "Uh, no, but I will be soon."

"Just set the tray on the crate next to the lamp when you're done. I'll come back and get it later."

She left the room, too. Bill ate the rest of his breakfast, but it didn't taste quite as good now.

The air of tension that gripped the settlement eased a little as the next few days went by, but it didn't go away completely. From the storeroom, Bill could hear some of the talk that went on between Eden, her father, and the customers who came into the mercantile. On the first day after Abner Williams's murder, that was all folks could talk about. Each day, the subject was less on their minds, but many of them still brought it up.

Eden refused to talk about it or the other killings, though, whenever Bill mentioned them. She claimed she had better things to occupy her mind, but he suspected she was still brooding about the murders.

Each day she unwrapped the bandages from Bill's leg to clean the wound and put fresh dressings on it. Bill couldn't see the injury all that well, since it was on the side of his leg, but Eden assured him it was healing nicely, with no sign of festering. Once again he told himself just how lucky he was.

On the morning of the fourth day, as he finished his breakfast, he told Eden, "I want to get up."

She shook her head. "No, it's too soon."

"You didn't even think about it."

"That's because I know it's too soon. The wound on your leg is nowhere near healed. You'll pull the stitches loose."

Bill smiled. "I'm not talking about running a footrace. I just want to get up and move around a little. If I keep lying on this cot all the time, my muscles are gonna be so weak I won't be able to get around."

"You haven't been laid up that long yet," argued Eden.

"It's *my* leg."

"That *I* worked on to save."

"Does your pa have any crutches for sale in his store?"

She didn't answer. He had to ask the question again, and when he did, she replied in open exasperation, "I think there's a set of them around here somewhere."

"Well, then, find them. I'll buy them."

"With what? There was no money in those trousers of yours when Mr. Sanders brought you into town."

"Listen, Hob'll pay you when he comes back to pick me up. However much your pa's been out on me, Hob can take it out of the wages I've got coming. I don't care if I don't have any money left to take back to Texas with me."

"You were going to take your wages back with you? From what I've heard, you Texans like to spend all your money on debauchery in Dodge City when you get paid off at the end of a drive."

"I reckon a lot of the boys do that, all right," said Bill, "but I was planning on saving up to buy a spread of my own in a few years. I might not ever be able to afford anything except some little greasy-sack outfit, but at least it'd be mine."

She looked at him. "You've never had a place of your own?"

"Not really. I told you, my folks died when I was a kid. Their farm went back to the county for taxes. I went to live with my aunt and uncle and a whole passel of cousins. None of 'em liked me much, so I sure never felt like that was home."

"Where was that?"

"Down in South Texas, between Victoria and Hallettsville. As soon as I got old enough, I took out on my own and drifted over into the Nueces country. That's where I met up with Hob. I cowboyed for him and some of the other ranchers around there, and when he put together that consolidated herd to drive to the railhead, I asked if I could come along. He said I could." Bill shrugged. "That's the story of my life."

"I'd like to hear some more."

He shook his head. "No, you wouldn't. You're just trying to use your feminine wiles to distract me from wanting to get up and walk around a little. Next thing you know, you'll be battin' those blue eyes at me."

"You noticed I have blue eyes?"

"How could I miss that?"

He didn't tell her that he had noticed her eyes first thing, along with everything else that made her so pretty.

"Now, how about those crutches?" he went on.

She blew out her breath and said, "You're the stubbornest Texan I've ever seen."

Bill grinned. "You haven't seen all that many Texans. I'm downright changeable compared to some."

"All right. I'll get the crutches for you. But if you fall and tear that wound open again, don't expect me to patch you up. You can go find somebody else to do your doctoring for you."

"I'll be careful," he promised her, although he didn't really believe her threat. He was sure she would still take care of him, even if he reinjured himself.

She left the room and came back a few minutes later carrying a pair of crutches. She leaned them against the wall and said, "All right, let's get you sitting on the edge of the cot first. Carefully, now."

He was already sitting up. He was wearing a pair of jeans she had done some cutting on so the left leg fit over the bandages. He moved his right leg off the cot and let it sink to the floor. Eden leaned over, took hold of his splinted and bandaged leg, and picked it up, swinging it around so it stuck out straight in front of him as he sat on the cot.

"All right, now you're going to stand up on your right leg," she said. "I'll help you."

She moved close in front of him and bent down to slide

her arms under his arms. That put her face right in front of his, and for a crazy moment he was tempted to lean forward just a little. That was all it would take for him to kiss her.

But he had promised Eden's father that he wouldn't do anything improper.

"Put your hands on my shoulders," she said. He did so as she tightened her arms around him. She was surprisingly strong, he discovered as she lifted him.

His right leg threatened to fold up under him when his weight came down on it. He was a mite light-headed, too. He had to clutch at her shoulders to keep from falling as he sagged against her.

This was the closest he had been to a woman in quite a while. He hoped desperately he wouldn't have any sort of reaction that might prove embarrassing. Being this close to her, he already felt bad enough about smelling like an old boar hog. He needed a nice cold creek to jump into and wash off. That might have the added effect of cooling off some of the feelings coursing through him, too.

"Sorry," he muttered, not sure what he was apologizing for. Eden could take her pick, he supposed.

"That's all right. Let me know when you feel steadier."

He stiffened his right leg under him. "I'm fine now," he told her.

"Hang on to me anyway." She had put the crutches where she could reach them. She got one of them and slid the curved wooden handle under his left arm. "Rest some of your weight on that."

Bill did so. It felt awkward, and having the crutch pushing up under his arm was uncomfortable. But it wasn't as bad as being confined to the cot, he told himself.

"All right, are you braced like that?" asked Eden.

He nodded. "Yeah. Hand me the other one."

She took the other crutch and placed it under his right arm. He reached down and wrapped his fingers around the hand grips on both of the crutches.

"Well, you won't fall over, at least not to the side, as long as you hold on to them," she said as she stepped back. "Now it's just a matter of not falling on your face or back." She cocked her head to the side. "How does that feel?"

"Not too bad," he lied. It was uncomfortable as all get-out, and he wasn't the least bit confident he could get around using these blasted things. But he wasn't going to let *her* see that.

His left leg felt heavy and useless as it hung beside the right one. "How do I walk?" he went on.

"You have to stay balanced on your right leg while you put the crutches in front of you," she said. "Then you put your weight on them and sort of swing yourself forward."

"Like this?" He did as she said. He felt a little disoriented again, and his left leg twinged as that foot bumped the floor, but he managed to move toward the door of the storeroom.

"That's good," said Eden. "You seem to have some natural balance and grace."

Bill grinned. "I don't know about the grace part, but the balance probably comes from spending more time on horseback than on my own two feet the past ten years. If you don't have good balance, you'll have a hard time staying in the saddle, especially on some half-wild mustang."

He took another step with the crutches. This was easier than the first one, and he felt his hopes rise.

But suddenly all his strength seemed to desert him. He swayed precariously on the crutches and might have fallen if Eden hadn't been there to spring forward and catch him.

"I knew it," she said as she steadied him. "I knew it was too soon."

"I'm all right," said Bill. "Just sort of . . . played out. Might be a good idea to sit down."

She helped him back to the cot. When he was lying down again, resting, he said, "Leave the crutches."

She snorted. "I don't think so. You'll get some crazy notion about getting up and walking around by yourself." Her voice softened. "But we'll try again later today."

Bill nodded. "All right. Thanks, Eden. When a fella's always done for himself, it's sort of hard to have to have somebody else do everything for him."

"I'm sure it is. You just have to be patient."

He didn't have time to be patient, he told himself. Hob and the boys would be coming back from Dodge before too much longer, on their way home to Texas. He had to start getting better, faster, if he wanted to be able to go with them.

Problem was, he thought as he looked at Eden, he wasn't sure he wanted to go anymore.

Chapter 7

By the time four more days had passed, Bill was getting around fairly well on the crutches. He had regained some of his strength, too. He could walk all the way to the front of the mercantile and back to the storeroom without getting too worn out. Eating Eden's cooking had been good for him, and he made sure she knew he felt that way.

It had been a little more than a week since the rustlers had hit the herd. Hob and the boys might've lost most of a day rounding up the strays that had scattered during the stampede and its aftermath, but even so, they should have reached Dodge City by now. That meant in another day or two, they would be showing up in Redemption looking for him.

He spent a lot of time thinking about what he would do when that happened. He was a Texan, born and bred, and like most Texans, the thought of spending the rest of his life somewhere else hadn't ever occurred to him. That just wasn't something he was interested in doing.

His plans were all laid out. Work as a cowboy, save as much of his money as he could, and buy some land of his own. Then, and only then, maybe he would start thinking about trying to find some gal who might want to share those plans with him.

A lot of cowboys had that dream. Most of them never achieved it. Most wound up broke, stove up, and hanging on as a cook or a horse wrangler or just doing odd jobs around a ranch, subsisting on the pity of the owner. For some reason, being a cowboy and saving money never seemed to go together.

Bill was determined to be different, and he had taken the first step by signing on with Hob for the drive. Now everything had gone to hell, and he didn't know what he was going to do. Every time he looked at Eden, he got more confused.

For one thing, he didn't know for sure how he felt about her. Sure, she was as pretty as the sun coming up on a spring morning, and just being around her made him feel better. She was smart, too, and had enough grit and good humor to her nature to make her interesting.

But for another thing, he didn't know how *she* felt about *him.* She had taken good care of him, and she seemed to like to josh around with him, sometimes in a mighty fresh manner. That didn't necessarily mean she liked him, though. Not enough to consider, well, marrying him or even letting him court her.

And if he stayed in Redemption, what in blazes would he do with himself? He didn't know how to work at anything but cowboying. He sat in the store and watched Eden and her father waiting on the customers, weighing out flour and sugar, cutting fabric, selling farm implements and tools, working their way through lists and filling up boxes with all sorts of things that folks wanted to buy. Bill watched them and thought, *I could do that.* Then he thought, *And it'd bore the hell outta me, too.*

So when he divided his thoughts on the matter into two columns and toted them all up, the reasons for going back to Texas outweighed the reasons for staying here in Kansas.

But if he knew how Eden really felt about him, that reason by itself might outweigh all the others put together.

That afternoon he was sitting in a chair near the potbellied stove in one of the back corners of the store when several burly, roughly dressed, bearded men came in. Since it was summer the stove wasn't lit, but Bill liked to sit there because it was out of the way and folks didn't pay much attention to him. Perry Monroe still glared at him from time to time, and many of the customers who came in gave him wary looks from the corners of their eyes, as if they were afraid he might start hollering and go on a rampage without any warning. After all, a Texan was about as unpredictable as a wild Indian, wasn't he? About as savage, in the minds of these Kansans, too.

The three strangers glanced at him as they approached the counter at the rear of the store, but that was all. Bill had seen their type before. They were freighters, bullwhackers, westbound with a long wagon train full of goods headed for New Mexico Territory and points west along the Santa Fe Trail. They stopped in Redemption to wet their whistles and get their ashes hauled, because it was a long, dry stretch for both of those activities west of the settlement.

As far as Bill could tell, in general bullwhackers were rougher, dirtier, and more profane than any of the cowboys he had ridden up with from Texas. There was no sign on the edge of town forbidding them entrance, though. He supposed that was because they visited Redemption in smaller numbers, and they didn't have herds of half-wild longhorns with them to cause trouble, either.

He wasn't sure what these three were doing in the store. Maybe they had run short of some provisions. He watched them, only idly curious, as they waited for Perry Monroe to finish tending to another customer, a sun-bonneted farmer's wife. Eden wasn't around at the moment.

"Mr. Monroe, did you hear that Helen Drake had a baby last night?" the middle-aged woman asked.

"No, ma'am, I knew she was expecting, but I hadn't heard that the blessed event had taken place," said Monroe. "Boy or girl?"

"A little boy. Pudge Drake rode over and told us this morning. The Drakes are our nearest neighbors, you know.

I thought I'd tell Wilbur to hitch up the wagon, and this evening we'll drive over there and see if there's anything they need. Pudge was wearing the biggest grin when he rode up on that old mule of his." The woman leaned closer to the counter. "You know, not to gossip, but I think he was a wee bit soused."

Monroe chuckled. "I'm not a bit surprised."

A rumble like the thunder of a distant storm came from one of the bullwhackers. He stepped up to the counter and said, "If you two have caught up on all the news, you got some payin' customers here, Gramps."

The white-bearded storekeeper glared at the stranger. "I'll be with you in just a minute, friend. Can't you see I'm helpin' this lady here?"

"I can see you're standin' around wastin' my time," snapped the man, "and I'm damn sick and tired of it."

The woman gasped, and Monroe lifted a hand and pointed a finger at the freighter. "I run a decent place here, mister," he said, "and I'll thank you to keep a respectful tongue in your head. Either that or get out."

"Come on, Blaisdell," said one of the other bullwhackers. "There are other stores in this town."

"Yeah, but I like this one." A leering grin stretched across the sunburned, whiskery face of the man called Blaisdell. "This is the one where that pretty little blonde works. I told her last time we come through Redemption that I'd stop and say hello to her again."

Monroe's face flushed with anger. "I remember you now!" he said. "You're the varmint who made my daughter cry because of the vile things you said to her when you came in while I wasn't here."

Bill's interest had perked up as soon as the bullwhacker mentioned Eden. Now anger welled up in him, too, when he heard Monroe say the man had made her cry.

"You three get on out of here," Monroe went. "I don't need any business from trash like you."

"You better be careful, Gramps," warned Blaisdell. "I don't cotton to bein' talked to like that."

"I'm not your grandfather, and I'm not scared of you. Get out, or I'll give you a thrashing!" Monroe was so mad he was shaking a little.

He was also a blasted fool, thought Bill. Blaisdell wasn't overly tall, but his shoulders looked almost as wide as an ox yoke and his arms were long and thick with muscle under the homespun shirt he wore. On Perry Monroe's best day, he couldn't have given a man like Blaisdell a thrashing.

Bill sat forward in the chair as the female customer turned and hurried out of the store. Nobody else was in the mercantile.

If it came down to a fight, a man who had to hobble around on crutches wouldn't stand much of a chance. But Monroe had helped him. Grudgingly, sure, but Bill was still in his debt. He couldn't sit by and do nothing if Blaisdell or either of the other two bullwhackers tried to hurt Monroe. He would feel that way even if Monroe hadn't been Eden's father.

"You talk too damn much, old man," Blaisdell said. Without warning, he leaned forward and his arm shot out over the counter. He grabbed Monroe's long white beard and jerked. Monroe howled in pain as Blaisdell hauled him forward onto the counter.

Bill heaved himself up on his crutches and yelled, "Hey!"

Blaisdell barely spared him a glance. He jerked his head toward Bill and told his companions, "Take care of that cripple. I'm gonna teach this mouthy old mossback a lesson."

He shifted his grip from Monroe's beard to the canvas apron he wore and held the old man while he swung a brutal backhand across his face.

Bill grated a curse as he clumped forward on the crutches. He was about to take a beating, he knew, but there was nothing he could do about it. Bum leg or not, he had to try to fight.

Maybe he could get in a couple of blows with a crutch, he thought. It might not be such a bad weapon.

One of the other bullwhackers growled, "Sit down, gimp. We don't want to hurt you."

Blaisdell hit Monroe again, this time with a fist. The storekeeper groaned as he lay half on the counter with Blaisdell holding him in place.

"Make your friend stop," said Bill, nodding toward Blaisdell.

"Nobody makes Clint Blaisdell do anything he doesn't want to do. Now, are you gonna butt out of this, mister, or do we bust that other leg for you?"

Bill judged he was close enough now. Bracing himself, he whipped up the right-hand crutch and thrust it forward like a spear, taking the nearest bullwhacker by surprise as he drove the tip of it into the man's belly.

As the man staggered backward from the unexpected blow, the third one lunged at Bill. Bill swung the crutch and tried to hit the man with it, but the bullwhacker blocked the blow with a forearm and swiped the crutch away from him. It slipped out of Bill's hand and clattered across the floor toward the front door.

A booted foot came down on the crutch to stop its slide. Marshal Frank Porter drew his revolver, earing back the hammer. The distinctive metallic ratcheting was loud enough to cut through the profane tirade coming from Blaisdell as he hammered punches into Monroe's face. Blaisdell froze with his fist pulled back for another blow.

"You're about a second away from me blowing a hole in you, mister," Porter told the bullwhacker. "Let go of Mr. Monroe and step away from the counter."

"Marshal, you stay out of this!" blustered Blaisdell. "This is between me and this old coot!"

"You're wrong as you can be. My job is to protect that man and his store. If that means splatterin' your brains all over the wall . . . well, I'm a man who does his duty at all costs."

The standoff held as seconds ticked by. The man Bill had jabbed in the stomach had staggered off to the side, catching himself against a cracker barrel. As he leaned against the barrel, his right hand stole toward a coiled bullwhip attached to his belt.

Bill saw the move and knew what the man intended. The bullwhacker was off to Porter's right. His body concealed his movements from the marshal.

Bullwhackers were deadly accurate with the long whips. They could flay a man's skin or pop an eye out of its socket. If this man struck fast enough, he might be able to knock the gun out of Porter's hand before the marshal could pull the trigger.

For a split second Bill thought about calling a warning to Porter. Then he realized there was no time for that. The whip was free and snaking out, writhing like a snake as it prepared to strike.

Bill threw his other crutch as hard as he could.

The crutch didn't hit the bullwhacker all that hard, but the whip tangled around it and fell far short of its intended target. Porter pivoted smoothly and fired. The bullet smashed into the bullwhacker's shoulder and spun him off his feet, screaming in agony.

Blaisdell let go of Monroe and started to charge toward Porter, but the marshal was too fast. He'd already swung his gun back in line. Blaisdell skidded to a halt as he found himself staring down the Colt's barrel.

Bill was left with only one leg to stand on. He windmilled his arms in an attempt to keep his balance as he reeled and hopped backward. It was blind luck that he came down hard in the chair where he had been sitting earlier. It was better than falling all the way to the floor.

The wounded man lay on the planks, whimpering. Porter motioned toward him with the gun barrel and told Blaisdell and the other bullwhacker, "Pick him up and carry him over to the jail."

"Jail! You can't throw us in jail! We're part of a supply train."

"You should've thought of that before you started assaulting citizens and trying to kill a lawman. Reckon your wagon boss will have to either do without your services or pay your fine."

Blaisdell snarled. "You tin star–wearin' son of a bitch."

"I can shoot you, too, you know," Porter said with a smile. "Shoot all three of you dead and say it was self-defense. I don't reckon Mr. Monroe or Tex here would claim otherwise."

Bill wasn't so sure about that. Killing the three bull-whackers when Porter had the drop on them would be pure murder, nothing less.

But he figured the marshal was just bluffing.

Blaisdell sighed and muttered to his companion, "Hell. I guess we better do what he says."

Porter covered them as they lifted the wounded man to his feet and helped him toward the door. The lawman glanced at Bill and threw him a wink, seemingly confirming that the threat had been a bluff.

"Thanks for your help, Harvey," said Porter. "That fella probably wouldn't have gotten me with that bullwhip . . . but he might have." He asked the storekeeper, "Are you all right, Mr. Monroe?"

"Yeah, yeah, madder than anything else," Monroe said as he came out from behind the counter. "He yanked a few hairs out of my beard and I'll have some bruises, but they'll heal."

"Well, I'll tend to these varmints and see that they get what's comin' to them." Porter ushered the prisoners out through the group of curious townspeople who had gathered on the store's front porch in response to the shot. He raised his voice and called, "Move along, folks, move along."

Monroe picked up the crutches and brought them over to Bill. "How about you, young fella?" he asked. "Are you all right?"

"Yeah, I think so." Bill touched his left leg gingerly. "It hurts a mite, but not enough for me to have busted anything loose again, and it doesn't look like it's bleeding."

"Well, I'm glad to hear that." Monroe frowned and gave him a curt nod. "Appreciate you stickin' up for me like that. Most men in the shape you're in wouldn't risk a fight."

Bill shrugged. *"De nada."* He could tell that Monroe was struggling to express his gratitude. The man still didn't like him and probably didn't trust him, either, but now at least a little of the debt went the other way.

Eden rushed in then, hurrying to her father and throwing her arms around him. "I heard there was a shooting!" she said. "Are you all right? Oh, no! There's blood on your face!"

"Just from being punched," said Monroe. "I'm fine."

Bill got the crutches under his arms and struggled to his feet. Eden turned to him, and he smiled as he waited for her to thank him.

"And you!" she said. "Brawling like a man who doesn't have an injured leg! What's wrong with you?"

Then she punched him on the shoulder. Bill didn't know what to say. All he could do was stare at her in surprise.

He suddenly had a feeling that if he was going to be around Eden Monroe very much, that was a feeling he'd better get used to.

Chapter 8

The wagon boss paid the fines levied against Blaisdell and the other two men by the local justice of the peace, Kermit Dunaway. The freighter complained bitterly about it, but he needed the two uninjured men. When he suggested leaving the wounded man behind, Marshal Frank Porter vetoed that idea.

"You just take him with you," the marshal said. "We don't want the likes of him in our town, even if he is wounded."

When Bill heard about that, it made him feel good. Redemption had taken him in, but not the wounded bullwhacker.

Of course, he reminded himself, that was because the wounded bullwhacker hadn't had the strong-willed Eden Monroe to stick up for him and offer to take care of him.

The wagons rolled out of Redemption late that afternoon, taking Blaisdell, the wounded man, and the other bullwhacker with them.

Eden was cool toward Bill the rest of the day. He told himself it was just because she'd been worried about him. Maybe that was a sign she really did care for him but didn't want to admit it, even to herself. That possibility didn't make the decision he was facing any easier.

That evening, after supper, Bill was alone in the store with Perry Monroe. Eden had brought Bill's supper to him and taken the tray back home when he was finished. Monroe would be closing up soon and heading for the house on a side street a couple of blocks away he shared with his daughter.

Bill was leaning against the counter with the crutch under his left arm while he toyed with the right-hand crutch, spinning it on its tip. A few feet away, the battered and bruised storekeeper bent forward over a piece of paper as he used a stub of a pencil to tote up a column of numbers. Monroe muttered to himself as he added the sums.

The clump of boots on the floorboards made Bill look up. He saw Zach Norris coming along the aisle toward the counter. The deputy's scarred face was set in its usual smirk.

"Evenin', gents," he drawled. "I'm makin' my rounds. You about ready to close up, Monroe?"

"Just as soon as I get this figuring done," replied Monroe.

Norris came up to the front of the counter and rested his hands on it. He looked at the paper, tilted his head to read the numbers, and asked, "Is that your day's take?"

"Yeah." Monroe's voice was curt and unfriendly. Nobody in town seemed to like the deputy. That included Bill, who had seen Norris in the store several times during the past few days. If Eden happened to be in the mercantile at the same time Norris was, his eyes followed her around with an intensity Bill didn't like.

"You're makin' pretty good money," said Norris.

"I do all right." Monroe's tone made it clear he didn't want to discuss his finances.

"And you know why?"

"Because I work damned hard," said Monroe.

Norris gave his head a lazy shake. "You make good money because there's law and order in this town. Folks ain't afraid to come here and buy what they need. If Redemption didn't have such good peace officers, people would start movin' out and nobody new would come in. The settlement would start to wither on the vine. Sooner or later it'd just dry up and blow away."

"Yeah, maybe." Monroe sounded distracted and impatient. "Is there something I can do for you, Deputy?"

Norris put his left hand on his chest. "Not for *me*. I don't need a thing. But from the way I hear it, those troublemakin' bullwhackers who came in here earlier today probably would've beat you within an inch of your life if not for Marshal Porter."

Monroe frowned across the counter at Norris but didn't say anything. Norris never even looked at Bill. He acted like the Texan wasn't there.

"What are you suggesting?" Monroe asked coldly.

"Well, if somebody was to do me as big a favor as Marshal Porter done you, I'd want to, I don't know, show my appreciation somehow."

"I thanked the marshal for doing his job. What was he supposed to do when one of my customers found him and told him there was trouble brewing?"

"Oh, he'd do his duty, sure enough, and never hesitate," said Norris with a nod. "That's just the way Marshal Porter is. Devoted to his duty. But I know for a fact it'd make him feel mighty good to have some concrete evidence that the people of this town truly appreciate him and everything he does."

"He gets paid good wages."

Norris grinned. "Everybody can always use a little bit extra, even a lawman."

Bill kept his expression neutral, even though he had a hard time believing what he was hearing. It sounded for all the world like Norris was trying to extort a payoff from Monroe, a payoff to Marshal Porter for doing his job and intervening in the trouble with the bullwhackers.

"I'll think about it," Monroe said in a grudging tone.

"You know, if it'd make things easier for you, you could just give me whatever you think's fair, and I'll pass it on to the marshal as a token of your gratitude."

That made it different, thought Bill. Norris wasn't really here on Marshal Porter's behalf after all. He was just trying to weasel a little cash out of Monroe for himself. Bill would have bet a hat—if he still had a hat—that any money Monroe might give to Norris would go straight in the deputy's pocket and Porter wouldn't know anything about it.

"I told you I'd think about it," said Monroe. He put the paper he'd been working on under the counter. "I need to close up now, Deputy."

"Sure," Norris said with a casual shrug. "Just thought I'd mention how nice it'd be if the marshal knew how much you folks appreciate him."

"I'll keep it in mind." Monroe put his hands flat on the counter and stared at Norris, obviously intent on waiting him out.

Grinning, Norris turned away. He stopped and finally looked at Bill. "How you doin', Harvey?"

"I reckon I'm all right," Bill said.

"I hear that even on crutches, you got mixed up in that fracas this afternoon." Norris chuckled. "Ain't that just like you Texans? If there's any trouble anywhere, you got to be right in the big middle of it, don't you?"

"Not me. I'm the peaceable sort."

"If you are, you're the first Texan I ever met that was. But you just stay that way, you hear? I expect you'll be leavin' town soon, so it'd be better if you didn't go messin' in things that don't concern you."

That sounded like a warning to Bill, and he knew the smart thing would be to let Norris have the last word. That way the deputy might go ahead and leave.

But he couldn't stop himself from saying, "Mr. Monroe took me in. I'm beholden to him. I couldn't stand by and let those hombres attack him."

Norris hooked his thumbs behind his gun belt and said, "But if it hadn't been for the marshal, you'd have got a whippin', too, wouldn't you? You'd ought to be thankin' him, too, if it wasn't for the fact that you're just a dirt-poor cowboy without a pot to piss in."

"Is there anything else you need, Deputy?" asked Monroe.

Norris shook his head. "Nope. I've said what I come in to say. You gents have a nice evenin'."

He walked out of the store, not getting in any hurry about it and leaving the front door standing wide open behind him.

Monroe came out from behind the counter and hurried to the front of the store to close the door before anybody else could come in, thinking the place was still open. When Monroe came back to the counter, Bill had both crutches under his arms and was standing straight again.

"I feel sort of bad about it, him being a lawman and all," he said, "but I don't like that fella."

Monroe snorted. "Nobody does. I reckon it'd be all right with most folks in Redemption if Marshal Porter was to fire him and run him out of town. I suppose we needed Norris at first, to help stop those trail herds from causing so much trouble, but I think Porter could handle the job by himself now."

"Do you think the marshal knows Norris was over here trying to get money out of you?"

"I'd like to believe that he doesn't."

That wasn't really an answer, but Bill didn't press the question. Monroe took off his apron, put on his hat and coat, and gave Bill a curt nod as he muttered, "G'night." He turned out all the lamps except the one in the storeroom where Bill was staying, went out the front door, and locked it behind him. Bill heard the key turn in the lock.

He started toward the storeroom, figuring he would turn in for the night, but he paused along the way and looked into a cabinet that had glass on the front and top of it. The cabinet had three shelves in it. On the bottom one lay a couple of double-barreled shotguns. The middle shelf held three new Winchesters, the Model '73.

And arranged on the top shelf were half a dozen handguns. Bill saw the cylinders and barrels gleaming dully in the light that came from the storeroom.

His pistol and his hat were lost, somewhere out there on the range where the herd had stampeded and he had been injured. His bloody, dirty, cut-up jeans had been discarded, and Eden had taken his shirt to wash it. He was dressed now in clothes provided by the Monroes, he ate the food they provided as well, and he depended on Eden to care for his injured leg. He was already so deeply in debt to them, he figured a little more wouldn't matter.

He went behind the cabinet, opened the door in the back, and reached in to wrap his fingers around the walnut grips of a Colt Single-Action Army revolver. As he lifted it and took it out of the cabinet, the weight of the weapon felt familiar in his hand. He'd carried the old pistol he'd lost for a good many years. It had never been as fine as this .44-caliber Peacemaker, though. Bill leaned on the crutches and spun the cylinder, pleased and impressed by the way it turned so smoothly and easily.

Carefully, he placed the gun on the glass top of the cabinet and went to the shelves on the back wall where Monroe kept boxes of ammunition. He took down a box of .44s and carried it back to the cabinet. Then he opened the box, plucked out five cartridges, and thumbed them one by one into the Colt's cylinder. He kept one chamber empty and let the revolver's hammer rest on it.

Bill slid the gun behind his belt and thought about Zach Norris. The deputy was known to be fast on the draw, and Bill was no pistoleer. He was a good shot and if he had a little time to aim he nearly always hit what he was shooting at, but if he got in a gunfight with Norris, he would almost certainly wind up dead.

Still, the weight of the gun behind his belt made him feel better.

At least, it did until he thought about what Eden was liable to say if she found out he was packing iron.

Chapter 9

By the next morning, Bill had convinced himself he'd been acting a little loco the night before. He was hobbling around on crutches, after all, and even at his best he'd never been a gunfighter, not by any stretch of the imagination. He had absolutely no need for a shiny new Colt .44.

But for some reason, he didn't unload it and put it back in the cabinet, although he could have before Monroe showed up to open the mercantile. The storekeeper didn't even have to know what Bill had done.

Instead he slipped the Peacemaker inside the waistband of his jeans when he dressed that morning, after Eden had changed the bandages on his leg, and he wore his shirt out so it draped over the gun butt.

Even so, it didn't take Eden long to notice, just as he suspected would happen. She caught a glimpse of the gun as he stumped out into the store's main room on the crutches.

"What in the world is that?" she demanded.

"What?" asked Bill.

She waved in the general direction of his waist. "That!"

Bill put a smile on his face. "And here I thought you were this unshockable gal who'd seen all there was to see."

"I don't mean—" She broke off with an exasperated glare and a shake of her head. "You know good and well what I mean, Bill Harvey. I'm talking about that *gun.*"

Behind the counter, Perry Monroe looked up. "Gun?" he said. "What gun?"

With a shrug, Bill surrendered. He pulled up his shirt a little so Monroe could see the Colt.

"Is that some of my merchandise?" Monroe went along the counter and stepped behind the glass-topped cabinet. "By God, it is! I must say, I didn't expect you to steal from me, Harvey, after everything we've done for you."

"I'm not stealing the gun," Bill insisted. "I'll see that you're paid for it, once Hob gets back here with my wages. I took a box of ammunition, too."

"But why?" Eden wanted to know.

Monroe frowned suddenly, pursed his lips, and gave a tiny shake of his head as if he didn't want Bill to answer that question. He must have figured out that Bill had helped himself to the Colt *after* Zach Norris's visit to the store the previous evening.

Eden was looking at him with fierce determination, and Bill knew she wouldn't let it go until he answered her. So he said, "You know what happened yesterday. You can still see the bruises on your pa's face, Eden. Those bullwhackers might not have been so quick to start trouble if I'd been armed."

"Somebody might've been killed, that's what you mean," she snapped. "It might have even been you. Haven't enough people died in Redemption lately?"

"I don't know anything about that," said Bill. "I just know that where I come from, a man stands up for himself and for his friends."

"This isn't Texas. That's what we have the law for."

Bill wanted to tell her the law only went so far . . . and sometimes the law was even part of the problem, as it was with Zach Norris.

But she wouldn't understand that. She would think he was just some wild Texan, some unreconstructed Johnny Reb.

"Anyway, you're no gunslinger," she went on. "You told me that yourself."

"Neither were those freighters. I'm not sure they were even packing iron. They just had those bullwhips."

"Which would have been enough to cut you to ribbons if they'd gone after you with them." Eden shook her head stubbornly. "No, Bill, I'm going to have to insist that you give my father that gun. I don't want you carrying it in this store."

"Wait just a minute." The sharply voiced words came from behind the counter. Monroe went on, "I reckon I've got something to say about this. If Harvey wants to carry a gun, it's all right with me. I might even start carrying one myself."

Eden stared at her father for several seconds before saying, "That's crazy. You're no more a gunman than he is."

"You don't know everything there is to know about me, girl. When I was a young man back in Missouri, before the war, there were some pretty rough times in those hills. I'll bet Harvey's seen his share of troubles, too."

Bill shrugged as if to agree with the storekeeper's point.

Eden opened her mouth to say something else, but Monroe stopped her by extending his hand toward her with the palm out. "You just hold on there," he said. "I'm still your father, and this is still my store. You'd do well to remember that."

"Fine," Eden said, her voice as chilly as a blue norther raking across the plains. "But I may not be around here as much in the future if you're going to insist on carrying guns. I don't want to get caught in the middle of some shoot-out."

"That's up to you," said Monroe. "I always said you didn't have to work here any more than you wanted to."

Bill didn't like the sound of it, though. He had gotten used to Eden being around, and he knew if he went even a day without seeing her, he would really miss her.

Then he asked himself what had happened to the footloose, reckless daredevil of a young cowboy he had been until that night on the trail he had run afoul of the brindle steer. Maybe he was becoming entirely too dependent on Miss Eden Monroe.

So he didn't try to stop her or even say anything as she turned and walked out of the mercantile with her back stiffened in anger.

Monroe shook his head as he watched her go. "She'll come around once she cools off, I reckon," he said.

"You've known her a lot longer than I have," said Bill. "Ever known her to quit being stubborn?"

For the first time, something he'd said drew a chuckle from the old man. "Well, come to think of it, not often," Monroe admitted. He grew serious as he went on, "That trouble with those bullwhackers isn't the real reason you're carrying that gun, is it, Harvey? Leastways, not the only reason."

Bill shrugged. "I just thought it might be a good idea."

"If you're thinkin' about Zach Norris, you'd better get that idea out of your head right now. He's snake-quick, boy." Monroe paused. "Anyway, he was just seeing if he could get his hands on a little extra coin. Now that he's made his pitch and been turned down, he probably won't try it again."

"You really think that's true?" A hunch struck Bill. "How do you know he hasn't tried the same thing with some of the other businessmen here in town? That'd help explain why nobody seems to like him."

Monroe shook his head. "You'd better hush up that sort of talk. Norris is a lawman, for God's sake."

"Been plenty of outlaws who pinned on a star at one time or another," Bill pointed out. He tapped his chest. "It's what's behind the star that matters."

"Yeah . . . and I've heard a few things, just rumors, you understand—" Monroe broke off with an abrupt shake of his head. "Look at me, standing around spreading foolish gossip when there's work to do. You better get off your feet, Harvey. Sooner you heal up, the sooner you can get out of my storeroom."

"And good riddance?"

Monroe snorted. "You said it, not me. Anyway, that trail boss of yours will be showing up any day now, and when he does it'll be just fine with me if you're ready to ride!"

*   *   *

But the days continued to pass, and there was no sign of Hob Sanders or any other members of the crew. Bill took to walking out onto the mercantile's front porch and lowering himself onto a bench there, so he could watch the street and see Hob riding into Redemption to reclaim him like a stray calf that had wandered off from the herd.

By the time another week had passed, the stitches had been removed and the wound on Bill's leg had scarred over. Eden declared that he could put more weight on the leg, although it would still be weak. Bill discarded the crutches and started using a cane that also came from the store. He still hobbled around, not light on his feet yet by any means, but it was a big relief getting off the crutches. He could wear regular jeans again, too, since his leg wasn't covered with bandages anymore.

Eden was still acting cool toward him. During that week she took care of his bad leg as well as she ever had, but they didn't talk as much as they did before, and they didn't joke back and forth with each other, either.

It was almost enough to make him quit carrying the gun. Anyway, he wasn't sure he actually needed the weapon. Zach Norris had been around the store some, but he hadn't said anything else about collecting some extra money "for Marshal Porter." Bill knew he hadn't imagined the vaguely threatening tone of the deputy's words that night, but maybe Norris had decided it wasn't worth the trouble.

Bill was sitting on the porch with the cane across his lap on a hot afternoon when the marshal came along the street and climbed the steps to the porch, which did double duty as the mercantile's loading dock. He thumbed back his hat and gave Bill a friendly nod.

"It's starting to look like that trail boss of yours forgot about you, Tex," he said.

As proud as he was of being a Texan, Bill didn't like being called Tex. Norris had picked up the habit, too, and both lawmen managed to invest the word with a certain note of scorn.

"Hob will be back to get me," Bill insisted. "He's just been delayed, that's all."

"Shouldn't have taken much more than a week to get that herd to Dodge, sell it, and get back here," said Porter. "It's been two weeks. A day or two more'n that, actually."

"Like I said, he's been delayed."

Porter took a pipe from his pocket and began toying with it. "Tell you what," he said. "You've been livin' off the Monroes' charity for a while now—"

"I'll see to it they get paid back." Bill's voice was hard and angry.

Porter grinned. "Don't get proddy with me, Tex. I know that's your nature, you boys who come from down there, but hear me out."

Bill didn't say anything, and after a moment, Porter continued.

"I was thinking that I could stake you. I'll take care of what you owe Perry Monroe, and I'll loan you enough money you can get yourself a horse. Your saddle's still down at Hartnett's."

"What'll I do with a horse?"

"Why, ride it back to Texas, of course," said Porter. "Don't you want to go home, son?"

There was a part of him that did, of course. But to be honest, he didn't have much waiting for him in Texas. Certainly nothing like Eden, who, even though she was peeved at him, was still the prettiest, nicest girl he had ever met.

"If I was to take off down there on my own, then sure enough Hob would show up a day or two later, lookin' for me."

Porter shrugged. "So? I'd tell him you already headed south. It probably wouldn't take him long to catch up to you."

That was true enough, Bill supposed. But he had another objection.

"If I did that, then I'd just wind up owing you instead of the Monroes."

"Yeah, but I wouldn't be in any hurry for the money. You could just send it to me here in Redemption whenever you got a chance."

"What if you weren't still here? I've heard that lawmen move around a lot."

Porter put the unlit pipe in his mouth, clamped his teeth on the stem, and said around it, "I'll be here, you can count on that. My days as a drifting badge are over. I'm in Redemption to stay."

A harsh note in the lawman's voice made Bill glance up at him. In a more normal tone, Porter added, "Well, you think about it, Tex. The offer's good anytime if you want to take me up on it."

He gave Bill a nod and walked off, going lightly down the steps and crossing the broad, dusty street in the general direction of the marshal's office and jail. Bill could see the squat stone building a couple of blocks away, on the other side of the street.

Perry Monroe came out onto the porch. "Saw you talking to the marshal," he said. "What did he want?"

"Oh, he was just passing the time of day," said Bill.

But he had a feeling that wasn't true. It was only a hunch. Maybe Porter's offer had been genuine and he was just trying to be helpful.

Something inside Bill told him that wasn't the case.

For some reason of his own, Marshal Frank Porter wanted him out of Redemption.

Chapter 10

With no way of knowing when or—although he didn't want to admit it—if Hob Sanders would return to Redemption, Bill decided he couldn't continue living on charity. He had to earn some money so he could start paying back Perry Monroe.

That wasn't going to be easy. He could get around pretty well, despite the weakness in his left leg that caused him to limp, but other than being a cowboy, he didn't really know how to do any kind of job. He would have to be taught. But he was smart enough to pick up on almost anything, he told himself, if somebody would just give him a chance.

Nobody seemed inclined to do that. People in Redemption remembered how much trouble Texans had caused in the past and they seemed to hold that against him, even though he hadn't had anything to do with that.

That wasn't the only reason finding work was difficult, though.

Since he'd been around horses all his life, Bill's first stop was the livery stable. Josiah Hartnett was running the place mostly by himself since the still-unsolved murder of his partner, Abner Williams, a couple of weeks earlier. Bill thought that would be his best chance of getting work. He could spend the nights in the tack room to take care of late-arriving customers, the way Williams had.

But Hartnett, a burly, red-faced man with gray hair and beard, shook his head immediately when Bill introduced himself and broached the subject of a job.

"I'm not hirin'," said Hartnett as he forked some hay into one of the stalls. "Sorry."

"I wouldn't ask for much in the way of wages," Bill said. "You probably know I've been staying with the Monroes, and I'd like to start paying them back for being so generous."

"Yeah, I know. Eden Monroe took you in like you were a stray dog." Hartnett's voice made it clear he considered Bill to be on about the same social level as a stray dog, too. "But that's her business and not mine. I'm not hirin'."

"I just thought you might need somebody to stay here nights, since Mr. Williams passed away."

Hartnett's hands tightened on the pitchfork he held. He turned toward Bill with an angry look on his face. Bill eyed the sharp tines of the fork warily.

"What do you know about what happened to Abner?"

The harsh question took Bill by surprise. "Why, no more than anybody else around here, I reckon. I just know what I heard about it. Somebody shot him in the back one night."

Hartnett jerked his head toward the office. "That's right. That's where I found him, right in there. Him and me was good friends. Worst moment of my life when I saw him lyin' there with that bloody hole in his back."

"Yes, sir, I expect it was."

Hartnett lowered the pitchfork. Bill was glad. For a second there he'd thought the liveryman was going to jab him with it.

"Anyway, I'm not hirin' anybody," Hartnett went on in a leaden voice. "I got an old hostler who helps me out sometimes, and that's enough. It's hard makin' ends meet these days, you know."

Bill didn't really understand that. Most of the stalls in the barn were occupied, and there were other horses in the corral he could see through the open rear doors. Hartnett ought to be making decent money, especially since he didn't have to split the profits with a partner anymore.

That thought made Bill's forehead crease in a frown. He wondered if Marshal Porter or anybody else had considered the fact that Hartnett stood to gain from Williams's death.

But that was a loco idea, he told himself. Hartnett seemed genuinely upset by what had happened to Williams, and besides, he was a family man, Bill recalled. He had been at home when Williams was shot and doubtless his wife and kids could prove that.

"Well, if you change your mind about the job, I'd appreciate it if you'd let me know," Bill said.

Hartnett grunted. "I won't."

Bill limped out of the stable. His next stop was the blacksmith shop, but the smith was just as adamant as Hartnett about not hiring anybody.

And like Hartnett, he claimed he couldn't afford to take on any more help, despite the fact that he seemed to be backed up with his work.

It was the same story everywhere else in Redemption. He visited every store and business except the ladies' millinery shop . . . and he was tempted to stop there just to see if he could make it unanimous. Several merchants made thinly veiled comments about him being a Texan, but that wasn't all of it. Without exception, they all claimed they couldn't afford to hire more help than what they already had.

That didn't make any sense, thought Bill as he made his way back to the Monroe mercantile. From the looks of it, Redemption was a thriving town. Yet, to hear the citizens tell it, everybody was struggling to get by.

Eden was behind the counter in the store. "Where have you been?" she asked as Bill came in.

"Looking for a job," he told her. "I'm tired of bein' a charity case."

"It's barely been two weeks since you suffered a major injury. You're in no shape to be working."

Bill shrugged. "I heal fast. Comes from spending most of my time working outside, I expect."

"You do seem to have something of an iron constitution," said Eden. "But there's still no need for you to worry about getting a job." She made a point of not looking at him. "After all, you'll be leaving soon, won't you?"

"I'm starting to wonder about that."

"Oh?"

"Yeah, it looks like Hob's not coming back to get me. Something must've happened to him."

It occurred to him that he ought to head for Dodge City himself and try to find out why Hob and the rest of the crew hadn't returned to Redemption after selling the herd. A cold lump of fear suddenly formed in Bill's belly. Maybe those rustlers had jumped them again, only this time the raiders had succeeded in wiping out the crew and stealing the herd.

He might have to take Marshal Porter up on that offer of a grubstake, he thought, but instead of heading south toward Texas, he would ride north to Dodge City.

Not yet, though. He was better, but he wasn't up to a long horseback ride this soon. Give it another week, he decided. If Hob hadn't shown up by then, Bill would head north.

Until then, the least he could do was help out a little around here. He went behind the counter and grabbed a broom leaning in the corner.

"What do you think you're doing?" asked Eden.

"The place could use being swept out," Bill replied, "and so could the porch. Thought I'd give you a hand and take care of the chore."

"You mean you want to work *here*?"

"Not for wages. So, I can't start paying back what I already owe. But at least I can work for my room and board the rest of the time I'm here."

"That's not necessary."

Bill placed his cane on the counter and gripped the broom instead. "I know it's not. It's just something I want to do."

Eden gave an exasperated sigh as he started sweeping, but she didn't try to talk him out of it anymore.

Monroe came in a few minutes later from some errand and frowned in surprise when he saw Bill sweeping. He didn't say anything, though, just went behind the counter, hung up his hat, and put on his apron. He told Eden, "You can go start supper now. I'll watch the store."

The mercantile wasn't busy. When Bill finished sweeping, he put the broom up and asked Monroe, "Any other chores need doing around here?"

"Did I hire you and forget that I'd done it?" asked Monroe.

Bill smiled. "No, sir, just consider me a volunteer. I like to earn my keep, so I thought I'd start helping out as long as I'm here." He shook his head ruefully. "I tried to get a real job so I could earn some wages and start paying you back, but it seems nobody's hiring in Redemption these days."

"I'm not surprised. Nobody can afford to hire extra help."

"That's what they kept tellin' me. It's surprising, too, because from the looks of it, most of the businesses here in town are pretty successful."

"Things aren't always what they appear to be," said Monroe.

"Yeah, I'm starting to figure that out. Redemption looks like a friendly little town, but everybody acts a little spooky, like a trail herd that's bedded down for the night when there are thunderstorms around. It doesn't take much to set 'em off." Bill shrugged. "I guess it's because of those killings."

"Wouldn't it spook you, knowing there was a backshooter around?"

"It would," Bill admitted. "It does. I hadn't really thought about it until now, but there's been a shooting about every two weeks, hasn't there?"

"And it's been two weeks since Abner Williams was killed." Monroe tugged worriedly at his beard. "Yeah, that's been on my mind."

"Maybe there won't be any more. Maybe that was the last one."

"Yeah. Maybe."

Monroe didn't sound convinced, though.

A couple of customers came in, then a couple more. Since the store had gotten a little busy, Bill decided to go ahead and ask one of the men if he could help him.

"You work here now?" the man asked.

"Just sort of part-time," Bill explained. "Something I can get for you?"

"Well, yeah. I came in for a box of .44-40s."

Bill got the cartridges from the shelf and set the box in front of the customer. "How much for a box of .44-40s, Mr. Monroe?"

"Two dollars," Monroe replied without looking around from the bag of beans he was weighing.

"That'll be two dollars," Bill told the customer, even though the man must have heard Monroe's answer as plainly as he did.

The man slid a pair of silver dollars across the counter, picked up the box of cartridges, and left. Bill put the coins in the cash drawer, as he had seen Perry Monroe do on countless occasions.

That was his first sale as a mercantile clerk. It wasn't too bad, he told himself. Of course, he would go plumb loco if he had do things like that all day, every day, for years and years to come. It was fine for some people—Monroe seemed to like running the store and dealing with the customers—but Bill wasn't made that way.

He carried a bolt of cloth to the counter for a lady, tucking it under his left arm since he used the cane with his right hand. He would have thought the cane would go on the same side as his bad leg, but he'd discovered through trial and error that it actually worked better the other way by taking some of the weight off his bad leg as he walked.

When he was through with that, he sold a bag of sugar to another customer and helped yet another pick out a shovel from the ones Monroe had hanging from hooks on one wall. Bill stayed busy enough that the time went by faster than he thought it would.

By supper time, though, business had slacked off, and the store was soon empty again except for Bill and Monroe. The storekeeper said, "Eden ought to be back pretty soon with a tray of food for you." He ran his fingers through his beard and frowned in thought. "You know, it doesn't really make sense for her to have to fix a tray for you and carry it over here every evening. Now that you can get around better, you could just walk over to the house with me after I close up and eat there."

"Join you folks for supper, you mean?" The invitation took Bill by surprise. He still got the feeling Monroe didn't like him all that much. Likely the man would always feel some resentment toward him because he was a Texan. But Monroe wasn't being downright hostile anymore, either. Bill smiled and said, "Sure, I'd like that."

"We'll start tomorrow, then. Might as well come over for breakfast in the morning, too. I'll tell Eden to expect you."

"All right. I'm much obliged."

"You've been on your feet a lot today. Look a mite tired. Why don't you go sit down? When Eden gets here with the food, I'll tell her you're in the storeroom."

"My leg does ache a little. It'll feel good to get off of it for a while."

Bill went to the storeroom and sat down on the cot. He kept a handful of lucifers on the crate next to the lamp and used one of them to light it. A book lay there, too, with a marker in it. Eden had found it for him. It was called *Ivanhoe* and was about knights and such in England, and while it was slow going in places, there were a lot of sword fights, too, and Bill liked those parts. He pulled the Peacemaker from the waistband of his jeans, set the gun on the makeshift table next to the lamp, then picked up the book to read a little while he waited for Eden to get there with his supper.

After a few minutes he heard somebody come into the store and lifted his head, thinking the newcomer was Eden. But then he heard a man's voice talking to Monroe and figured it was just a late customer. Bill went back to his book.

He looked up again when he heard Monroe say angrily, "I won't do it. I can't do it. You're asking too much!"

The other man's voice was low enough Bill couldn't

make out the words, but it had a menacing edge to it that came through loud and clear. Bill set the book aside and stood up, grasping his cane and using it to help him make his way to the partially open door of the storeroom. Whoever was out there couldn't see him, but now he could hear the man clearly enough to identify him.

"You better think long and hard about what you're doin'," said Zach Norris. "You know how much good law enforcement is worth."

"I know how much so-called law enforcement costs," snapped Monroe. "I'm not sure it's the same thing."

"Well now, that's just a downright rude thing to say. You know how many times I've risked my life for you, old man? You got money in the bank, don't you? You might've lost every penny of it if I hadn't shot it out with those robbers. And what about those trail herds? They'd have pounded this town into the dust if the marshal and me hadn't stopped 'em."

"I know. Everybody knows. And we're grateful to you. That's why we've gone along with these . . . these extra levies of yours, even though it's not right. You get your wages from the town, Norris. We shouldn't have to pay you protection money on top of it!"

Norris's voice was angry as he said, "You're actin' like there's something wrong with payin' your peace officers what they're worth. I'm startin' to feel insulted, Monroe. You're a damned fool, old man, if you don't know a good thing when you see it."

"I can't give you any more," said Monroe. "I gave you what we agreed on. That's all."

Bill's heart pounded as he stood there just inside the storeroom, leaning on his cane. Norris must have thought the place was empty except for Monroe, so he had spoken plainly. And what Bill had just overheard went a long way toward explaining a lot of the tension and uneasiness he had witnessed in Redemption. The deputy was forcing the settlement's business owners to pay him extra so he would "protect" them . . . but the real danger he'd be protecting them from was him.

As far as Bill was concerned, that made Norris an outlaw, tin star or no tin star.

Now, from the sound of it, Norris had upped his demand to Perry Monroe. Bill wondered suddenly if the same thing had happened to Abner Williams, and to John Lightner, Walter Tompkins, and the baker named Hendrickson before him.

He wondered where Zach Norris was on the nights those men had been murdered.

"Is that your final word on it?" Norris was saying now. "You sure you know what you're doin', Monroe?"

"I've given you all I can afford to give you. I'm sorry."

"You're fixin' to be a whole lot sorrier, old man."

Monroe cried, "No!" and Bill heard a rush of footsteps as he shoved the door all the way open. He went through it as fast as he could on his bad leg and got out there in time to see that Norris had gone around behind the counter. The deputy had hold of Monroe's apron with his left hand, and a gun was in his right.

He wasn't about to shoot the storekeeper, though. Instead Norris had raised the heavy revolver and held it poised, ready to strike. He was going to pistol-whip Monroe.

Unless Bill stopped him.

Chapter 11

Bill was on the verge of yelling at Norris and charging him, although he knew a cane was a mighty poor match against a gun. An already-drawn gun, at that.

But before he could move, a scream came from the front of the store, accompanied by a crash and clatter of dishes. Bill looked in that direction and saw Eden standing just inside the door with a horrified look on her face and the scattered debris of his supper at her feet where she had dropped the tray.

Norris's head jerked toward the scream, but his gaze stopped on Bill along the way. His face contorted in a snarl, and he said, "Get out of here, Tex, and take the girl with you."

"Leave him alone," Eden pleaded. "Let my father go."

"Get out, I said, or the old man'll get hurt a lot worse!"

Bill took a step toward the counter. He lifted the cane and held it in front of him in both hands, ready to strike out with it.

Instantly, Norris swung the gun toward him. "Keep comin', cowboy, and you're a dead man," he said.

"Bill, no!" cried Eden. "He'll kill you."

A harsh laugh came from Norris. "Damn right I will."

"Let go of Mr. Monroe," Bill said. "Let go of him, or I'll fetch the marshal."

"No, don't do that!" said Monroe. His voice was choked with fear. "Harvey, you take Eden, and both of you clear out of here."

"Dad, no!" Eden said, and at the same time Bill said, "Sorry, Mr. Monroe, I can't do that."

"Damn it, this is still my store! I'm in charge here, and I say the two of you should get out! I got . . . business to discuss with . . . with Deputy Norris here."

A grin spread across Norris's face, pulling on the scar. "Is that so? We're talkin' business now, are we, Monroe?"

The storekeeper swallowed. "We are."

Norris lowered the gun a little and let go of Monroe's apron. Monroe took a shaky step back and straightened the apron and his shirt.

Bill began, "Mr. Monroe, I heard—"

"I don't care what you heard," the older man cut in. "What goes on in this store is my business, not yours or anybody else's. Both of you go on now, and close the door behind you on your way out."

"Now you're talkin' sense," said Norris. He smirked at Bill. "You heard the man, Tex. You ain't wanted here. Run along, and take Miss Monroe with you."

Eden's chin lifted defiantly. "I won't go."

"Yes, you will," her father said. "Harvey, I'm asking you, as one man to another . . . get my daughter out of here."

Bill understood then. Monroe didn't know what was going to happen here, but whatever it was, he didn't want Eden to see it.

Bill knew, as well, that if he tried to interfere with the deputy, Norris would shoot him. It would be different if he had a gun, too, instead of just the cane. He had left the revolver in the storeroom when he had hurried out here. He couldn't stop Norris with a cane.

And he probably couldn't stop him with a Colt, either, Bill realized, but at least it would be closer to a fair fight. Attacking Norris now would be suicide.

Knowing that didn't keep Bill's mouth from filling with a bitter, sour taste as he slowly lowered the cane and said, "I reckon we'd better get out of here, Eden."

Her eyes widened in surprise as she looked at him. "No! Bill, how can you say that?"

"Your pa's the boss, and he told us to leave."

"That's right." Monroe summoned up a shaky smile. "It'll be all right, honey. You take Bill on home and give him some supper to replace what you dropped. I'll be along directly. It won't take long for Deputy Norris and I to finish our business, will it, Deputy?"

"Not long at all, now that you're bein' reasonable," drawled Norris.

The tightly wound tension inside Bill eased just slightly. Norris was more interested in money than anything else, and now that Monroe was talking like he would go along with the increased payoff, Norris might be willing to forego the violence he'd been about to commit.

That was the chance Bill would be taking, anyway, if he left with Eden.

But if they stayed, there was no telling what Norris might do. Thinking about that, Bill began edging along the aisle toward Eden. Keeping her safe was his main concern right now.

Obviously she didn't feel the same way. "I won't go," she warned Bill as he approached. "I'll start screaming, so everybody in town will hear."

Norris shook his head. "Oh, you don't want to do that, Miss Monroe," he said. "I can sure tell you, you don't want to do that."

It would be easy enough for Norris to kill all three of them, thought Bill. He could gun them down, duck out the back of the store, and circle around to pretend he had just heard the shots and was coming to investigate. Nobody would know any different, and even if they did, probably they would be too scared to say anything.

"Don't you raise a ruckus," said Monroe in a voice that trembled slightly. "Please, Eden. I'll be fine. Just go on home."

Bill reached her side, stepping around the dropped food to take hold of her arm. At first he thought she was going to jerk away from him, but then a dull sheen of defeat came over her eyes, and she didn't struggle.

"All right," she said. "If that's what you want."

"It is," declared Monroe. "Don't worry."

"Yeah, you got nothin' to worry about, Miss Monroe," Norris said smugly. "Your pa will be fine. After all, the law's here to keep him safe, right?"

Eden looked mad enough to explode, as well as being scared. She allowed Bill to steer her out the door, although she went grudgingly.

Once they were on the porch, he looked up and down the street. At this hour, there weren't many people around. Most folks were at home having supper. A few of the businesses were still open, and of course the saloon down the street still had customers.

"You head for home," he told Eden. "I'll see if I can find the marshal."

It was Eden's turn to clutch his arm. "No," she said. "That won't help."

"Why not?" asked Bill.

She shook her head. "Just trust me, it won't." She looked fearfully at the closed door and went on, "There's nothing we can do now except hope that my father will be all right."

"Well, I can do more than that, now that you're out of harm's way. I'll get a gun somewhere—"

Eden's fingers tightened on his arm until her grip was almost painful. "No," she said in a soft but intense voice. "No. Norris would kill you, Bill, and I . . . I don't want that."

She was afraid for him, just like he had been afraid for her. Bill couldn't help but think that meant something, but this was one hell of a way to find out for sure she cared about him.

There hadn't been any shots from inside, or any more loud voices, for that matter. "Come on," Bill said to Eden. "We'll go to your house, like your father told us, and then I'll come back here to make sure he's all right."

"You won't try to fight Norris?" When Bill hesitated in answering, she said, "You have to give me your word."

He nodded. "All right. I won't try to fight Norris."

"Then I'll go."

They went down the steps at the end of the porch and started along the regular boardwalk in front of several darkened businesses. With each step, the ball of self-disgust in Bill's stomach grew. He couldn't believe he had left Perry Monroe back there to face the trouble with Norris alone. It wasn't in Bill's nature to run away from a fight, and he sure as hell wasn't in the habit of abandoning his friends. That was the way he thought of Monroe, whether the storekeeper returned the feeling or not.

As they walked, with Eden holding back a little to accommodate Bill's limping pace, Bill said, "You didn't want me to go find the marshal because you think Porter knows what Norris is doing."

"How could he not know? Norris is his deputy."

"And you've known all along that Norris is collecting bribes from the business owners in town."

"I've heard rumors." There was a bitter edge to Eden's voice. "We've all heard rumors. But everybody is scared to come right out and talk about it. My father wouldn't even tell me what was going on. I had to find out by going through his books and seeing that he's not clearing as much profit as he ought to be. I asked him to tell me where the money was going. At first he wouldn't do it, but finally he admitted he's been paying off Norris to leave him alone."

Bill asked the question that had been dogging his brain. "What about those men who were killed?"

"Again, it's just rumors, but . . . there was talk that they tried to stand up to Norris. I heard that Abner Williams even threatened him with a pitchfork."

"I'll bet everybody went along with whatever Norris wanted for a while after each of those murders," muttered Bill.

"Well, of course they did. Can you blame them?" The two of them turned a corner. Bill let Eden lead the way, since she knew where she was going. She asked, "What was going on in there tonight? Why was Norris there?"

"To ask for more money." Quickly, Bill told her everything he had overheard from the storeroom.

She said, "When I came in and saw . . . saw Norris threatening my father, I knew it had to be something like that. He's getting greedier and greedier. He's going to bleed the whole town dry before he's through."

"Folks have got to stand up to varmints like that," said Bill. "If the whole town told Norris to go to hell, he couldn't do a thing about it."

"Except start killing people. You don't know how fast and deadly with a gun he is, or how utterly ruthless. That's why I can't let you fight him. He'd kill you. I don't doubt it for a second."

Neither did Bill, but the feeling that he should have fought back anyway still gnawed at him.

Hob wouldn't have walked off and left him with Norris, the way he had walked off and left Perry Monroe. If Norris killed the old man, Bill was going to have to live with that guilt for the rest of his days, and that would be the end of any hope he might have of making a life with Eden. Love couldn't exist side by side with such guilt. She would come to hate him, just as he would hate himself.

"Here's the house," said Eden, motioning toward the neat, whitewashed structure. It was bigger than a cottage but wasn't exactly imposing. Just the sort of place where a moderately successful businessman in a small Kansas town would live with his daughter.

"All right, go on inside," Bill told her. "I'll be back in a little bit."

"You gave me your word you won't try to fight with Norris," Eden reminded him.

"Yeah, I know." That didn't mean he was going to keep the promise, thought Bill. Eden might be angry with him for breaking his word, but he might just have to live with that.

Or die with it.

The place even had a picket fence around the front yard.

Eden opened the gate but didn't go in. She stood there watching Bill as he turned and limped back toward Main Street. He could feel her eyes on him.

His leg ached, not too bad but more than enough to remind him that he'd been badly injured and had been laid up for a while. He had been on his feet quite a bit today, too, first looking unsuccessfully for work and then helping out in the mercantile as much as he could. His gait was slow and awkward.

A humorless grin tugged at his mouth. Sure, he was in fine shape to be taking on a gunfighting deputy who was probably also a cold-blooded, back-shooting murderer. But there was only one way to stop the bile filling his throat, and that was to face up to the challenge awaiting him.

When he turned the corner onto the boardwalk fronting Main Street, though, he saw a familiar figure coming toward him. Perry Monroe had put on his hat and coat, as he always did when he closed up the store and headed home. When Bill saw the storekeeper, he knew Monroe must have given in to Norris's demands and paid the extra money to the crooked deputy. That was the smart thing to do, Bill supposed, and although he hated to admit it even to himself, he was relieved that he didn't have to face off with Norris and try to avenge the old man.

But what would Norris do next time? How much money would he demand when he came around again, as he inevitably would?

Bill couldn't answer those questions, but for tonight, at least, violence had been averted. Another killing had been prevented.

His cane thumped against the planks as he hurried ahead to meet Monroe. He said, "Mr. Monroe, it's me, Bill Harvey. Are you all right?"

As if to answer the question, Monroe suddenly stumbled, let out a groan of pain, and pitched forward.

Chapter 12

Bill was close enough to reach out and grab Monroe's arm as the storekeeper fell. Monroe's weight sagged against him and threatened to knock him off his feet. Bill's grip on the cane tightened as he braced himself. Monroe looked at him, and in the dim light filtering down the street from the windows of businesses that were still open, he saw dark blotches on Monroe's face that had to be blood. Streaks of the stuff ran down into Monroe's white beard.

"Norris," Monroe gasped. "He . . . he . . ."

"How bad are you hurt?" asked Bill. "Are you wounded? Did he shoot you?"

Bill hadn't heard a shot, but maybe Norris had muffled the report somehow.

Monroe shook his head. "Not . . . shot," he managed to get out. "Just . . . beat up . . . Said he was gonna . . . teach me a lesson . . ."

Monroe seemed to be a little steadier on his feet now. Bill shifted his grip so he had an arm around the older man's waist and said, "Let's get you home where Eden can take care of you."

"No!" protested Monroe. "Don't want her . . . to see me . . . like this."

"I understand, but somebody needs to clean you up and make sure how bad you're hurt. She's the best one to do that."

Monroe didn't argue. He stumbled along beside Bill with the Texan supporting him and making sure he didn't fall.

They made a fine pair, thought Bill. A half cripple and a beat-up old man. He hoped they wouldn't run into any more trouble along the way, because they sure weren't in any shape to handle it.

Nothing happened as they slowly made their way to the Monroe house. Light showed in the windows, so Bill knew Eden had gone inside and lit the lamps. She must have pulled a curtain back and been watching for them, because as they reached the fence gate, she came out of the house and rushed toward them.

"Dad!" she cried. "Oh, Dad, what happened?"

"Norris," Monroe said. "Our deputy marshal."

"Let's get him in the house and get him cleaned up," suggested Bill. "Then he can tell us about it."

Eden got on one side of her father and Bill on the other. Together, they helped Monroe onto the porch and into the house. In the lamplight, his face looked even worse. The bruises from the run-in with the bullwhacker Blaisdell had faded, but now he had new ones, plus a gash on his forehead and one on his cheek that had leaked blood down his face and into his beard.

Bill and Eden lowered Monroe into an armchair in the parlor. Eden said, "I've got some hot water on the stove. I'll go get it and a cloth. Can you watch him, Bill?"

"Sure." Bill nodded as he straightened.

"No need to watch me," muttered Monroe. "I'm not going anywhere."

Eden hustled off to the kitchen. When she was gone, Bill lowered his voice and asked, "Norris pistol-whipped you anyway, didn't he?"

"Yeah. He hit me twice. Said I'd know better than to argue next time he came to see me."

"He hit you even though you gave him the extra money?"

"If I hadn't done that, he wouldn't have stopped with hitting me twice. He would have killed me."

Bill didn't doubt it. He had seen the look in Norris's eyes. The deputy had been primed to kill. He might have even been disappointed it hadn't come to that.

Eden's footsteps returning to the parlor made both men fall silent. She bustled into the room carrying a basin of water with steam rising from it. A clean cloth was draped over her arm. She knelt beside Monroe's chair, set the basin on the floor, and dipped the cloth in the water. Bill stepped back to give her some room. Monroe winced as Eden began to dab at the cut on his forehead.

"Norris hit you with his gun, didn't he?" she asked.

"Yeah. The sight tore those gashes in my head."

"That son of a bitch."

Monroe frowned. "Here, now. There's no call for you to use such language."

"I'm not a little girl," she snapped. "Anyway, where do you think I learned that language? You raised me."

Even under the circumstances, that brought a wry chuckle from Perry Monroe. "True enough," he said. "I sure did."

"And you can't deny that the description is an apt one."

"Yeah, that's true, too."

Eden cleaned the blood away from the wounds and frowned at the one on her father's forehead. "That's bad enough it ought to be stitched up by a real doctor."

"There's not one closer than Dodge City." Monroe glanced at Bill, who stood to the side watching. "If there was, Harvey wouldn't be here."

Eden ignored that comment and said, "I'll bandage it and sew it up so it'll heal, but you know my stitching isn't the neatest. You'll have a bigger scar than you would have if it was tended to properly."

Monroe waved a hand. "Just do your best, girl. It'll be fine. I'm too old and grizzled to care about anything like a scar."

Since Monroe was steadier and seemed to have his wits

about him now, Bill decided it wouldn't hurt anything to discuss the situation. He said, "Does anybody know whether Marshal Porter is part of this, or is it possible Norris might be doing it on his own?"

"Porter's never said anything to me about it. He always acts like he's completely honest. And he's been a good lawman as far as keeping order in the town and stopping those cattle drives from ruining us."

"But you remember what Mr. Hendrickson said," Eden reminded him as she got out the needle and thread she had used on Bill. "He told several people he was going to complain to the marshal if Norris didn't leave him alone."

"Hendrickson is one of the men who was killed, right?" asked Bill.

Eden dropped the bloodstained cloth in the basin. "That's right. He owned the bakery. He . . . he was the first one shot in the back."

"And you think Porter did it?"

Monroe shook his head. "There's no way of knowing. I don't reckon it'd be a good idea to walk up to Marshal Porter and ask him if he's a no-good backshooter. If he's not, he'd be mighty insulted. And if he is . . ."

Monroe didn't have to finish that statement. Bill and Eden both knew what he was getting at.

"Norris could be doing this on his own," Eden went on, "but I don't believe it. I think it's both of them."

"So do I," her father agreed.

"What are we going to do about it?"

They looked at Bill in surprise. "What *can* we do about it?" asked Monroe wincing as Eden started stitching up the cut.

"Bill seems to think the citizens should stand up to Porter and Norris," said Eden.

Monroe started to shake his head again but stopped as Eden tugged the thread snug. "That'd be a good way to get dead in a hurry, just like those other fellas."

"Not if everybody acted together," Bill insisted. "Get your guns and march down to the marshal's office. Confront

Porter with what Norris has been doing and see how he reacts. If he backs Norris, you'll know he's been crooked all along. If he's innocent, he'll arrest Norris, or at least run him out of town."

Monroe tugged at his bloodstained beard, keeping his head still this time as Eden put a knot in the final stitch. "It's all well and good to talk about doing that, but folks'd be risking their lives if they really tried it."

"People risk their lives doing what's right all the time."

"Not in Redemption. We're peaceful folks here. Why do you think we hired Porter and Norris in the first place?"

"To do your fighting for you," said Bill, trying to keep the disgust out of his voice. He had no room for feeling superior to anybody, he told himself. Not after what had happened earlier tonight. Not after he had abandoned Monroe to whatever fate Norris had in mind for him. The fact that that hadn't turned out to be fatal didn't really change anything, nor did the argument that Bill had just been trying to make sure Eden was safe.

He had turned tail and run. No two ways about it. He was a coward.

And from the sound of what Monroe was saying, so was everybody else in Redemption.

"You're right, that's why we hired them. If we'd had the gumption to stand up to you Texans ourselves, maybe we wouldn't be in this fix. But we didn't, and so here we are." Monroe sighed. "I reckon we'll just have to keep on figuring out ways to pay off Norris and still get by."

"Couldn't you at least send for the county sheriff?"

"Porter's got a good reputation as a lawman. Who do you think a fellow badge toter would believe, us or him?"

Monroe seemed to have an answer for everything. That was because it was easier to give up than to fight.

"All right," Bill said. "This is your business, not mine."

Monroe nodded. "That's right."

"Anyway, as soon as Hob shows up, I'll be leaving town."

Or else I'll be going to look for him, if he doesn't show up, Bill added to himself.

Eden looked up at him. "You've made up your mind? You're leaving Redemption?"

He nodded and said, "That's right."

What he didn't tell her was that when he left town, he intended to ask her to go with him.

Chapter 13

Once Eden had finished tending to her father's injuries, she went to the kitchen to warm up what was left of their delayed supper. Monroe said to Bill, "There's no point in you walking all the way back to the store to sleep. We have a spare room. Eden can make it up for you."

"I'm much obliged," said Bill, "but I don't want to be any bother."

"No bother," Monroe told him. "I reckon you'll conduct yourself like a gentleman and not a wild cowboy?"

Bill felt a flush of irritation at the question and the way Monroe had phrased it, but he shrugged it off. "You don't have any reason to worry," he told the storekeeper. "Not about me, anyway."

"Good." Monroe sighed. "I got plenty of other worries. There are bills coming due, and paying Norris what he asked for took some of the money I had set aside for them."

Bill didn't say anything. He was done arguing about what the townspeople should do.

Supper was a somber affair. While they were eating, Monroe told Eden he had asked Bill to stay there at the house. She nodded and said, "That's a good idea. Our spare room isn't very big, but it'll be more comfortable than that storeroom, I'm sure. And the walk from here to the store every day will probably help strengthen your leg. It's healed enough that some exercise will be good for it."

Bill thought so, too. And Eden was right about the bed in the tiny spare room being more comfortable than the cot. He slept better than he had since coming to Redemption.

At least, he did until the face of Zach Norris began haunting his dreams and turned them into nightmares. He couldn't get the deputy's evil smirk out of his head and wound up staring at the darkened ceiling while his heart pounded in his chest.

Everything that had happened didn't affect Eden's talent as a cook. After an excellent breakfast the next morning, Bill and Monroe headed for the mercantile. Monroe sported fresh bandages on his head and face, along with some colorful bruises.

"Won't people be curious about what happened to you?" asked Bill.

Monroe grunted. "People in this town have learned not to be too curious about anything. It doesn't pay."

When they reached the mercantile, Bill went into the storeroom and emerged a moment later carrying the Colt Peacemaker he had left there the previous evening.

"Do you have a holster to fit this?" he asked Monroe.

The storekeeper frowned. "I'm not sure it's a good idea for you to be carrying a gun, Harvey. A man who packs iron is always tempted to use it."

"And sometimes it's a good thing he does," Bill said.

Monroe shrugged and gestured toward a bin on the left-hand side of the store. "Got some holsters and other leather goods in there," he said. "Take your pick, if you can find one that suits you."

"I'll pay you back."

"No need." Monroe gave a humorless laugh. "Making an actual profit on this place seems to be a thing of the past."

Balanced on his cane, Bill rooted through the bin full of holsters and belts. He found a plain brown gun rig that was made all together. When he buckled it on, it fit perfectly around his lean, horseman's hips, and the revolver slid easily into the holster.

"How's it feel?" asked Monroe.

Bill nodded. "Good." He drew the Colt a couple of times, not trying to be fast about it or anything like that, just smooth and easy.

"You use the cane with your right hand," Monroe commented. "That's your gun hand."

"Yeah, I know. That's why I'm gonna stop using the cane as soon as I can."

"That's going to be a while yet. Eden says you'll need it for a couple of weeks, maybe longer."

"We'll see," Bill said. He had beaten all of Eden's predictions about his health so far. Maybe this one would be the same way.

It was a busy day in the store. Bill helped out from the start this time. It didn't take him long to learn where everything was and how Monroe liked to have things done. He didn't know the customers, of course, although some of them were starting to look familiar to him. He had been around Redemption long enough now that he was beginning to recognize faces, even if he couldn't put names with them just yet.

Zach Norris didn't come in, but Marshal Frank Porter showed up at the store that afternoon, strolling along the aisle toward the counter. He stopped, frowned in surprise as he looked at Monroe, and said, "Good God, Perry, what happened to you?"

Awkwardly, Monroe touched the bandage around his head that covered the gash above his eye. "Just an accident, Marshal."

"You look like you've been pistol-whipped, man. You weren't robbed, were you?"

"No, of course not," Monroe replied with a shake of his head.

"Well, if anybody gives you trouble, you let me know. That's what I'm here for, after all, to protect you good citizens of Redemption."

Bill watched the lawman closely as Porter spoke, trying to detect any signs of either malice or sincerity. All he saw was the bland, unruffled calm with which Porter always carried himself. The marshal must have been a good poker player, because he didn't give away a blasted thing.

Porter turned toward him. His somewhat bushy eyebrows rose in surprise as he looked at the gun belt strapped around Bill's hips.

"Packing iron, Tex?" he asked. "Can't say as I'm surprised. You Texans have always been a wild bunch."

"A lot of Texas is still wild country," said Bill. "A man needs to go armed to protect himself and those he cares about."

Porter rested his hands on the counter. "You see, that's the big difference between there and here. Kansas is a civilized place. Common, everyday folks don't need to carry guns here in order to be safe. Trouble doesn't crop up all that often, and when it does, they have lawmen like me and Deputy Norris to protect them. Why don't you take that gun off and put it away? You're liable to make folks nervous, wearing it out in the open like that."

"There's no ordinance against wearing a gun in town, is there?"

Porter pursed his lips and slowly shook his head.

"Or any state law against carrying weapons?"

"Nope," said Porter.

"Well, then, I reckon I'll keep it on, Marshal. I've carried a gun for a long time. Don't really feel right without one."

"Suit yourself." Porter's voice was curt. He turned his head and gave Monroe a nod. "See you, Perry. I hope you get to feeling better."

"I'll be fine, Marshal, don't worry," Monroe said.

Porter left the store. Bill moved closer to Monroe and said quietly, "It's damned hard to figure that man out. I can't decide if he's in on the payoffs with Norris or not."

"He didn't like the idea of you wearing a gun, that's for sure," said Monroe.

Bill rubbed his chin. "Yeah, I know. And that's a mite suspicious . . ."

* * *

Several days passed uneventfully. The walking Bill was doing, plus the work in the store, made his leg ache considerably at night, but he could also tell it was getting stronger. He had hopes of discarding the cane before too much longer.

There was still quite a bit of tension in Redemption, but the citizens seemed to have relaxed slightly. Bill figured they had been expecting another murder, and when one didn't occur on the same schedule as the others, they allowed themselves to hope the killings were over. Of course, the merchants still had to deal with the fact they were being forced to pay off Zach Norris and perhaps the marshal, but they were getting used to that.

Bill was behind the counter one afternoon when he saw Eden at the front door. She had been about to come into the store, but she stopped and looked back, as if someone had called her name. Bill watched as she moved back out onto the porch, and he noticed when her back suddenly stiffened like something had happened to upset her. He moved around the counter and started toward the front of the store.

As he reached the door, Eden turned toward the building again with an angry look on her face. She was also blushing furiously. Bill looked past her and saw Zach Norris standing in the street, grinning up at the porch.

"Eden, what happened?" Bill asked her quietly.

"Nothing," she replied without looking at him. "Just go on back inside, Bill."

Norris laughed and said, "Aw, honey, I didn't mean to embarrass you. I figured you'd be flattered."

"What did he say?" Bill asked through clenched teeth.

"*Nothing,*" Eden repeated. "Please, let's just go inside."

Bill ignored the plea and stepped around her. "You better learn to show some respect when you're talking to a lady, Deputy."

"Why, I thought I was. All I said to Miss Monroe was that I'd sure like to find her waitin' for me in my bed some night. That's respectful, ain't it?"

Bill switched the cane from his right hand to his left. Eden clutched at his arm and said in a low, urgent voice, "It's all right, Bill. I don't care. Really."

"Well, I do," he said. He shrugged off her hand and moved to the edge of the porch. "You're supposed to be a lawman," he snapped at Norris, "and yet you go around threatening folks and saying shameless things to young ladies. Where I come from, a man like you wouldn't wear a badge. He'd be horsewhipped!"

Norris shifted his stance so his right hand was closer to his gun. The smirk on his face disappeared as he said, "Well, you ain't in Texas anymore, you rebel trash. Up here, nobody cares what you think. And you better have a care how *you* talk to a peace officer. I can throw you in jail for disturbin' the peace, you know." The cocky grin flashed across his face again. "Or put a bullet in you for resistin' arrest, if that's the way you want it."

"I'm not worried about you shooting me," said Bill. "My back's not to you."

Norris's face paled, making the scar stand out even more. "You son of a bitch," he said. "You want to back that big mouth of yours?"

Bill didn't answer the question directly. Instead he said, "Eden, get in the store."

She tugged at his arm. "Forget it, Bill, please. Just come on with me."

"I'll be in directly. Go on."

He didn't take his eyes off Norris as he spoke, nor did he move his hand even the slightest fraction of an inch toward the Colt on his hip. He wasn't going to give the deputy any excuse to slap leather as long as Eden was potentially in the line of fire.

Once she was out of the way, though, he figured he would draw. Norris would kill him, he didn't have much doubt about that, but all he wanted right now was to stay alive long enough to get lead in the deputy, too. He had backed down before, and he wasn't going to do it again.

But, *damn*, he was going to miss being alive. Being able to feel the warm sun on his face and wrap himself around a good meal and enjoy how it felt to stretch his muscles when he woke up in the morning. Feeling a good horse rocking along beneath him and the bite of a cold beer as it washed the dust out of his throat. Singing a hymn in church on a Sunday morning. Watching the sun go down in the evening.

Feeling Eden's body under his hands and tasting her lips for the first time.

All those things flashed through his mind in an instant, and he knew he was about to throw them away because of nothing more than his own stubborn pride.

But without his pride, those things and all the other good things in life would be just ashes and dust. A man who traded his honor for mere survival lost everything in the end, anyway.

A sob came from Eden. "Bill . . ." she said, her voice breaking.

"Go," he whispered, still not taking his eyes off Norris.

He didn't have to look around to know that this confrontation had drawn some attention. As if from far away, he heard people shouting. The prospect of somebody dying violently would always bring folks on the run. Redemption was no different from any other place in that respect.

"You sure you want to do this, Tex?" Norris goaded him.

"You've had folks around here buffaloed for too long, Norris."

The deputy was about to make some other mocking comment, but at that moment a new voice demanded, "What the hell's going on here?"

"Marshal, you've got to stop them!" Eden said. "They're going to kill each other over nothing!"

A chill went down Bill's back. He didn't know where Porter had come from, but the man was behind him now. He didn't dare look away from Norris, but an even bigger threat might be lurking at his back.

"Zach, what is this?" asked Porter, his voice sharp with anger.

Norris nodded toward Bill. "Gonna teach this mouthy Texan a lesson, Marshal."

"Like you taught Perry Monroe a lesson by pistol-whipping him?" By God, somebody was going to get that outrage out into the open, even if it had to be him, thought Bill.

Porter clucked his tongue. "That's a mighty serious accusation, Harvey," he said. "You have any proof of what you're sayin'? Did you see my deputy attack Mr. Monroe?"

"No, I wasn't there," Bill began, "but Monroe told me—"

"Perry told *me* that nothing of the sort happened," Porter cut in. "Don't you think if what you're sayin' is true, he would have made an official complaint about Deputy Norris?"

Bill knew at that moment that despite what he had hoped, Frank Porter was just as crooked as his deputy. Porter had probably known all along that Norris was extorting money from Redemption's businessmen. It might have even been his idea.

And Porter was just as likely as Norris to be responsible for some or all of those murders.

Bill kept his right hand in plain sight and rock steady. He knew if it wavered even a little, Norris or Porter or maybe both of them would pull their guns and kill him. They would claim he'd been trying to draw on them and say they were acting in self-defense, and nobody would dare to question them. A few moments earlier he had been willing to die in a showdown with Norris, but now he wasn't.

Somebody had to do something about the crooked lawmen, and it looked like the job was falling to him. Nobody else in Redemption was going to act.

But in order to see justice done, he had to stay alive, had to bide his time.

Monroe gave him his chance. The storekeeper had emerged from the mercantile, and now he said, "Marshal, I don't know what's wrong with the boy. He's crazy. Deputy Norris never attacked me. A, uh, crate fell off a high stack and hit me in the face. That's all."

Porter sounded satisfied with himself as he said, "Now, see, that's a reasonable explantion. I appreciate you speakin' up like that, Perry." The marshal moved up on Bill's left. "Are you drunk or something, Harvey? I know how you Texans like your whiskey."

Bill swallowed hard. "Yeah," he said, his voice tight from the effort he was making to control it. "Maybe I'm drunk."

From the street, Norris put in, "I say we haul him to jail anyway, Marshal, for spreadin' ugly rumors about a peace officer."

Bill knew if he ever wound up in Frank Porter's jail, he would never come out alive. If they tried to arrest him, he would have no choice but to fight.

"No, I don't think that's necessary," Porter said easily. "You've learned your lesson, haven't you, Harvey? You won't be spreadin' any more lies?"

"That's right," Bill said.

Porter turned to the crowd and raised his voice. "You heard the man, folks. It was all just a misunderstanding. Let's all go on about our business now."

The group of townspeople began to disperse. Eden moved up on Bill's right side and took hold of his arm.

"Come in the store with me," she said. "Please."

He nodded, his face stony and expressionless. "Sure."

Porter went down the steps and said to Norris, "Come on, Deputy. We have things to do, too."

Norris turned and fell in step beside the marshal. But as he walked away, he glanced back over his shoulder at Bill and gave him an ugly grin.

"Let's go, Bill," Eden said softly as she urged him toward the door. "It's over."

"Yeah," he said.

But he knew it wasn't over.

Not even close.

Chapter 14

"What were you thinking out there?" demanded Eden when they got inside the store. "Norris came within a hair of killing you."

"Maybe I would've killed him," said Bill. "You ever think of that?"

Her answer was blunt in its honesty. "No, I didn't. You're not a gunfighter, Bill. You've admitted that."

"Well, maybe not, but I'm not all that slow, either. I'll bet I'd have ventilated him before I went down."

"But you still would have died."

Bill couldn't argue with that conclusion.

Monroe shook his head wearily. "You should've kept your mouth shut," he said. "Accusing Norris of attacking me like that, right out in the open where folks can hear it, won't do any good."

"Why not? It's true, isn't it?"

"Don't you understand? What's true doesn't matter. The only important thing is what you can do about it, and in this town, nobody can do anything."

"You people can't," said Bill, without bothering to keep

the scorn out of his voice. "But a crew of Texas cowhands could stand up to Porter and Norris, you can bet a hat on that."

"You're asking us to put our future in the hands of a bunch of wild cowboys?" Monroe slapped a hand on the counter. "By God, it's the likes of them that got us into this mess to start with! If not for you Texans, we never would've had to hire Porter and Norris in the first place!"

"Yeah, well, how much of a toll did your mayor demand when he went out to talk to those trail drivers? I've got a hunch it was highway robbery."

"I never said anything about a toll—"

"But there was one, wasn't there?" asked Bill. "The town wanted the drovers to ante up before any of the hands could come in and pay a visit to the saloon or to the Stanley woman's whorehouse."

Monroe glared at him. "I'll thank you not to mention certain things in front of my daughter, sir."

"Dad, I know whores exist," said Eden. "They're even in the Bible, for goodness' sake."

"Nothin' good about those painted hussies," muttered Monroe. "Anyway, all the mayor did was ask those Texans to drive the herd around the town. That's all I know about, anyway."

"You ask him sometime," Bill said. "You ask him if he said anything to the trail boss about paying extra for the privilege of letting his punchers come into town. You might be surprised by the answer."

"That doesn't have anything to do with anything! You still played hell by challenging Porter and Norris like that. You think they won't try to do something about it?"

"Like shooting me in the back?"

"That's exactly what I mean."

Bill shook his head. "I'm not gonna give 'em the chance. I'm getting out of here tonight."

"Running out on us, are you?" Monroe asked with a sneer.

"No. Going for help. Hob Sanders and the rest of the crew

are somewhere between here and Dodge. I'm going to find them, and we'll come back here and deal with those two crooked lawmen."

"You'll be fugitives if you do," warned Monroe. "No matter what else they are, Porter and Norris have badges pinned to their shirts. Any man who guns them down will be guilty of murder in the eyes of the law."

"The town council hired them, right?"

"Yeah."

"Then the town council can fire them," said Bill. "They can appoint somebody else marshal, somebody like Hob Sanders, and then he can deputize as many men as he wants."

"Like the rest of that bunch of cowboys?"

"They won't be afraid of Porter and Norris," Bill said, well aware of the sting his words probably carried. At the moment, he didn't particularly care about hurting the store-keeper's feelings.

Monroe surprised him by tugging at the white beard and frowning in thought. "I don't like the idea," he said slowly, "but it might work."

Eden said, "You're talking about a war between those cowboys and Porter and Norris. And if the Texans win, then who's going to control them? They might turn around and go on a rampage. They could loot the whole town!"

"You've got us all wrong, Eden," Bill said. "I promise you, you'll be a lot safer with Hob and his men than you ever will be with a couple of murdering owlhoots like Porter and Norris."

She shook her head. "I don't know . . . Anyway, there's no guarantee you can even find them, and on top of that, you're in no shape to make a long horseback ride. Not yet."

"I was thinking I might take a wagon." Bill played his hole card. "And I was hoping you might come with me, Eden."

Both Eden and her father stared at him in shock. "Come with you?" she finally repeated. "What do you mean?"

"Just what I said. You'll be better off out of Redemption until this is all over."

"I'm not going anywhere," she said without hesitation. "This is my home."

"I know that. But like you said, there's gonna be a lot of trouble, and . . . I don't want to see you get hurt."

Frowning darkly, Monroe added, "I hate to agree with the boy, Eden, but you'd probably be safer in Dodge, even as wild as it is. Porter and Norris will put up a fight."

"And when they do, everybody else in Redemption will have to take their chances." Stubbornly, Eden shook her head. "No. I'm . . . touched . . . that you want to keep me safe, Bill, but I won't run out on the town."

She was showing more backbone now than anybody else in Redemption had for a while, he thought. If everybody in town had been that muleheaded, Porter and Norris wouldn't have been able to take over as easily as they had.

But that was in the past and couldn't be changed, just like a lot of other things.

"You really think you could find somebody to help us?" asked Monroe.

Bill nodded. "It might take a day or two, but I believe I can."

"Take my wagon, then."

Eden looked at her father. "You're going to help him with this crazy idea?"

"Those two so-called lawmen will clean out the town if somebody doesn't stop them," said Monroe. "They'll bleed us all dry and ride out leaving Redemption just a husk of a settlement. I don't want to see that happen."

"Neither do I, but—"

"I wish you'd go with Harvey."

Bill couldn't resist asking, "With a wild Texan?"

Monroe glared at him. "Don't push your luck, son. Maybe I've misjudged you and maybe I haven't, but these are desperate times. I reckon they call for desperate measures."

Eden crossed her arms over her chest and returned glare for glare. "I'm not going," she insisted. "And you can't make me."

A wistful smile crossed Monroe's bearded face. "You sound just like you did when you were a little girl. You'd get like that, and because your mama had died, I'd let you have your way most of the time. Maybe I shouldn't have, but it was all I could do." He looked at Bill. "I won't force her to go with you. But I will give you my word I'll look after her."

Eden snorted. "For years now, it's been me looking out for you."

Monroe didn't deny that. He went on, "The wagon's parked behind the store, and the team is down at Hartnett's. I'll tell Josiah to bring the horses down here and hitch them up as soon as it's dark. You can slip out of town then. Best not to let Porter and Norris know you're going."

Bill nodded. "I was thinking the same thing."

"Can you follow the trail north to Dodge in the dark?"

Bill thought about the broad trail that had been pounded into the Kansas earth by millions of hooves belonging to Texas longhorns, and he chuckled. "I can follow it," he said.

"I figured as much." Monroe gestured toward the glass-topped cabinet. "Get one of those Winchesters and take it with you. They use the same rounds as the Peacemaker. Better take an extra box of cartridges, too."

Eden looked back and forth between them. "You two have lost your minds," she said.

"No, maybe I'm just thinking straight for the first time in quite a spell," said Monroe. He started for the cabinet. "Think I'll get one of those Greeners and load it."

Bill didn't know where the man's newfound courage had come from. Sheer desperation, maybe.

Or the realization that a man could go along with evil for just so long before he risked being no better than that himself.

He turned to Eden. "You're sure you won't come with me?"

"I'm sure. And you're bound and determined to do this?"

"I am."

"Then you have to promise me you'll be careful."

"Sure, I—" Bill began.

The promise was cut off by Eden's lips as she stepped forward, came up on her toes, and pressed her mouth to his.

Instinctively, Bill's arm went around her and pulled her

tighter against him. His pulse thundered inside his head. The feel of Eden's body molded to his sent the blood racing through his veins, and her lips were warm and moist and even sweeter than he'd thought they would be, when he allowed himself to think about such things.

They broke apart as Perry Monroe snapped closed the shotgun he had taken from the cabinet, after thumbing a couple of shells into its twin barrels. The old man cleared his throat, shook his head, and said, "Well, I reckon now you've got an even better reason to come back here, boy."

"Yeah," Bill whispered as he looked into Eden's blue eyes. "I reckon I have."

Chapter 15

Since it would still be several hours before Bill left Redemption, he expected Eden to try to talk him out of going. She didn't, though, and he couldn't help but wonder why.

Maybe after thinking about it she had realized he would be running an even greater risk by staying in town. Monroe was right: now that Bill had defied Porter and Norris and openly accused them of being criminals, they would have to do something about him. As far as they were concerned, his words had painted a target on him.

Smack-dab on his back, in fact.

They might think it over for a little while before they came after him, though, so the sooner he got out of Redemption, the better. He wasn't running away this time, because he would be back, but when he returned he wouldn't be alone. If he couldn't find Hob and the boys, at this time of year he was bound to run into some other Texas cowboys headed home from the railhead. Once he had explained the situation to them, even if they were strangers, he was confident they would help him.

After all, a Texan might wait for the right time, but in the end he never ducked a good fight . . . as General Santa Anna and his army had found out to their everlasting regret on the plains of San Jacinto.

Monroe left the store for a while, and when he came back he said quietly to Bill, "I had to tell him the plan, but I've got it fixed up with Josiah Hartnett. He'll have the team hitched to the wagon as soon as he can after dark."

"He'll keep his mouth shut about what I'm doing?" asked Bill.

Monroe gave a curt nod. "Josiah's suspected all along that either Porter or Norris killed his partner. He'll do his part, don't worry."

Bill stepped out the back door of the store and put the loaded Winchester on the floorboard of the driver's seat, covered with a blanket. That way he wouldn't have to go inside to get it later.

Monroe closed the store a little earlier than usual that day. All three of them walked to the house together, and as they went inside, Eden said, "I'll get supper started. If you're going to be driving all night, you'll need some food before you go. I'll pack some breakfast for you to take along, too."

Bill nodded. "I'm obliged."

"You don't have to thank me," she said. "You're risking your life for us, and it hasn't been even a month yet since you were badly injured. You shouldn't be fighting our battles for us."

Somebody had to, thought Bill, but he refrained from saying that. Anyway, the people of Redemption weren't fighters. They were settlers. There was a difference, and he supposed one group was just as important to the world as the other.

Maybe even more so, because when the fighting was over, as it inevitably would be, there would always be a need for people to keep the world running day after day.

A strained silence hung over the table at supper. Bill was aware that outside, dusk was settling down over the town. He would have to leave soon.

Eden knew that, too, and she frowned as he pushed his empty plate away. "I can get you some more," she offered.

Bill shook his head. "I appreciate it, but I'd better get started. No telling how far I'll have to go before I run into somebody who can help us."

He got to his feet, using the cane to help him rise, and glanced toward the window. It was dark outside. If he went out the back door of the house and stuck to the alleys, he thought he could reach the rear of the mercantile without anybody seeing him.

It would be a good idea to get as far from Redemption as he could before the crooked lawmen realized he was gone.

"Wait just a minute," said Monroe as he stood up. He left the room and came back holding a wide-brimmed, flat-crowned hat made of brown felt. It had a black band around it. Monroe held the hat out to Bill and went on, "You'll need something to keep the sun off your head while you're on the trail."

Bill took the hat and nodded. "Much obliged, Mr. Monroe," he said. He settled it on his head, pleased with the fit. A smile touched his mouth. With a hat on his head and a Colt on his hip, he was starting to feel like a cowboy again, instead of a cowboy pretending to be a store clerk.

"Now, here's how you need to go to get back to the store," said Monroe. He gave Bill directions for the best route. "Stick to that, and nobody should spot you."

Eden still sat at the table, her head down and her gaze on the plate in front of her. Bill hesitated, waiting for her to say something or at least look at him. But she remained silent, eyes downcast.

"Well, I, uh, reckon I'll be going now," he finally said.

Monroe stuck out a hand. "Good luck."

Bill shifted the cane to his left hand and shook with the storekeeper. Monroe glanced at Eden and shrugged. Bill gave a little shake of his head. If she didn't want to say good-bye, he wasn't going to force her to.

He walked into the kitchen. Monroe said, "I'll blow out the lamp, so nobody can see you leaving."

Bill waited at the door. The lamp went out, and as it did, Eden rushed in from the dining room. She threw her arms around Bill and hugged him tightly, as if she didn't intend to let go.

He returned the embrace as best he could. She lifted her head and kissed him again. It was as hot and sweet and urgent as the first time. As she pulled back slightly, she whispered, "You come back safe."

"I will," he promised.

Once this was all over, once the threat of Porter and Norris had been taken care of, they would have to sit down and figure out what they were going to do next, thought Bill. He knew Eden wouldn't want to leave Redemption and her father and travel all the way to Texas to be the wife of an almost penniless cowboy.

But he was equally certain he couldn't stay here and continue clerking in the Monroe mercantile. Perry Monroe had warmed up to him a little, and no doubt he would be willing to provide a job for a son-in-law, but Bill didn't want that. He couldn't live that way.

Not even for Eden.

He was getting way ahead of himself, of course. A lot of other things had to happen first, and he had no guarantee he would survive the showdown with Porter and Norris. It would be better to concentrate on dealing with that threat first. Getting too distracted by thoughts of the future could make the present even more dangerous.

He hugged Eden again, then slipped out the door before she could stop him. Monroe closed it behind him, leaving him in the thick shadows behind the house. Bill turned to his left and began making his circuitous way toward Main Street and the mercantile.

He didn't see anyone. Redemption didn't quite roll up the sidewalks at sundown, but close to that. The saloon was open, along with a few of the other businesses, but most folks were at home, either having their supper or getting ready to turn in for the night. This was the sort of town where people went to bed with the chickens.

When Bill reached the alley behind the store, he saw the dark shapes of horses looming in front of the wagon. Josiah Hartnett had made good on his promise. The team was hitched up and ready to go. Bill put a hand on the floorboard and felt the hard shape of the Winchester under the blanket. Nobody had bothered it.

He put his cane on the seat, took hold with both hands, and placed his right foot on the step. Since his left leg was still weak, he had to haul most of his weight up with his arms and shoulders. With a grunt of effort, he swung himself onto the seat.

The reins were looped around the brake lever. Bill untied them. He had driven a wagon plenty of times while he was growing up and working on his aunt and uncle's farm. He clucked to the horses and slapped the reins against their backs. They pulled against the harness and the wagon lurched into motion with a creak of wheels.

Bill stuck to the alley until he reached the edge of town. Then he headed northeast over the prairie. The main cattle trail was half a mile in that direction.

It didn't take him long to get there. The team handled well, and the wagon was in good shape. It rolled easily over the plains.

Bill turned on the seat and looked behind him. The moon wasn't up yet, so all he had to go by was starlight. He didn't see anyone following him. It appeared he'd been lucky and had gotten out of Redemption without anyone knowing he was leaving except Eden, Perry Monroe, and Josiah Hartnett. And they wouldn't be telling anybody.

The ground was packed so hard by the millions of hooves that had pounded it down, driving on it was almost like driving on a paved city street, Bill supposed. He didn't know for sure that was true, because he hadn't actually ever driven on a paved street. Keeping to the trail made for an easy ride, though, and he was grateful for that because it didn't jar so much on his bad leg.

The stars wheeled through the black sky overhead while he put several miles behind him. He didn't want the team to get worn out, so he reined the horses to a halt and gave them a chance to rest for a few minutes.

As the wagon rocked to a stop, Bill stiffened on the seat. He heard the swift rataplan of hoofbeats somewhere behind him. A rider was coming up fast.

That didn't necessarily mean the horsebacker was after him, he told himself, but the possibility was worrisome enough that he twitched the reins and got the horses moving again.

"Sorry," he muttered, even though the animals couldn't understand him. "Wish I could've let you rest more. Maybe in a little while."

The rider might veer off to one side or the other. Or maybe he would pass the wagon and continue on toward Dodge. Bill didn't know, but he could hope.

That hope turned out to be futile. He heard the sharp crack of a rifle as the horseman closed in behind him. His head jerked around, and he saw a spurt of orange muzzle flame in the darkness as the man fired a second round.

This shot came close enough Bill heard the whine of the bullet as it passed over his head. He turned around again and slapped the reins hard against the backs of the team as he shouted at them. The horses broke into a run.

Bill had no doubt the man trying to kill him was either Frank Porter or Zach Norris. Nobody else in Kansas had any reason to want him dead.

Even on the beaten-down cattle trail, the wagon bounced quite a bit as the team stretched out into a gallop. Bill knew the horses couldn't keep up that pace for very long, and even if they could, it wouldn't matter, because they couldn't pull the weight of the wagon and outrun the pursuit. The horseman would catch up sooner or later, most likely sooner.

So Bill did the only thing he could. He hauled back hard on the reins, dragging the team to the left at the same time. The turn was so sharp it caused the wagon to tip. As the wheels left the ground, Bill reached down and grabbed the Winchester from the floorboards.

He leaped clear, sailing into the air as the wagon went over with a grinding crash.

It was a risky move, but it was better than letting the gunman catch up and kill him. He made sure he came down on his good leg. His momentum carried him to the ground, where he rolled over a couple of times in the dust of the trail before coming to a stop.

The horses had broken free of the wagon and were racing off into the night. A few yards from Bill, the overturned vehicle lay on its side, a couple of its wheels still spinning freely in the air.

He planted the rifle butt against the ground and heaved himself to his feet. He was shaken up and breathless, but his bad leg seemed to be all right. Limping heavily, he ran to the wagon and dropped behind it just as the hoofbeats of the pursuer's horse welled up like thunder somewhere close by.

A muzzle flash split the night again. Bill heard the bullet thud into the thick planks of the wagon bed. He brought the Winchester to his shoulder and fired, aiming at the place where he'd seen the jet of orange flame. A horse screamed, and a man gave a hoarse yell of alarm.

Bill figured his shot had knocked the would-be killer's horse out from under him. The man might be all right, though, and would definitely still have murder on his mind.

That hunch was confirmed a second later when a pair of shots blasted out. These came from a handgun. The man must have dropped his rifle when he was thrown from the wounded horse.

Both slugs hit the wagon but failed to penetrate. The vehicle gave Bill good cover. He fired twice, squeezing off the shots as fast as he could work the Winchester's lever, then crouched behind the wagon again.

His daring move of deliberately wrecking the wagon was paying some benefits now. Out here on this broad, open trail, there was no cover to be found except the overturned wagon, and he held that ground. He wasn't out of danger, though. The killer could always circle around and try to get behind him.

A mocking voice floated out of the blackness. "How you doin', Tex? Bust that bum leg of yours when the wagon turned over?"

Norris. Well, that came as no surprise, thought Bill. He didn't bother answering, nor did he fire toward the sound of the voice. Norris was probably hugging the ground, and it would be sheer luck if Bill hit him. They were in a standoff of sorts.

But it would end when the moon came up in a little while. Once the silvery illumination washed across the plains, Bill would be able to see his enemy and pick him off.

Norris had to be aware of that, too. He needed to end this fight before moonrise. He wasn't done goading Bill just yet, though.

"I'll bet you thought you got out of town without anybody knowin', didn't you?" Norris taunted. "Hell, the marshal knew you'd run. He set me to watching the back of Monroe's store. Said to let you leave town and follow you, whichever way you went, then take care of you once you were far enough away from the settlement. He didn't know if you'd head north or south. You were gonna go to Dodge to look for some help, weren't you, cowboy?"

Bill still didn't answer. He didn't see any point in it.

"You had to know we wouldn't let you get away with that," continued Norris. "Frank and me, we got us a sweet deal in Redemption, and we're not just about to let some two-bit cowpoke with shit on his boots ruin it for us. It's about to get a lot sweeter, too." The crooked deputy chuckled. "Yes, sir. If killing some of those stubborn old fools wasn't enough to convince everybody not to buck us, what's gonna happen to Eden Monroe tonight sure will."

The words hit Bill like a punch in the gut. His first impulse was to empty the Winchester toward the sound of Norris's hateful voice. He forced himself to wait.

"Wish Porter had come after you and left me in town so I could have first crack at her, but, hell, he's the marshal, after all. Reckon he deserves to have her first. Anyway, I'll get my turn later, after I've killed you. It'll be that much better, takin' her while I'm tellin' her all about how I shot her Texas cowboy full of holes."

Norris was trying to prod him into doing something stupid. Bill knew that, and with a supreme effort of will, he forced himself to be calm. All he had to do was wait until the moon came up, and then he could kill Norris at his leisure.

"Yeah, right about now Marshal Porter will be gettin' to the Monroe house," said Norris. "What do you think pretty little Eden will do when Porter puts a gun to her pa's head? She'll do anything he tells her to, that's what! And I'll bet Frank's got plenty in mind to do to that little blond slut." He laughed. "Right now, Tex. I'll bet she's gettin' it from him right now!"

Chapter 16

Something snapped inside Bill. With a howl of anger, he
straightened from his crouch behind the wagon and started
firing at sound of Norris's voice, cranking off round after
round.

But Norris wasn't there anymore. He was up and sprint-
ing to Bill's left, and Colt flame bloomed in the darkness as
gun thunder rolled out. A sledgehammer blow struck the rifle's breech and ripped it out of Bill's hands. The impact sent
him stumbling backward. His bad leg went out from under
him and dumped him on his ass.

He knew he had only heartbeats before Norris was on
him, blasting slugs into him at close range. His hand went to
the holster on his hip. If he could just draw the Peacemaker
in time, he might still have a chance . . .

The holster was empty.

The next instant, Bill realized he was sitting on something hard. The gun had slipped out of the holster and landed
underneath him as he fell. He rolled to the side and slapped
at the revolver as he heard a rush of footsteps and another
shot blasted. The slug kicked dust from the trail into his face.
The grit that landed in his eyes half blinded him.

But the gun was in his hand now, his fingers wrapped around the walnut grips, and acting almost completely on instinct, he tipped the barrel up, squeezed the trigger, and thumbed off three shots. The gun roared and bucked in his hand as flame lanced from the muzzle.

In those garish shards of light, he saw Zach Norris driven backward as at least one of the bullets slammed into him. Norris howled in pain.

Using his free hand, Bill pushed himself up and fired again, but he couldn't tell if he hit anything. He heard Norris scrambling away. No more shots came from the crooked deputy. Bill crawled behind the wagon again and lay there with the gun in his hand. His heart was pounding so hard it felt like it was going to break out of his chest.

A moment later, hoofbeats sounded in the night, starting nearby but then diminishing rapidly to the west. Norris was fleeing. Bill could hardly believe it. He must have wounded Norris badly enough the deputy didn't want to continue this fight. And he must not have killed Norris's horse after all, he figured out after a moment. He had probably creased the animal and caused it to fall, but it was able to get up and Norris was still able to ride it.

Bill reached in his pocket and took out several .44 cartridges he had placed there. Working by feel, he opened the revolver's cylinder, dumped the empties, and thumbed in the fresh rounds. He regretted losing the Winchester, but at least he had a full wheel in the Colt. Just because Norris had lit a shuck right now didn't mean he wouldn't be back.

Bill swallowed hard as he thought about the vile things Norris had said. Maybe the deputy had been lying, just trying to get his goat so he would do something foolish. That was certainly possible.

But it was equally possible Norris had been telling the truth. Marshal Porter might be at the Monroe house even now, carrying out that sordid plan.

Bill's pulse had slowed a little while he was reloading the gun, but it began to race again with fear for Eden. He had to get back to Redemption somehow.

But he was several miles out of town, on foot, with a bad leg to boot. It might take him the rest of the night to walk back there, if he could even make it that far without his leg giving out completely on him. He looked disgustedly at the wagon. Maybe wrecking it hadn't been such a good plan after all.

There were other horses out here besides Norris's mount, he reminded himself. The team had torn loose from the wagon when it overturned and bolted off into the darkness. But the four horses probably hadn't gone very far. They had been spooked by the shooting, but once they were away from it, they might have calmed down. They might have even stopped to graze once they were off the wide cattle trail where more grass grew.

Bill climbed to his feet. Looking for the horses was worth a try.

Carrying the revolver, he walked around the wagon, looking for his cane. He found it where it had flown out of the vehicle during the wreck; he picked up his new hat as well. Switching the Colt to his left hand for the time being, he took the cane in his right and started in the direction the horses had taken when they ran off. He moved as fast as he could.

With Eden possibly in danger, he didn't have any time to waste.

He reached the edge of the trail in a few minutes and continued west, acutely aware that this was the direction in which Norris had fled. The man might be lying in wait somewhere out there in the darkness, ready to ambush him. Or he might have fallen off his horse and bled to death by now, or anywhere between those two extremes. Bill had no way of knowing. All he knew for sure was that he had to get back to Redemption.

After a few more minutes, he spotted some dark shapes up ahead. Moving carefully and quietly, he approached them. The moon was beginning to creep up over the eastern horizon now, brightening the sky. Bill recognized the four horses. They were still yoked together, although the violence of the crash had torn their harness loose from the wagon tongue.

Bill had worked with horses most of his life. He began talking softly to them as he came closer. These were draft horses, without much wildness left in them. He was able to walk right up to them and catch hold of the harness on the closest one.

He had ridden bareback for years as a kid before getting his first saddle. That wouldn't be a problem. Getting onto one of the horses wasn't be an easy task, though, without stirrups. He was sweating heavily by the time he managed to clamber onto the back of one of the horses.

He took a clasp knife from his pocket and cut the animal free from the other horses. Knowing they would follow him, he cut the others loose from each other as well.

Then using the cut harness for reins, he turned the horse he was riding toward Redemption and dug his heels into its flanks, sending it south at a fast trot.

That gait caused pain to shoot through his bad leg, but he didn't care. All that mattered was getting back to town . . . and Eden.

Not wanting to risk getting lost, he angled back to the east a little and soon picked up the cattle trail again. The moon was completely above the horizon now and provided plenty of light. Bill was able to move faster on horseback than he had been while driving the wagon in the other direction, so it didn't take him as long to cover the several miles back to the settlement. Less than half an hour had gone by when he spotted the faint yellow glow of a few lighted windows ahead of him.

That prompted him to push the horse to a gallop. He aimed straight for the settlement now.

He wasn't exactly sure how to reach the Monroe house from this direction, so he lost a few valuable moments riding along Main Street looking for the cross street where the house was located. The delay chafed at him.

Everything was closed down now except the saloon. Light still spilled over its batwings and through the big front windows. For a second, Bill considered stopping there to see if he could get anyone to help him, but he discarded the idea. He had taken this battle on himself, and he would fight it alone. He would have surprise on his side, because Frank Porter probably expected him to be dead by now, gunned down by Norris.

Bill passed the marshal's office and jail. The door was closed and the windows were dark. The hope that Norris was lying had lingered in Bill's mind, and he would have been relieved to see that Porter was in his office.

But the marshal wasn't here, and Bill no longer had any doubt where he was.

He recognized the corner where the street he was looking for crossed Main. As he rode around it, he glanced back and saw that the other three horses were no longer following him. They must have stopped at the livery stable, recognizing it as their home, he thought.

That was good. If Porter was at the Monroe house, as Bill believed, he wouldn't hear a whole group of horses approaching. He'd be less likely to pay any attention to a lone rider, and if he did, he'd probably think it was Norris returning to Redemption from his mission of murder.

Bill pulled the horse to a stop and slid down from its back while he was still several houses away from the Monroe house. He went the rest of the way on foot, using the cane in his left hand now since he had the Colt in his right.

A light burned in the parlor window, but the rear of the house was dark. Bill circled it to come in from that direction. The hinges on the front gate creaked a little when it was opened, and he didn't want to take a chance on even that small sound warning Porter.

He hoped Perry Monroe had left the back door unlocked after he'd gone out that way earlier in the evening. When he reached the door, he set his cane on the ground and took hold of the knob, turning it slowly and carefully.

It turned, and the door swung open an inch.

Bill eased it open more, just wide enough for him to slip inside. The kitchen was dark. No one had relit the lamp back here after Monroe turned it out.

He closed the door soundlessly, then stood there in the

dark and listened intently. He heard voices coming from the front of the house.

Praying that the floorboards wouldn't squeak under his feet, he started along the hall in that direction. He heard a man's voice, and a woman's, and then the woman let out a sob that almost made him charge recklessly down the hall. He had to force himself to proceed cautiously.

"You don't have to do this, Porter." That was Perry Monroe speaking. Bill could make out the words now. "I already paid Norris the extra he asked for, and I will from now on, even if I go broke doing it."

"This isn't just about the money anymore," said Porter. "That cowboy defied us, and he's obviously sweet on Eden here."

"Yeah, but you said Norris went after him to kill him."

Monroe's words prompted another sob from Eden.

"You can't hurt him by hurting her, not if he's already dead," Monroe went on.

"You gave him food and shelter and a job." Porter's voice was relentless. "You got to learn a lesson, too, Perry. After tonight, you won't even think about defyin' us again, and you'll make sure all your friends feel the same way." A grim chuckle came from the crooked marshal. "Most of them have wives or daughters or both. You tell 'em they better cooperate with the law, or I won't be responsible for what might happen."

"The law." The bitter, angry voice that spoke belonged to Eden. "You're not a lawman, Porter. You're a thief and a murderer and . . . and a low-down snake!"

"You won't feel that way when I get through with you, Miss Eden. You're gonna enjoy yourself, whether you want to or not."

Bill was almost at the entrance to the parlor now, willing his bad leg not to give in to the weakness in it and cause him to make any noise. The rage he felt toward Porter threatened to erupt into an out-of-control blaze, but somehow he managed to contain it.

"There's been enough talkin'," snapped Porter. Bill heard

the ominous sound of a gun being cocked. "Get your clothes off, Eden, and get over here, or I'll put a bullet in your pa's brain."

In a voice wracked with strain, she said, "I can't . . . you can't expect me to . . . not in front of—"

"Oh, yeah. Your pa's gonna watch the whole thing. I'm just sorry that damned cowboy of yours isn't here to see it, too."

Bill thought he had the three of them located in the room by the sound of their voices. He had to act now. He pulled in a deep, silent breath, then stepped into the entrance to the parlor, leveled his Colt at Porter, and said, "I'm here, Marshal, but you're the one who's gonna get your brains blown out if you don't drop that gun."

Chapter 17

Porter, standing to Bill's right, turned sideways to him as he aimed a revolver at Perry Monroe, who stood to Bill's left. Eden was straight ahead, facing him. The four of them formed a rough diamond shape in the parlor.

Porter looked surprised, but only for a second. Then a smile appeared on his face.

"You don't want to do that, Tex," he said. "You can't shoot me fast enough to keep me from killin' Monroe. I don't reckon Miss Eden would ever feel too kindly toward you again if you were responsible for her pa's death."

"He won't be," said Monroe. "It's you who's to blame for this, Porter. Shoot him, Bill."

Actually, Bill had given some thought to doing just that, while he was standing out there in the hall listening to Porter's vile demands. He had considered stepping into the parlor and pulling the trigger without warning Porter or giving him a chance to surrender.

But even though Porter deserved it, Bill didn't have it in him to kill somebody in cold blood.

"I don't care what happens to me," Monroe went on. "Just shoot this son of a bitch like you would a snake."

Porter chuckled. "That's not gonna happen, Perry. Look at the boy. If he was gonna pull the trigger, he would have done it by now. He's scared I'll kill you if he does. He's scared that I'll live long enough to get some lead in him, too. But that's not what I'll do, Tex. I won't kill you. I'll kill *her*."

Bill's heart raced.

"I'll do it right now, too," continued Porter. "You think you can stop me? I'm pretty fast. You miss with that first shot and I'll have time to kill Eden and Monroe and probably you, too. You dead sure of your aim, son? You better be, if you're gonna do this."

Emotions warred inside Bill. He knew he was letting Porter get to him, but there was truth in what the crooked lawman said. If he shot Porter in the body, Porter would live long enough to get off at least a couple of shots. The only thing that would put him down fast enough was a bullet in the head, and even that might not be enough to save Perry Monroe.

And the head was a smaller target. Bill might miss completely, even at this range. If he did, he and Eden and Monroe would die in the space of a couple of heartbeats.

Eden was standing in front of the fireplace. Leaning against the wall within reach of her hand was the shotgun Monroe had loaded earlier, Bill noticed. As if she had noticed him looking at it, her eyes suddenly flicked down and to the side, toward the double-barreled weapon.

Bill wanted to tell her not to try it, but he was too late. She was already reaching for the shotgun.

Porter must have seen the motion from the corner of his eye, because he suddenly cursed and jerked toward her. Bill fired at the same instant, as Porter swung his gun toward Eden, but the lawman was moving, too, and the bullet from Bill's Colt plowed a shallow furrow in the side of Porter's neck.

The impact was enough to make him stagger as he pulled the trigger. The bullet he sent in Eden's direction missed her and smacked into one of the stones that formed the fireplace instead. She had the shotgun in her hands now and was trying to lift it. Bill drew a bead on Porter's back but didn't pull the trigger. Porter was between him and Eden, and if the bullet went all the way through the marshal, it could hit her, too.

Porter lunged forward and grabbed the scattergun's twin barrels. He shoved them toward the floor and clubbed at Eden's head with the gun in his other hand. She jerked aside and took the blow on her shoulder, but it was still enough to make her cry out in pain.

Monroe tackled Porter from behind and drove the crooked lawman off his feet.

Bill jammed the Peacemaker in its holster as he leaped toward them. He couldn't risk a shot now, not with Porter, Eden, and Monroe all tangled up together in front of the fireplace. As he closed in on them, Porter twisted in Monroe's grip and slammed his gun into the old man's bearded jaw. Monroe rolled to the side, stunned.

Bill planted his bad leg and swung the other one in a kick aimed at Porter's gun hand. The toe of his boot caught Porter on the wrist and knocked the revolver out of his grip. It clattered to the floor and slid across the parlor.

Before Bill could draw his own gun again, Porter lashed out with a kick of his own. It landed on the knee of Bill's bad leg and knocked it out from under him. Bill fell heavily.

Eden had dropped the shotgun when Porter hit her in the shoulder with his gun. Porter lunged for the fallen weapon. Bill reached out desperately, snagged the marshal's shirt collar, and jerked him back. Porter's hand fell short of the shotgun. Bill went after him, swinging punches.

His fists hammered against Porter's face and body. Bill had been in several bare-knuckle, no-holds-barred brawls, but his recuperation had weakened him, and the blows didn't land with as much power as they would have otherwise. Porter was an experienced fighter as well, and his fist shot up and smashed into Bill's cheek with enough force to send him rolling across the rug on the parlor floor.

Bill came up against the legs of a small table that sat against the wall. He grabbed the table, lifted it, and swung it down across Porter's back, where it landed with shattering force. Porter's face hit the floor. Bill still had one of the broken table legs in his hand. He swung it like a club, intending to bash Porter's brains out.

Porter rolled aside at the last second. The table leg slammed into the floor instead, sending pain shivering up Bill's arm. Bill managed to hang on to the table leg and slashed at Porter with it, forcing the lawman to keep rolling. Porter came up on his knees and dove at Bill while the Texan was off balance from the missed swing with the table leg.

The two of them sprawled on the rug. Porter was on top now, hooking vicious punches into Bill's midsection. He aimed a knee at Bill's groin. Instinct made Bill twist aside just in time to take the blow on his thigh, but unfortunately, it was his bad leg. Pain exploded through him.

The agony he felt made his vision blurry, but he could still see well enough to see Eden attack Porter from behind, wrapping her arms around his neck and trying to drag him away from Bill. Brutally, Porter drove an elbow back into her body and knocked her away from him.

But even though the respite had lasted only a second, that was long enough for Bill to suppress the pain. He reached up and closed both hands around Porter's neck. He hung on tightly as he pulled Porter's head down, while at the same time lowering his head and driving it upward. The top of his head crashed into Porter's face and flattened his nose with a crunch of cartilage and a spurt of blood. Porter howled in pain. He tried to pull away, but Bill wouldn't let go. Harder and harder, he dug his fingers into Porter's throat. He was going to squeeze the very life out of the man.

Porter wasn't finished, though. He slammed his fist twice into Bill's leg, and the fresh bursts of agony that resulted were bad enough to make his grip on Porter's neck loosen. Porter tore free. Blood bubbled and streamed down his face from his ruined nose.

He went for the shotgun again, and this time he got it. Gritting his teeth against the pain, Bill pulled himself to a sitting position to look for another weapon, and Porter was still on his hands and knees when Zach Norris suddenly appeared at the entrance to the parlor. The deputy had a gun in his hand. As the revolver swung toward Bill, Norris yelled, "I'll get him, Frank!"

Norris pulled the trigger.

Porter lurched upright at the same instant, the shotgun gripped in his hands, and the bullet from Norris's gun punched into his back. Porter jerked under the impact. His eyes widened with shock and pain. He stood there for a second, blocking Norris's line of fire, before his mouth opened and more blood welled out to join the crimson flood from his nose. The shotgun slipped from nerveless fingers, and he pitched forward.

Bill caught the shotgun as it fell. Porter's body sprawled across his legs. Bill pointed the Greener toward the door. Norris leaped for cover as the twin muzzles loomed at him. Bill fired the right-hand barrel and sent a charge of buckshot slamming through the entrance and into the wall on the other side of the hallway. The shotgun's boom was deafening.

Porter moved a little, raising his head. His eyes rolled and bulged in their sockets as his mouth worked but no sound came out. Then his eyes rolled back even more, and his head fell forward as death claimed him.

Bill kept the shotgun pointing toward the door with one hand while he used the other to take hold of Porter's collar and haul the lawman's corpse off his legs. He fought his way to his feet, stiffening his throbbing left leg under him to keep it from collapsing. He watched the parlor entrance. At the first sign of movement, he intended to fire the shotgun's other barrel. Awkwardly, he made his way toward the hall.

Eden was crumpled not far from her father's motionless body. Bill wanted desperately to check on both of them, but Zach Norris was still a threat. In the brief glimpse Bill had had of the deputy, he had seen blood on Norris's shirt. Bill already knew he had wounded Norris during their fight on the cattle trail, but obviously the wound hadn't been a fatal one. Norris had circled back to town and come to the Monroe house, figuring he would find Bill there.

But caught up in the heat of battle, Porter hadn't realized what was going on and had lunged up right in the path of the bullet Norris intended for Bill. That was justice, thought Bill, the backshooter being gunned down from behind, but it didn't end matters.

Norris was still loose, still a deadly threat.

Bill reached the entrance and turned the corner, thrusting the shotgun ahead of him. The hall was empty, and at the far end of it, through the kitchen, the rear door stood open. It looked like Norris had fled again, rather than face the shotgun's second barrel.

But Bill couldn't be sure of that. He advanced slowly along the hall until he could see into the kitchen. He worried the shotgun blast in the parlor had damaged his hearing enough that he couldn't hear Norris, even if the deputy was moving around. Bill lurched into the kitchen, quickly swinging the scattergun from side to side.

No sign of Norris. Bill closed the door with his foot. He didn't have the key to lock it, but he shoved a table in front of it. That would slow down anybody who tried to get in that way and maybe give him some warning.

He turned and hurried back to the parlor. Eden was kneeling beside her father now, shaking him. "Dad! Dad!" she said. She looked around at Bill. "He won't wake up!"

Bill tried to kneel, but he lost his balance. He sat down on the floor next to Perry Monroe. "Let me take a look," he muttered as he set the shotgun down. He took hold of Monroe's shoulders, rolled the man onto his back, and placed a hand on his chest. After a second, he felt the steady beat of Monroe's heart.

"Is . . . is he dead?" asked Eden.

Bill shook his head. His long brown hair hung in his face. He tossed his head to get it out of his eyes and said, "No, he's alive, Eden. He's alive." He took hold of her hand and placed it over Monroe's heart. "You can feel for yourself."

"Oh, thank God!" Eden exclaimed with a gusty sigh of relief.

"Porter walloped him pretty hard, but I reckon he'll come around in a little while. Are you all right?"

Her face was wet with tears. She nodded and said, "Yes,

I . . . I'm fine. It hurt when Porter hit me, and I couldn't breathe for a minute. But I'm all right now." She glanced at the dead lawman. "What . . . what happened to him? Did you kill him?"

Bill realized she hadn't seen Norris. The shooting had happened quickly, while she was in pain and trying to catch her breath.

"No, Norris did."

"Norris? I thought Porter said he sent Norris after you."

"He did," said Bill. "He ambushed me on the trail. But I wounded him, and he took off. He said Porter was coming after you, so I lit a shuck back here and made it to town first. Norris showed up and tried to shoot me, but Porter got in the way of the bullet."

A laugh edged with hysteria came from Eden's mouth as she rocked back and forth. "Norris shot Porter? In the back?"

Bill nodded. "Yeah."

Eden kept laughing, and Bill had started to wonder if he was going to have to slap her to try to bring her out of it when Monroe suddenly moaned and started moving around a little. Instantly, Eden forgot all about the ironic circumstances of Porter's death and leaned anxiously over her father.

"E-Eden . . ." rasped Monroe as his eyes fluttered open. "Eden?"

"I'm here, Dad," she said as she caught hold of his right hand in both of hers. "I'm all right, and you will be, too."

Bill picked up the shotgun and used it to help him climb to his feet. His leg hurt like hell, but when he looked down at it, he didn't see any bloodstains on his jeans. The wound caused by that brindle steer hadn't broken open again, and the leg still worked so he knew the bone wasn't busted, either. It just hurt.

As he took a step toward the hall, Eden looked up from her father and asked, "Where are you going?"

"Norris is still out there somewhere," Bill said, "and there's no telling what he might do. I got to find him and stop him."

"You can't! You're hurt."

Bill shook his head. "I set off this whole ruckus by convincing Porter and Norris they had to get rid of me and tighten the screws on the town even more. That's why Porter came here tonight to . . . to . . . Well, he wanted to send a message to everybody in Redemption that they'd better go along with whatever he and Norris wanted, or things would get even worse."

"That's not your fault," Eden argued. "That was them, all them. They were pure evil."

"Norris still is," said Bill.

From the floor, Monroe whispered, "Let the boy . . . go, Eden. He's the closest thing we've got . . . to real law . . . in Redemption now."

Bill hadn't thought about it like that. Porter and Norris were still the town's only duly sworn lawmen. Norris had killed Porter, but if Bill tracked down Norris and killed him, would that make him a murderer in the eyes of the law?

He would just have to take his chances, he decided. Somebody had to go after Norris, and he was the only one who could do it. With Eden calling out to him to stop, to come back, he limped out of the parlor, through the foyer and the front door, and onto the porch. His step might not be firm, but his determination was.

A lot more lights were showing in windows now, he noted as he moved through the yard and opened the gate. People had heard all the shooting from the Monroe house and had gotten up to ask themselves what was going on. They hadn't come to investigate, though. They were still safely behind closed doors.

He wished he had found some shotgun shells, reloaded the chamber he had emptied, and brought some spares with him. But he still had one barrel of the Greener ready to go, as well as the rounds in the Colt on his hip. That would have to be enough.

But how was he going to find Norris? The deputy could have gone anywhere.

A sudden burst of gunfire sounded from Main Street, and Bill knew he had the answer to that question.

Chapter 18

Bill hurried toward the sound of the shooting as best he could. He might not be able to get around very well for a while after this. Might even have to lay up at the Monroe house and recuperate for a few days, he thought. He could afford to do that . . . if he lived through this night of violence.

The shots stopped as he reached Main Street. He peered along it, looking for Norris, but he didn't see anybody moving around. The saloon was still the only building that was lit up. Bill looked at the yellow rectangle falling into the street from the saloon door, and his eyes narrowed as he saw what appeared to be a cloud of smoke or fog drifting through the light.

It was smoke, he thought.

Powder smoke.

Grim lines were etched in Bill's face as he started toward the saloon. That was where he would find Zach Norris. He was convinced of that.

As he passed the livery stable, a voice called softly to him. "Harvey! Bill Harvey! Is that you?"

As tightly wound as his nerves were at that moment, Bill had to make an effort not to turn and fire at the sound. Instead he controlled the impulse and said, "Yeah. Who's that?"

One of the double doors in front of the stable was open slightly. It swung back more and the burly figure of gray-bearded Josiah Hartnett appeared. He stepped out and asked in a whisper, "What're you doin' here? Perry said you were going to Dodge to get us some help."

Bill's reply was curt. "Those plans got changed. What do you want?"

"Deputy Norris rode by here a few minutes ago. He looked crazy, like some sort of wild animal. He went to the saloon and charged in there, and then there was a bunch of shooting."

Bill nodded. "I heard. Porter's dead, and Norris knows he's not gonna be able to run roughshod over this town anymore."

"Porter's dead?" repeated Hartnett, sounding like he couldn't believe it. "What happened? Did you kill him?"

"No. Norris did, by accident when he was shooting at me. Norris is wounded. He tried to kill me out on the trail north of town earlier tonight."

"Then what's he doing in the saloon?"

"I don't know. Maybe he's planning on taking off for the tall and uncut, and he wants a stake first. The saloon is the only place open he could rob at this time of night."

Hartnett nodded. "Yeah, there might be quite a bit of cash in the till. Plus he could hold up all the customers, as well. You might be onto something there, Harvey." He nodded at the Greener in Bill's hands. "Are you goin' after him?"

"Yeah," said Bill. "Somebody's got to end this."

He waited a moment, thinking Hartnett might volunteer to come along with him, but the liveryman didn't. Stifling a snort of disgust, Bill turned away.

At that moment, a man's body came flying through one of the saloon's front windows with a huge crash of shattering glass.

Bill's hands tightened on the shotgun, but nothing else happened. The man lay on the boardwalk in front of the saloon, moaning for about a minute before he climbed laboriously to his feet and started stumbling toward Bill and Hartnett. His face and hands were covered with dark splotches of blood from cuts inflicted by the broken glass.

The man wasn't Norris. Bill could see him well enough to know that, although he didn't recognize the man. As he came closer, Bill called, "Hold it."

The man stopped short and held up his bloody hands. "Don't shoot! Whoever you are, don't shoot! I'm lookin' for that Texan. Have you seen him?"

"That's Benjy Cobb, the swamper," said Hartnett. "Benjy, it's me, Josiah Hartnett. Harvey's right here with me."

The man took a couple of shaky steps closer. "You . . . you're the Texan?" he said to Bill.

"That's right. Norris is in there, isn't he?"

Cobb groaned. "He came in and started shootin', like he'd lost his mind. He was plumb kill-crazy. He gunned down poor Pete, the bartender, and Fred Smoot. There were some bullwhackers in there who had guns, and they tried to fight back, but Norris just shot 'em like dogs. Then he grabbed me, and I thought for sure he was gonna k-kill me, too."

Cobb was shaking so bad he could hardly talk. Hartnett said, "Come in the barn. I got a bottle of whiskey. That'll settle your nerves."

"Wait a minute," snapped Bill. "What did Norris do?"

"He . . . he gave me a message." Cobb swallowed. "A message for you. He said he wanted me to go find you and deliver it. Then he slung me through the front window."

"What message?"

"That if you don't come down there and . . . and have it out with him . . . he's gonna burn the whole town to the ground!"

Hartnett gasped in horror. Bill understood the feeling. Fire was the most feared disaster in frontier settlements like this, and with good reason. More than one town had been wiped off the face of the earth by an out-of-control blaze.

Norris could do it, too. He was in a saloon, where there was plenty of fuel for a fire. All he had to do was bust a bunch of bottles of whiskey and set the rotgut ablaze. The building would burn so fiercely it couldn't be put out, and it was right up against other buildings so the conflagration would spread without any trouble.

"I figured he just wanted to rob the place, so he'd have some money to get away," Bill said.

"Oh, he emptied the till," said Cobb. "But if you ask me, mister, what he really wants is to kill you."

"And if he does, he'll take over and run things like Porter did, only worse. Porter was bad enough, but Norris is loco." Nobody would be safe in Redemption with Norris running rampant. Eden probably least of all. Bill took a deep breath and said to Cobb, "You go on in the barn with Mr. Hartnett. He can clean up those cuts and give you that drink of whiskey."

"Wha . . . what're you gonna do?"

"Norris is waiting for me. Reckon I'll go see him."

"He'll kill you!" said Hartnett. "He's faster with a gun than anybody I've ever seen."

"He's already tried to kill me twice tonight," Bill pointed out with a faint smile. "Let's hope the third time's not the charm."

He started toward the saloon, leaving the two men gaping after him.

All he wanted was to get close enough to Norris to put the shotgun's remaining load of buckshot in him. Bill was no gunfighter, but a man armed with a Greener didn't have to be.

Norris would be expecting him to come up to the front of the saloon, and Bill didn't plan to do that. When he came to the mouth of an alley, he ducked into it and hustled through the thick shadows to the rear of the buildings.

He had never been in the saloon, but most businesses had a back door. He was counting on that being true here. If he could get behind Norris, he wouldn't hesitate to blast him. That would make *him* a backshooter, he thought wryly, but he didn't care. All that mattered was ending Norris's threat, once and for all.

The saloon was one of the few buildings in town that had an actual second story instead of just a false front. From what Bill had heard, Fred Smoot, the owner of the place, had a few girls working up there, providing a little competition for Miss Alvera Stanley's young ladies. The second floor made it easy for Bill to tell from the back which building was the saloon.

It had a rear door, all right, and the door was unlocked. Bill eased it open and stepped into a windowless room cloaked in stygian blackness. He felt around until his fingers brushed a stack of crates. This had to be the storeroom where Smoot kept his extra liquor.

Carefully, so he wouldn't knock anything over and warn Norris someone was back here, Bill made his way across the room and felt around for another door. After a moment, he found one. No light showed underneath it, so he thought it would be safe to open it. When he did so, he spotted yet another door at the end of a short hallway, on the right-hand wall. The glow of lamplight seeped around its edges and at its bottom.

That was the door leading into the saloon's main room where Norris waited with his hostages. Bill limped toward it. The pain in his leg had subsided to a dull throb. He stopped when he reached the door and leaned forward to press his ear to it.

He heard at least one woman crying. A man cursed in a low, monotonous voice. And after a moment, Zach Norris snarled, "Shut the hell up!"

The man said, "I . . . I think I'm gonna bleed to death if I don't get some help soon, Deputy."

"I said shut up, Smoot! You think I care if you bleed to death? You think I care about any of you pissants in this damn town? I hope that cowboy doesn't show up, so I'll have an excuse to burn it down!" Norris paused, then added, "I'll give him five more minutes. Then things are gonna get mighty hot around here."

Bill knew he was going to have to risk opening the door and taking a look. He had to know where everybody in the room was. You couldn't just bust in and let loose with a shotgun. That was a good way to kill innocent people. He didn't want anybody else to die tonight except Norris.

He held the Greener in his right hand and used his left to turn the knob as silently as he could. The door opened toward him. He eased it back a half inch and put his eye to the narrow gap.

He couldn't see much. A man's unmoving legs were stretched out on the floor behind the bar with a pool of blood around them. That would be the bartender Norris had killed, thought Bill. He could see a thin slice of the room but no people. He opened the door a little wider, and as he did, Norris stalked through his field of vision, waving a revolver.

"You people didn't know when you were well off," the deputy ranted. "Marshal Porter and I kept law and order in this town. Law and order, by God! We risked our lives to do it. And all we asked in return was to be paid. All we asked was for you people to make it worth our while."

He was crazy, all right, trying to justify all the killing and violence. He swung around, and Bill pulled back. Norris might not notice the door being open an inch or so, but he'd sure see an eye staring at him.

Norris kept stalking and ranting. He passed through Bill's view a couple more times, moving from right to left and then back again.

There didn't seem to be anybody to the left, closer to the front windows. Norris had probably herded his prisoners toward the back of the barroom. That meant Bill could get between Norris and the hostages if he timed his move to coincide with Norris's pacing. He steeled himself and got ready.

A moment later, Norris passed in front of the bar again, cursing. "Damn that stupid Texan!" he bit out. "His time's up, damn it! I'm gonna—"

Bill had both hands on the Greener now. He got his toe

in the gap alongside the door and threw it open, lunging through as he thrust the twin barrels of the shotgun at the crazed deputy.

"I'm right here, Norris!" he yelled.

Then he pulled the trigger.

Chapter 19

Again, the thunderous roar of the shotgun assaulted Bill's ears. The air in the saloon was already thick with the reek of burned gunpowder, and the shotgun blast added to it as smoke geysered from the left-hand barrel along with the charge of buckshot.

Norris screamed as he went down, twisting to the floor from the impact of the lead ripping into his left arm and side. Bill had hoped to blow a huge hole clean through Norris, but the deputy's lightning-fast reflexes had prevented that. Norris had been turning and diving aside even as Bill pulled the trigger, and the range was so close the charge hadn't had time to spread out much. The buckshot was still clustered as it struck him, and only the edge of that cluster brushed him.

Norris rolled on the sawdust-littered floor and came up on one knee. Bill heaved the empty shotgun at him as the gun in Norris's hand blasted. The bullet whipped past Bill and shattered the mirror on the wall behind the bar. The next second the heavy shotgun crashed into Norris's chest and knocked him over backward.

Bill dragged his Colt out of its holster and thumbed back the hammer. He pointed the gun at Norris and fired, but the bullet chewed splinters from a floorboard mere inches from the deputy's head. Bill dropped behind the bar as Norris fired again and more glass shattered, this time one of the whiskey bottles on the back bar. The strong-smelling stuff splattered all over Bill.

The hostages were screaming and yelling as they broke away, running upstairs or out the door through which Bill had come in, scrambling to get out of the line of fire and find someplace safe. At least they would have a chance to escape now, thought Bill as he rose up and triggered another shot at Norris just as the man dived behind an overturned table.

Whiskey dripped from Bill's hair into his eyes, blinding him momentarily. He had to duck behind the bar again and paw at his eyes in an attempt to clear his vision. More bottles shattered above his head as Norris continued shooting. Whiskey showered down like rain, drenching him.

Suddenly, Bill smelled smoke and realized what Norris was trying to do. He heaved up from behind the bar and saw something burning flying through the air toward him. Norris had set his own hat on fire and flipped it toward the bar. He was trying to ignite all that spilled whiskey.

And since Bill was soaked with the stuff, he would go up in flames like a human torch if the burning hat touched him.

He slapped his free hand on the bar and levered himself up, rolling across the hardwood as the burning hat sailed over him. He fell hard in front of the bar and heard a whoosh as the hat landed behind the bar and the puddles of whiskey caught fire. A bullet slammed into the floor in front of Bill's face. He felt the sting of splinters as they dug into his cheeks. Luckily, they missed his eyes.

He looked up and saw Norris making a break for the door. Norris slapped the batwings aside and dived through them as Bill fired again. The fleeing man never broke stride, so Bill knew he had missed.

Grating a curse between clenched teeth, Bill scrambled to his feet. Flames leaped up behind the bar. He could go after Norris, or he could try to put out the fire.

It wasn't a very hard choice. The fire was the more immediate threat, and the more devastating one as well.

Bill saw that one of the saloon girls hadn't fled. She hunkered behind a table, obviously too terrified to move. He pouched his iron and said to her, "Gimme your dress!"

She blinked at him, clearly not understanding.

He didn't have time to explain. He lunged at her. She screamed as he grabbed her and dragged her to her feet. His hands hooked in the low neckline of her gown and ripped apart as hard as they could.

He tore the dress off of her and turned to the bar, dashing behind it. Using the dress like he would a blanket, he slapped at the flames as he fought to smother them. It was hard not to panic because he knew if the fire licked out and touched him, he was a goner. He suppressed the natural fear and worked frenziedly as heat from the flames beat at his face.

He didn't even notice at first that someone was beside him, helping him. Then he realized Josiah Hartnett was there, using a horse blanket. Benjy Cobb appeared with a bucket of water and dumped it on the fire. Somebody else, a townsman Bill didn't recognize, crowded in as well, wielding a blanket.

They were doing a better job than he was, he realized. He was just getting in the way. He staggered back, holding the charred dress he had torn off the saloon girl. He would have to apologize to her, he told himself, but that could wait.

A sickly sweet smell filled the air. Bill knew the fire must have reached the corpse of Pete the bartender. That stink was human flesh burning. But the men battling the flames were bringing them under control now. They had stopped the blaze before it reached the rest of the whiskey bottles on the back bar.

Redemption was saved . . . at least from this threat.

Bill dropped the gown and started toward the batwings. He dug cartridges out of his pocket and reloaded the Colt as he stumbled across the room.

"Harvey!" called Josiah Hartnett. "Where are you going?"

"After Norris," Bill said over his shoulder.

Hartnett hurried out from behind the bar and caught up to Bill just as the Texan pushed through the batwings. "He's gone," said Hartnett. "When I was comin' down here, I saw him run out, climb on his horse, and gallop out of town. Looked like he was hurt pretty bad and could barely stay in the saddle."

For a second, Bill had trouble comprehending what Hartnett had just told him. Norris . . . gone? The deputy wouldn't just take off like that while his hated enemy was still alive, would he?

But Norris had a history of fleeing when the odds weren't overwhelmingly on his side, Bill recalled. It had happened twice already tonight, out on the trail and then in the Monroe house. Norris was wounded, too, maybe seriously since Bill had grazed him with that shotgun blast. He had started the fire to delay pursuit, as much as anything else.

Bill looked into the night and sighed. "I'll have to try to pick up his trail, come morning."

"Why?" asked Hartnett. "Let him go. He's not coming back here. He wouldn't dare. Anyway, I'm hopin' he's hurt bad enough he'll just crawl off somewhere and die, like a sick dog."

Bill slid the Peacemaker back in its holster. That was a good thing to hope, he thought, but he'd feel a lot better if he knew for certain Zach Norris was dead.

He lifted his head as the sound of hoofbeats came to his ears. Was Norris coming back to raise more hell already?

No, this wasn't just one rider, but several. They were approaching Redemption from the north. More trouble, Bill wondered?

Hartnett heard the riders, too. "Who the hell could that be?" he asked.

"I don't know," said Bill. "But I reckon I'll find out."

He stepped down from the boardwalk and limped into the street, turning so he'd be facing the riders when they came into town. From the corner of his eye he saw people emerging from the saloon to watch as he waited. They weren't the only ones, either. Up and down Main Street, citizens of Redemption began to appear, curious to see what was going to happen next on this night of violence.

As Bill looked toward the end of the street, he tried not to think about how badly he hurt all over. His leg still throbbed, and the rest of his body was going to be bruised from the battering he had taken tonight. And it might not be over yet. He wasn't quite sure how it had become his responsibility, but if those strangers riding into town were bent on causing trouble, he knew he would have to try to stop them.

He could make them out now, three men on big horses coming toward him at a steady, unhurried pace. Bill put his hand on the butt of his gun as they moved into the light. He called out, "That's far enough, whoever you are. What's your business in Redemption?"

One of the men chuckled, and the familiar, gravelly tones of Hob Sanders said, "I could ask the same thing of you, son. What in blazes have you been up to since we left you here?" Hob sniffed. "You smell like a distillery, and by God, you sound like a lawman."

The realization that his friends had returned at last struck Bill like a physical blow. Everything would be all right now, he told himself. Hob was here. If there was any more trouble, Hob would take care of it.

That was the last thing Bill thought before the sheer willpower that had been keeping him going finally ran out. He felt his legs folding up beneath him, tasted dust in his mouth as he fell in the street. Then all that went away and left black emptiness in its place.

Chapter 20

For the second time in less than a month, Bill woke up to find himself in a strange place. His disorientation lasted only a moment, though, before he recognized his surroundings and realized where he was.

He was stretched out in the bed he'd been using in the spare room of the Monroe house. The sheets were smooth and cool and soft and felt wonderful against his skin. He just lay there and enjoyed the sensation for a few seconds.

Then his jaw tightened. Damn it, he was *naked* again.

His hands went to the sheet lying on top of him and pulled it higher. That brought a laugh from the doorway.

"You're the shyest cowboy I've ever seen," said Eden as she stood there smiling at him. "And I do mean seen."

Bill's face got warm, but he had more important things on his mind than being embarrassed. "What happened?" he asked. "Are you all right? What about your pa?"

Eden became solemn as she replied, "My father is sleeping. I think he'll be fine. But he's far from a young man, and he's absorbed a lot of punishment lately. I really hope things settle down now."

"You and me both," said Bill. "You didn't tell me how you're doing."

She moved her left shoulder and winced. "I'm pretty sore where Marshal Porter hit me with his gun, but nothing seems to be broken. And I'll have a nice bruise on my stomach from his elbow."

"That son of a—" Bill choked off the curse. "He had it comin', for hurting you like that."

"He had it coming for a lot of reasons," Eden said as she came closer to the bed. "Before you got here, he boasted about how he's the one who shot all those men, starting with Mr. Hendrickson, the baker. He was a madman."

Bill shook his head. "No. Norris might be loco, but not Porter. Porter was just poison mean. Pure evil hiding behind a friendly smile."

"He was a good lawman once."

"Was he?" asked Bill. "Or has he been doing things like this all along? Did he pull the same scheme in the other towns where he worked?"

Eden sighed. "We'll probably never know."

"Any sign of Norris since he rode out of town?"

She shook her head. "No. Your friend Mr. Sanders said he and some of his men would try to trail him in the morning."

"That's what I was gonna do."

"Well, you can forget about that," said Eden. "You're lucky your leg's not badly injured again. You're not going to do anything for at least the next week except rest it."

Bill frowned. "It hurts, but I reckon it's all right."

"And let's keep it that way. I'm afraid you're already going to have a slight limp for the rest of your life."

That wouldn't matter. Plenty of cowboys had limps. When you were in the saddle, it didn't matter.

Of course, thought Bill, that depended on whether he actually went back to cowboying . . .

He was in love with Eden Monroe. He knew that now, knew it beyond a sliver of a doubt. The question was what was he going to do about it.

Weariness gripped him, along with the soreness he felt all over. Figuring out the future could come later. He had put it off for this long, so he supposed a while longer wouldn't matter.

"How many people did Norris kill tonight?"

"Four. Five if you count Porter. Pete Baxter, the bartender at the saloon, and three freighters who were there and fought back when he came in to hold up the place. Fred Smoot's badly wounded, but he's still alive. It'll probably be a few days before we know if he'll pull through."

Bill blew out his breath and shook his head. "I sure wish I'd been able to put Norris under. A fella like that doesn't need to be walking around drawing breath. He'll be a menace to folks as long as he's alive."

"Maybe Mr. Sanders can find him and . . . see that he's dealt with properly."

Bill knew Hob well enough to have a pretty good idea how that would go. Norris would wind up with a bullet in the head or a hang rope around his neck, whichever was more convenient.

"Speaking of Mr. Sanders," Eden went on, "he's in the parlor and wants to talk to you. He said for me to let him know if you woke up." She smiled again. "I wanted a few minutes with you myself first, though."

Bill nodded. "I appreciate that. But I want to talk to Hob, too."

"I'll get him," she said.

But she didn't leave the room right away. Instead, she came over to the bed and leaned down to press her lips to Bill's forehead. He wanted to reach up, put his arms around her, and pull her down on top of him so he could kiss her properly, but he knew she'd fuss at him if he did that.

"I'll be right back," she said as she straightened.

Bill closed his eyes and waited, not opening them again until he heard Hob's boots on the floorboards. He looked up at the trail boss, who came into the room carrying his battered old black hat in front of him in his left hand. Hob looked back at Eden and nodded, saying, "Much obliged, ma'am."

"Howdy, Hob," Bill said as his friend and employer pulled a ladder-back chair closer to the bed and sat down.

"You look like you been drug through half the briar patches in the Indian Nations, boy," he said.

"Feel that way, too," replied Bill. "But I reckon I'll be all right."

"As bad hurt as you was when we left you here, I sure didn't expect to come back and find you up and around yet, let alone fightin' and shootin'. Miss Monroe tells me you pretty much saved the town's bacon tonight. Those two so-called star packers were really a couple o' lobo wolves."

Bill nodded. "Yeah. They've been forcing the businessmen in town to pay them off and killing the ones who wouldn't go along with it."

Hob shook his head. "They were no better'n common owlhoots, if you ask me. Just like those damn rustlers that hit us again betwixt here and Dodge City."

"They hit the herd again?" asked Bill, his eyes widening in surprise.

"Yeah. They raided us again two nights later, and that time they managed to make off with half the herd."

"No!"

Hob nodded grimly. "That's one reason it took us so long to get back here. I left a few of the boys to keep an eye on the cows we still had and took the rest of the crew after that bunch o' thieves. They headed west through the sand hills and into the breaks along the Colorado line. We had to chase 'em for damn near a week 'fore we caught up to 'em and took the herd back."

"Did you kill them?"

"I wish," Hob said fervently. "We burned a heap o' powder, but ever' last one o' the sons o' bitches got away." He glanced at the door, as if worried that Eden might be standing there and hear his profanity. The door was empty, though.

"Well, at least you got the cattle back."

"Yeah, but losin' that time cost us some money. Another herd that started from Texas after we did got to Dodge before us."

Bill understood. The price per head dropped a little with each herd that reached the railroad.

"But we got the herd there and sold it," Hob went on, "so I got your wages for you. Full share, too."

Bill shook his head. "That's not right. I didn't make the whole drive."

"Now don't argue with me, boy," said Hob with a glare. "The whole crew voted on this and decided you was to have a full share, and that's the way it's gonna be, you hear?"

Bill had to chuckle. "Sure, sure. I don't want to start a riot." A thought occurred to him. "Who was that with you when you rode in? I wasn't seeing too good by then."

"Too much gun smoke in your eyes, I expect. That was Dorsey and Santo. The rest of the boys have already headed back to Texas. They went a-stragglin' out of Dodge as soon as I'd paid 'em off and they blew out most o' their dinero." Hob grinned. "Lord, I don't know what me and all the other trail bosses'd do if cowboys ever got the good sense to save some o' their money. Nobody'd sign on for a hellacious job like herdin' cows from Texas to Kansas if they wasn't poor."

"I plan on saving my wages," said Bill.

"I know that, and I'm proud of you for it, son. Reckon it might've been a blessin' in disguise that ol' brindle steer got you like he did. Kept you from goin' to Dodge and bein' tempted to waste your wages on heathen pursuits."

Bill was curious. He asked, "Are you sure it was the same bunch of rustlers who hit the herd the second time?"

"Damn sure," Hob replied with an emphatic nod. "Durin' the raid, Dorsey caught a glimpse of that fella with the long blond hair, the one who started the stampede the first time."

Bill frowned. "I told you about that? I don't recall."

"That's 'cause you was outta your head at the time, before we got you here to Redemption. You talked a heap, mostly cussin' that long-haired fella who shot at you. Wish I could've ventilated the son of a buck for you. From what I heard in Dodge, he's the leader of that bunch. They been raisin' hell around here ever since the herds started comin' north this year. They've hit half a dozen other herds, killed some good Texas cowboys, and made off with several thousand head o' beef."

"Really? I hadn't heard anything about it while I was here."

"No, I don't reckon you would. All the herds go around this settlement now. All the drovers know they ain't wanted here." Hob's mouth twisted a little. "This is a town full o' farmers and storekeepers."

Bill wanted to explain that it wasn't exactly like that in Redemption. There were a few small ranches in the vicinity, along with the farms, and there was the freight wagon traffic, too.

But for the most part Hob was right, and Bill understood why the trail boss felt a mite scornful of the folks who'd settled here. It was sure different from Texas. Not bad, necessarily, just . . . different.

"Anyway, from what I heard, those rustlers have been cleanin' up," Hob went on. "We ain't far from the Colorado border. They drive the stolen cows over there and sell 'em to buyers who don't care where they come from. There's a good steady market for beef in Colorado, what with all the minin' goin' on over there."

That made sense, thought Bill. Miners got hungry, too, just like everybody else.

Hob turned his hat in his hands. "Dorsey and Santo and me figured we'd try to trail that Norris hombre, come mornin'. A hydrophobia skunk like that hadn't ought to be runnin' around loose. Fella can't try to kill one o' our boys and get away with it."

"I appreciate that, Hob," said Bill, "but it's not really your responsibility."

"Is it yours? I saw the way you walked out in the street to meet us a while ago. You didn't know who was ridin' in. Could've been anybody. But you marched right out there like it was your job to protect this town."

"Well . . . they took care of me when I was hurt. They still are."

Hob shook his head. "Looks to me like it's Miss Monroe

and her pa who're doin' that. Any o' these other sodbusters and broom pushers back your play when you went up against them crooked lawmen?"

Bill had to sigh. "Not really. But they helped put out the fire Norris started in the saloon."

"Hell, anybody'll fight a fire when it's threatenin' to burn down his home. Anybody but a worthless polecat, that is. Way I see it, you don't owe these folks anything."

"Neither do you," Bill pointed out. "You owe them a whole lot less than I do. But yet you're talking about going after Norris."

"Because of what he did to you, and outta sheer common decency. Somethin' these folks in Redemption don't seem to have a whole passel of."

"You're wrong about them," said Bill. "They're not like us, but it takes all kinds, I reckon."

Hob didn't look convinced, and Bill knew there was no point in arguing with him.

Besides, he was mighty tired, and as that thought crossed his mind, Eden appeared in the doorway as if she knew what he was thinking.

"Bill needs to rest now, Mr. Sanders," she told Hob.

He got up right away and nodded. "Yes'm. You've been doin' such a good job of takin' care of him, I'm sure not gonna argue with you."

She smiled. "A good job? Look at him! He was nearly killed half a dozen times tonight."

"Yeah . . . but he wasn't. He's still alive and kickin'. Leastways he will be once that bad leg gets a mite stronger. Seems to me like he's growed up a lot since we left him here. He ain't a wild young cowboy no more."

"Then what am I?" asked Bill in a sleepy voice as he struggled to keep his eyes open.

"I don't rightly know yet," said Hob. "I ain't sure you do, either. But when you figure it out, you'll let us know."

Chapter 21

West of Redemption, the flat plains of Kansas gradually gave way to a range of low, sandy hills stretching north almost all the way to the Arkansas River. Between the sand hills and the Colorado border, the terrain consisted of rocky ridges and shallow gullies that weren't good for much of anything. The dirt was too poor for farming, and the grass was too sparse for grazing cattle.

The only real use for these badlands was to shelter men who were on the run from the law.

The camp was dark and quiet, but guards were posted on the ridge overlooking it in case anybody came along. The rustlers had been holed up here for a while, licking their wounds and lying low after the battle with the Texans. The men were disgusted by the fact that those cowboys had caught up to them before they could push the stolen stock across the Colorado line and sell it. Another day would have seen the job done successfully.

The only good thing to come out of the debacle was that none of the gang had been killed. Some of the men were shot up pretty bad, but they were recovering and expected to live.

Dock Rakestraw sat with his back against a rock and smoked a quirley, cupping it in his hand so the orange glow of the coal couldn't be seen. He was called Dock not because he had any medical training, but because his real first name was Dockery. He was the leader of the bunch, but he took his turn standing guard along with everybody else. The men respected him because of that.

They also feared him because he was the toughest, meanest son of a bitch among them, and he liked it that way.

His long blond hair fell past his shoulders, but nobody made sport of it because none of them were as fast on the draw as he was. Tall, lanky, with long arms and big hands, he was built to kill with a gun. It came natural to him.

He frowned and pinched out the quirley as he suddenly leaned forward. A faint sound drifted to his ears. He couldn't make it out at first, but after a moment he realized he was hearing the hoofbeats of a slow-moving horse. Somebody was riding toward the outlaw camp, but whoever it was, they weren't getting in any hurry about it.

Rakestraw picked up the Winchester lying beside him and stood up. He made the sound of an owl hooting to alert the other two guards on the ridge.

The camp lay just beyond the point where two of those hogbacks pinched together. It was easily defended against attack from the east, the direction from which those hoofbeats came. Rakestraw went down the slope, sliding a little, and hurried over to a slab of rock that loomed near the opening between the ridges.

With the rifle held ready to bring to his shoulder and fire if need be, Rakestraw waited until he could see the man on horseback. Of course, he couldn't make out many details. Even though the moon was up, floating high in the sky, not much of the silvery illumination penetrated into the shadows cloaking the gap. The rider and his horse were just an irregular patch of deeper darkness drawing slowly closer to the camp.

Rakestraw socketed the rifle butt against his shoulder, leveled the sights on the stranger, and called out, "That's far enough, mister! Speak your piece! Who are you, and what're you doin' here?"

The voice that replied was drawn thin and tight with strain. "D-Dock? Is . . . is that you?"

Rakestraw had to think for a second before he realized who the voice belonged to. He said, "Zach?"

"Y-yeah. Can you . . . gimme a hand? I'm damn near . . . shot to pieces."

Rakestraw lowered the rifle and rushed out from behind the rock. He reached the horse just as the man who was hunched over and swaying in the saddle started to topple. Rakestraw hurriedly set the Winchester down and reached up to grab Zach Norris in time to keep the crooked deputy from crashing to the ground.

Turning his head, Rakestraw called into the camp, "Somebody come help me! It's Norris!"

Several members of the gang came running. Rakestraw handed Norris over to them and ordered, "Careful with him. He's wounded. Find a place where you can make him comfortable."

Leading Norris's horse, Rakestraw followed the men into camp. Somebody stirred up the embers of the fire, which had been built in a circle of good-sized rocks so the flames couldn't be seen. Once it was burning again, it cast a faint, flickering glow over the bedroll where the men lowered Norris's body.

Rakestraw turned the horse over to one of the other men and hunkered next to his friend and fellow outlaw. Several years earlier, both of them had ridden with the same bunch, holding up trains and stagecoaches over in Missouri. Then they'd drifted apart, and the next thing Rakestraw had heard about Norris, his old partner was wearing a badge.

That hadn't sounded right to Rakestraw, and sure enough, it wasn't. Norris had gotten word to him through the grapevine that stretched across all the dark trails ridden by men outside the law, and the story told by Norris's message was a good one. It seemed Norris had lucked onto a sweet deal, partnering up with a veteran lawman who had slowly but surely abandoned the law and become just as crooked as Norris himself was. They had cleaned up a town called Redemption and for all practical purposes had established themselves as rulers of the community. The settlement was near the main cattle trail from Texas, and if Rakestraw and his men wanted a free hand to raid the herds with a guarantee of no interference from the local law, Norris and Porter could provide it . . . for a small share of the profits, of course.

The arrangement had worked out well for everyone involved, for several months now. But obviously, something had happened, because even in the dim firelight, Rakestraw could see the dark bloodstains blotched on Norris's clothes.

Norris's pain-wracked eyes fluttered open. Rakestraw leaned over him and asked, "What the hell happened to you, Zach?"

"A damn . . . Texas cowboy . . . happened to me." Norris forced out the words with great effort. "Hombre from . . . the herd you hit . . . a few weeks ago."

Rakestraw's mouth tightened in his beard at the memory of that night. He had reacted too quickly, firing at one of the damn cowboys who had ridden up on him and setting off the stampede before all of his men were in position. Norris didn't know they had raided the herd again, more successfully this time, only to have that effort backfire on them when the blasted Texans caught up to them.

One of the other men said, "Dock, we better get those clothes off him and see how bad he's hurt. Maybe we can patch him up."

Rakestraw doubted Norris would live much longer, no matter what they did. The deputy had lost a lot of blood.

But it wouldn't hurt to try, he supposed.

"Yeah, that's a good idea. Somebody give him a drink of whiskey, too. I reckon he needs it."

One of the men brought out a bottle and handed it to Rakestraw. He used his teeth to pull the cork and spat it on the ground. He slipped his other hand behind Norris's head and raised it a little as he brought the bottle to the deputy's lips. Norris choked a little on the fiery liquor as Rakestraw tipped some into his mouth, but he swallowed most of it greedily.

A violent life lived outside the bounds of normal society had taught most of these men how to patch up bullet wounds in themselves and others. A grizzled old-timer known as Ozark Joe moved in and used a bowie knife to cut away some of Norris's clothes. Dried blood caused the fabric to stick to the wounds, and Norris made hissing sounds of pain as Joe worked them free.

"Somebody get a torch burnin'," said Joe. "I'm gonna need better light than this."

"Gimme some more . . . whiskey," pleaded Norris.

Rakestraw glanced at Joe. "Is it gonna hurt him?"

"Nope. Fact is, it'll probably help when I go to diggin' around to see if he's still got any lead in him."

Rakestraw lifted the bottle and poured more of the whiskey down Norris's throat. Norris coughed and gasped, but his voice was stronger when he said, "You want to hear about it, Dock?"

"Yeah," said Rakestraw, "go ahead and tell it, Zach."

Norris did, using the story to distract himself from the pain while Ozark Joe cleaned the wounds and probed them for bullets. Rakestraw listened with interest as Norris told how the trail boss had brought Bill Harvey to Redemption and left him there to recuperate with the Monroes.

"You've seen Eden Monroe," said Norris through lips tight with pain. "She's enough to make any man forget about bein' hurt."

Rakestraw nodded. "Yeah, she's a mighty pretty girl."

The boss of the gang, along with several of the other outlaws, had visited Redemption from time to time for supplies and a chance to visit the saloon and the whorehouse. They went in one or two at a time, never more than three, and each man knew the signal—a tug on his left earlobe—that told the local lawmen he was part of Rakestraw's bunch. That way, Porter and Norris had known to leave them alone. That was part of the arrangement, too.

"She nursed him right back to health," Norris went on,

"and the better he felt, the proddier he started to get. Frank said he was afraid we'd have to do something about him, and sure enough, he tried to leave town tonight. Frank figured he was gonna try to find some help, maybe some real law, so I went after him to kill him."

"But it didn't work out that way," Rakestraw guessed.

"Son of a bitch got lucky. He winged me and got away from me. Headed back to Redemption. I followed him but, uh, didn't get there in time to stop him from killin' Frank."

Something about the slight hesitation in Norris's voice made Rakestraw wonder if the deputy wasn't quite telling him the full story of the night's events. But the details didn't matter, he supposed.

"Damn Texan had a shotgun," continued Norris. "He peppered me with some buckshot. I barely managed to get away."

Ozark Joe looked over at Rakestraw and said, "I coulda told you about the buckshot. I already dug half a dozen pellets outta him. Looks like the slug that hit him went clean through, though. That's good."

"You think he'll make it?"

Before Joe could answer, Norris reached up and clamped a clawlike hand on Rakestraw's arm. "Damn right I'll make it," he ground out. "I got to. I got a score to settle with that cowboy."

Ozark Joe shrugged. "He lost a hell of a lot of blood, but it ain't really as bad as it looked at first. If he don't get blood poisonin', he might pull through."

"I'll pull through," said Norris. "Count on it. That's why I came lookin' for you, Dock. I had a pretty good idea where your camp was, and I knew I had to find you."

"We're glad to patch you up, Zach, but what else do you want from us?" asked Rakestraw, allowing a hint of a chill in his voice now. "Seems to me that under the circumstances, with Porter dead and you shot up, you can't be of any help to us anymore. Why should we help you settle your score with that Texan?"

"Because there's a whole town just sittin' there waitin'

for you to help yourself to everything in it!" said Norris as his hand tightened on Rakestraw's arm. "There's no law in Redemption anymore, and the settlers are the biggest bunch of sheep you ever saw. You and your boys can ride in and loot the place, all the way down to the ground!"

"We could've done that anytime," Rakestraw pointed out. "There was never any *real* law there."

"That's where you're wrong. Frank would've tried to stop you. He didn't want anybody shearin' those sheep but him and me. But he's dead and I don't care. I just want to kill Harvey. Wait until I'm on my feet again, and we'll hit Redemption like Quantrill hit Lawrence!"

"Well, it sounds like an interestin' idea . . . but why wait for you to heal up? Why not go ahead and raid the town now?"

"Because you and I are friends, Dock, and because you wouldn't even know what happened there if it wasn't for me. You owe me that much."

Rakestraw didn't like owing anybody anything, and he liked it even less when they pointed that out. But Norris was right. Friendship didn't amount to much in the lawless world in which they lived, but it wasn't completely without meaning, either.

Besides, it was getting later in the season and there would be fewer herds coming up the trail from Texas, and by now word would be getting around about the rustling going on in these parts. The drovers would be more cautious. After what had happened last time, it might be wise not to raid any more of the herds, mused Rakestraw. Maybe it would be smarter and more profitable to drift over into Colorado and hold up a few mine payrolls or ore shipments. It would be a good idea to have a nice stake before they started in on that, though.

Looting Redemption could give them that stake, and more besides.

"All right, you got a deal," said Rakestraw as he reached his decision. "On one condition."

"Name it," said Norris, wincing as Ozark Joe used some of the whiskey to clean out the buckshot holes in his side.

"I'm takin' the Monroe girl with us when we leave."

"Oh, hell, I don't care. Take her with my blessin', Dock. I just want to teach those bastards a lesson, and I want to kill Bill Harvey."

"Well, then," said Rakestraw as a cruel smile curved his mouth, "it looks like we both stand a good chance of gettin' what we want."

Chapter 22

After everything that had happened the night before, it struck Bill as odd that the next morning could dawn as normally as any other morning. When he limped out of the Monroe house after breakfast, over Eden's strenuous objections, Redemption looked just the same as it always had, at least since Bill had been there.

There was one fundamental difference, though, even though it wasn't apparent right away.

Frank Porter and Zach Norris were gone, and so was the air of fear that had hung over the town for so long.

"I don't know what you think you're doing," said Eden as she followed Bill onto the porch, where he stood next to the railing leaning on his cane. "You need to be resting."

"I know that. But you said yourself my leg didn't look too bad this morning."

Eden snorted. "Not as bad as I expected it to. That's not saying much, though."

"Your pa's in worse shape than I am," Bill pointed out. "He's older, and he's gotten walloped with a gun too many times lately."

Eden wore a worried expression as she nodded and said, "I know. It's going to take him a while to get back to normal."

"And he can't run the store while that's going on. So I'll do it."

She stared at him for a moment before saying, "You can't run the store. You don't know how."

"I've been helping out there for a while. I know how your father does some things, anyway, and what I don't know, I reckon I can figure out, especially with your help. You handle the books, don't you?"

"Well, yes, that's true."

"So you see," he said, "all you need is somebody to keep the place open and wait on customers, and I can do that."

Eden frowned as she considered the idea. After a few seconds, she sighed and nodded.

"I suppose you can," she admitted. "It's not easy work, but it's not all that strenuous, either. I'll help you all I can, but I'll have to be here a lot, too, looking after Dad."

Bill nodded. "I realize that. It'll work out, Eden, you'll see."

She moved closer and leaned her head on his shoulder. Quietly, she said, "I can't even bring myself to think about where we'd all be if it wasn't for you, Bill."

"Then don't think about it," he told her. "I'm here, and I'm not planning on going anywhere anytime soon."

"Not back to Texas with Mr. Sanders?"

Bill slid his free arm around her shoulders. "Nope. I reckon not." After a moment, he went on, "But speaking of Hob, I'd better go find him—"

"It's too late for that," said Eden. "He and the other two men came by here early this morning, before you were awake, to check on you. Mr. Sanders asked me to tell you that he and the others were starting on Norris's trail at first light."

Bill stiffened. He couldn't help it. He wanted Zach Norris brought to justice, and Hob would see to that if anybody could. But Bill wished he had been able to go along on the manhunt, too. The score he had to settle with Norris was a personal one, several times over.

At Eden's urging, Bill went back inside and rested for a while. He sat in the parlor while Eden helped her father into the room, saw that he got settled comfortably in an armchair, and covered his legs with a blanket. Perry Monroe had regained consciousness the night before, but he spent a lot of time just staring straight ahead, not saying anything. Bill hoped those blows to the head hadn't damaged Monroe's brain, but when a man had been pistol-whipped, that possibility couldn't be ruled out.

"Bill's going to go down to the store in a little while and open it for us today," Eden told Monroe. "Isn't that nice of him?"

The old man grunted to show he'd heard what Eden said, but that was his only response. He didn't even glance at Bill.

As he looked at Monroe, Bill hoped even more fervently that Hob, Dorsey, and Santo caught up with Norris. The deputy deserved to pay for the evil he had done.

When Bill felt a little stronger, he walked to the mercantile, unlocked the doors, and went inside. Again he was struck by how familiar everything looked, despite the fundamental changes that had occurred the night before. Main Street still looked like Main Street. The only business that appeared to be closed was Smoot's saloon. Bill didn't know how the wounded Fred Smoot was doing today, but it would take some time and effort to repair the fire damage inside the saloon.

Bill had seen people watching him from the boardwalks as he limped along to the mercantile, so he knew it wouldn't take long for word to get around town about him opening the store. Sure enough, the first few customers arrived a short time later. The women all smiled shyly at him, while the men wanted to shake his hand and slap him on the back. They offered their congratulations on ridding Redemption of a menace.

Bill was uncomfortable with the praise for a couple of

reasons. The first was that by nature, he wasn't a prideful sort.

The second, and more troubling, was that he had to bite his tongue to keep from asking these folks why they hadn't done something about Porter and Norris when they found what sort of crooks those two so-called lawmen really were. It wasn't his job to pass judgment on anybody, he told himself. He had done what he felt he had to do, and he supposed the citizens of Redemption had, too.

The store was busy enough to make the day pass quickly. Eden came in several times to check on him and to bring him lunch. When he asked her how her father was doing, she just smiled sadly, shook her head, and said, "About the same."

Late that afternoon, Bill heard the familiar jingle of spurs and looked up to see Hob Sanders coming into the store. The leathery trail boss looked tired and worn down, and judging by the solemn expression on his craggy face, he wasn't bringing Bill good news.

"Sorry, son," Hob began without preamble. "We lost that varmint's trail in the sand hills. Wind was blowin' too much to leave any tracks for more'n a little while. We spent hours castin' back and forth in those badlands on the other side of the hills, but we never could pick up the trail."

Bill felt disappointment go through him, but he said, "I know you did your best, Hob, and I appreciate it."

"We saw quite a few drops of blood on the ground before we lost him. You winged the son of a buck pretty good, looked like. I reckon there's a better than even chance he's layin' out there somewhere in the badlands as buzzard bait."

"I'd like to think so," said Bill with a nod.

"We can ride on over toward the border again tomorrow," Hob offered. "Might take a few days, but we'll find him."

Bill shook his head. "I can't ask you to do that."

"You ain't askin'. I'm offerin'. We got no reason to hurry back to Texas."

"Except for the fact you've got the money for that herd, and some of it goes to the other ranchers who threw their stock in with yours. Your wife's waiting for you, too, and

I'll bet Dorsey's wife and kids are missing him pretty bad by now."

Hob rasped his fingers along his silvery-stubbled jaw. "Well, you got a point there," he admitted. "And that cantina Santo favors there in Victoria might go broke without him around to soak up his share o' tequila."

Bill leaned his hands on the counter and said solemnly, "Go home, Hob. You've done all you can for me. Shoot, if you hadn't brought me to Redemption in the first place, I reckon I'd be in a shallow grave somewhere out there on the prairie by now."

Hob regarded him intently. "Are you comin' back with us? If it's too far for you to ride horseback, we can get a wagon for you."

Bill didn't have to think about it. He had reached a decision without a lot of brooding about it. He shook his head and said, "I'm staying here."

A grin tugged at Hob's mouth under the drooping mustache. "That yeller-haired gal, eh?"

"I can't just leave her to take care of everything by herself. Her pa's not doing very well, and she'll need help with him and the store."

"So you're tradin' a brushpopper's chaps for a storekeeper's apron, eh?" Hob couldn't keep a hint of disapproval out of his voice. Bill didn't take offense at it, though. Some things were just out of the comprehension of a man like Hob who had spent his entire life riding the range.

"For a while, I reckon."

Hob nodded slowly. "Well, it's a good man who knows what he wants and goes after it." He stuck a hand across the counter. "I wish you the best of luck, son." As they shook, he added, "Write us a letter ever' now and then and let us know how you're doin'. I'll read it to the boys who can't read. And we'll stop by when we bring the herd up next year." Hob chuckled. "Reckon there's a good chance you'll have a young'un on the way by then . . . if it ain't here already."

"I don't know about that," said Bill, feeling his face grow warm.

Hob clapped a hand on his shoulder. "I do. Good luck to you, Bill. We'll stop by here in the mornin' and pick up some supplies 'fore we ride out."

When Bill got back to the house that evening after locking up, Perry Monroe was still sitting in the parlor. Bill tried to tell him how business had gone that day, but Monroe didn't seem to pay much attention. The only time any life came into his eyes was when Bill explained how Hob, Dorsey, and Santo hadn't been able to find Zach Norris. Anger glittered in Monroe's gaze at the mention of the crooked deputy's name.

Bill thought that was a good sign.

The three Texans rode out in the morning after stopping at the store to pick up those supplies Hob had mentioned and say their farewells to Bill. Eden was there and solemnly shook hands with the trail boss.

"Thank you for bringing Bill to Redemption, Mr. Sanders," she told him. "If he hadn't been here . . ."

"You're the one who nursed him back to health so he was able to tangle with those two hombres," Hob pointed out. "So you deserve a lot of the credit, too, ma'am." He grinned at Bill and added, "So long, kid. See you next year. And don't forget what I told you."

"I won't," said Bill.

"What did he mean by that?" asked Eden once the three men were gone.

Bill shook his head. "Nothing. Hob just thinks he's a fortune-teller, that's all."

Eden frowned at him in puzzlement, but Bill didn't offer any further explanation.

As after any disaster—and the rampage Porter and Norris had gone on came pretty close to fitting that description—normalcy slowly reasserted itself. For Bill, that meant walking back and forth to the store every day, keeping the business going, sharing his meals with Eden, and gradually recovering from the ordeal and getting his strength back. By the time a couple of weeks had passed, his bruises had all healed, and his leg didn't hurt except for when he was on his feet for too long at a stretch. He had a slight limp and figured he always would, but it didn't slow him down and wasn't very noticeable.

The saloon reopened. Fred Smoot had survived the shooting, but he'd lost the use of his legs. Josiah Hartnett, who had experience building wagons, built Smoot a wheelchair, so he was able to get around a little.

Bill got to know the citizens of Redemption and could call just about all the customers by name when they came into the store. Best of all, Perry Monroe began to perk up a mite when Bill talked to him in the evenings about what had happened at the mercantile that day. He talked more, showed more of an interest in what was going on, and Bill wasn't surprised when Monroe announced one morning that he was going to the store, too.

"Are you sure you're strong enough, Dad?" Eden asked him.

"It's my store, isn't it?" replied Monroe with a touch of his old fiery nature. "Lord knows what sort of shape this *Texan* has let it get into while I was gone."

The sparkle of humor in the old man's eyes kept Bill from taking offense at the comment. He drawled, "Reckon it might be better than it was before," which drew a snort of disbelief from Monroe.

The town council had put a padlock on the door of the marshal's office. Bill had noticed it several times and wondered what they were going to do for a lawman. Things had been mighty quiet and peaceful in Redemption since that night of violence, but he knew it couldn't stay that way forever. Right now, folks were sort of holding their breath, as if they realized how lucky they were and how much worse it could have been, and they were afraid to do anything that might change the precarious balance.

Then one afternoon, after Perry Monroe had already gone home for the day, the mayor, Roy Fleming, and the justice of the peace, Kermit Dunaway, came into the store and marched down the aisle to the counter like they were on a mission. Fleming owned the bank and looked like a politician, with a round, always-smiling face. Dunaway was stocky, too, with heavy jowls and graying red hair. He favored an old-fashioned beaver hat.

Bill frowned as he watched them approaching the counter. Some instinct stirred inside him, warning him this might be trouble.

"Howdy, gentlemen," he said with a nod. "Something I can do for you?"

"We're here to offer you a job, Bill," said Fleming.

Bill shook his head and waved a hand to indicate their surroundings. "I sort of, uh, have a job already, Mayor," he said. "I've been helping Mr. Monroe run the store."

"We know that, but Perry's doing better now, thank the Lord, and we've got something more suited to you, I think."

"What would that be?" asked Bill, although he had a hunch he already knew the answer to that question.

Judge Dunaway slapped a hand down on the counter in front of Bill, and when he took it away, a five-pointed tin star lay there.

"We want you to be the marshal of Redemption," said Mayor Fleming.

Chapter 23

For a moment, all Bill could do was stare at the badge. Even though he'd been halfway expecting it, to hear the idea put into words actually made it more difficult to grasp. He had never in his life thought of becoming a lawman. Not once.

Back home in Texas, his only experiences with the law had been unpleasant ones. He had been hauled to jail a few times for brawling and drinking too much. Nothing serious, just the sort of wild-oat sowing most young fellas went through on their way to growing up.

But that certainly hadn't made him want to pin a tin star to his shirt.

"Well? What do you say?" prodded Judge Dunaway.

Bill nodded toward the star. "Is that Porter's badge?"

"Yes, it is."

"I can't wear it." Bill's voice was flat and decisive.

"Oh, come on, Bill," said Fleming. "At least give the offer some thought."

"I'm thinking about it. But no matter what I decide, I won't wear *that* badge. Not after Porter did."

The two older men looked at each other in understanding.

The judge said, "Because you think he brought dishonor to it."

"That's right."

"Well, hell, Bill," said Fleming with a note of impatience in his voice. "We'll get you another badge. In fact, there's probably a spare in the desk in the marshal's office. If that's the only problem—"

"It's not," said Bill. "What in blazes makes you folks think I'm fit to be a marshal?"

"You got rid of Porter and Norris, didn't you?" asked Dunaway.

"Norris killed Porter by accident." Bill had told the truth about that from the start and never tried to claim credit for something he hadn't done. "And we don't really know what happened to Norris except he lit a shuck out of town."

"The wolves have scattered his bones by now," said Dunaway. He took a cigar out of his vest pocket and clamped it between his teeth, leaving it there unlit as he went on around it, "The fact is, youngster, you're the only one in this whole blasted town who had the guts to stand up to those two killers. It pains me to admit it, but it's the truth."

Bill didn't argue with that. Instead he said, "I don't have any experience being a lawman."

"You protected the community," said Fleming. "And after Norris escaped, when those friends of yours from Texas rode in, you went out into the street to meet them without knowing who they were. Half the town saw you, Bill. If they had been outlaws, you would have met them head-on."

Dunaway nodded. "Sounds like a lawman's instincts to me."

"You're forgetting one important thing . . . I'm not a fast gun."

"But you *can* use a gun," said the judge. "You've proven that. Hell, maybe you're not as fast on the draw as Wild Bill Hickok. We know that. You don't have to be. This is a peaceful town now, and with Porter and Norris gone, it'll stay that way. All you'll have to do is keep things from getting out of hand at the saloon and maybe throw a troublesome bullwhacker or buffalo hunter in jail overnight to cool off. You can handle that without being a gunfighter."

What Dunaway said was probably true. Most frontier lawmen carried shotguns for a good reason. No matter how drunk or upset a man was, staring into the twin barrels of a Greener usually calmed him down in a hurry and made him come along peacefully. Gunslinging peace officers like Porter and Norris got all the notoriety, but actually they weren't all that common.

"What about the trail herds?"

"They've already stopped coming through town," said Fleming. "The men in charge know they're not welcome here, so they avoid us now."

"Actually, that's one thing we worried about when we considered offering you the job," said Dunaway. "Whether or not you'd be able to tell your fellow Texans they're not welcome in Redemption."—

"But we figure you're one of us now," added Fleming.

Bill bristled at the mayor's smug comment. "Don't be so sure of that," he said. "I've thought all along that you're making a mistake by keeping the cowboys out of town. The herds, sure, there's no reason to have thousands of cattle tromping right up Main Street. But when they bed down nearby, the saloon and the other businesses in town would do well to let some of the men come in and spend money."

"And shoot up the town and cause riots," said Fleming. "Haven't you heard what they did to me when I tried to talk to them?"

Bill spoke bluntly. "Yeah, and what I never did hear was whether you tried to charge them a toll or a special tax to come into town."

The mayor looked uncomfortable. "The council decided it was fair—"

"No, the council decided it was a good way to gouge the trail bosses out of some extra cash."

Fleming's usual affable expression vanished. "See here, young man—" he began.

"Oh, let it go, Roy," said Dunaway. "The boy's smarter

than you're giving him credit for, and you might as well admit that we got greedy. And we paid the price for it, too. You got roughed up, the town got a bad name, and worst of all . . . that whole mess was what led us to bring Porter and Norris here."

Fleming continued to glare for a second, but then he shrugged and said, "I'm not admitting anything. But maybe if we had a Texan for a marshal, somebody who knows how to talk to those trail bosses, he might be able to come to some other sort of agreement with them."

Dunaway chuckled. "Now that's not a bad idea, come to think of it. Maybe the town council should reconsider that no-Texans ordinance, especially if, like you said, we've got one for a marshal."

"We're still getting ahead of ourselves," said Bill. Using one finger, he pushed the tin star back across the counter toward the local men. "Before I give you an answer, I'll have to think it over and talk to somebody."

Fleming and the judge looked at each other and nodded in understanding. "Of course," Fleming said. "You ask Eden what she thinks. It's a wise man who knows how to consider the counsel of a woman."

"I didn't say it was her I had to talk to," Bill protested.

"No, you didn't." Fleming smiled, indicating that he knew good and well who Bill had meant. "You talk to whoever you need to. But don't take too long making up your mind, Bill. Like I said, Redemption is a peaceful settlement now, but even peaceful settlements need somebody to keep them that way."

The men picked up the badge and left the store. Bill thought about the job they had offered him . . . and what Eden might say when she heard about it.

They had spent a lot of evenings sitting together in the rocking chairs on the porch of the Monroe house, talking quietly about anything and everything. Bill had told her all about his life, which really hadn't taken that long, and she had told him about her family and how she and her father had wound up in Redemption.

During those times, the promise of the kisses they had shared in moments of desperation had grown into something deeper and stronger, an understanding that they intended to face the future together, whatever it might bring.

Bill had never thought that future would include the town council offering him the job of marshal, but there it was anyway. Life had a habit of not waiting very long before it threw even more changes at a fella.

The rest of the day seemed even longer than usual before Bill could close the store and head back to the Monroe house. He still didn't think of it as "home," despite all the time he had spent there during the past month. He supposed if he asked Eden to marry him, and she said yes, the place really would be home. Since her father was in poor health, he wouldn't expect her to leave him to take care of himself.

Bill didn't use a cane anymore. Sometimes his leg still got tired and achy, but the cane didn't help all that much. He didn't wear an apron while he was in the store, either, and whenever he left to walk back to the Monroe house, he strapped on his gun belt and settled the flat-crowned brown Stetson on his head. People he passed on the streets gave him friendly nods now, even though anybody could tell just by looking at him that he was one of those wild Texas cowboys.

But he wouldn't be with a badge pinned to his shirt.

He wasn't cut out to be a merchant. He knew that and always had. Helping out at the mercantile was just that . . . helping out. He'd assumed that maybe someday he would have a spread of his own down in Texas, and he still might. But for now, he found the idea of being a lawman surprisingly appealing. It was a job where every day would be a little different, and while it held the prospect of danger, it promised excitement as well.

Sometimes life didn't require a plan. Sometimes a man just stumbled into what he was meant to do. Maybe that was what had happened here in Redemption.

Eden was sitting on the porch when he reached the house. At first he thought she was just enjoying the evening air before going in to supper, but then he realized she was waiting for him. She said, "I heard that Mayor Fleming and Judge Dunaway came into the store this afternoon."

Gossip sure got around town fast, thought Bill. He climbed the steps to the porch, thumbed his hat to the back of his head, and nodded. "That's right," he said. "Nothing unusual in that, I reckon. Both of them have been in the store plenty of times."

"But usually not together," said Eden. "And not looking like they had town business on their minds."

Bill wasn't quite sure how anybody could have figured that out just by looking at the two men, but there was no denying Eden had the right idea in her head. He took his hat off and sat down in the chair beside hers.

"They offered me a job," he said straight out. He wasn't the sort to hem and haw about a thing, especially if it was important. "They want me to be the marshal."

"But you're not a lawman."

"Reckon they think after what happened, I'm the closest thing to it in these parts."

"You defended the town, that's true."

Eden sounded calm. That was worrisome in a way, he thought. When she was in tight control of herself this way, he couldn't tell how she really felt.

"What did you tell them?" she went on.

"That I had to think about it." He looked over at her in the fading light. "And that I had to talk to you."

"It's your decision, Bill."

He shook his head as he leaned forward in the rocking chair. "Not completely. You know how I feel about you, Eden—"

She held up a hand to stop him. "We haven't exactly had a normal courtship."

Bill thought about everything that had happened, all the blood and death, and said slowly, "No, I reckon we haven't."

She smiled. "I'd like for *something* to be normal about it."

He realized she was talking about the fact he hadn't asked her father for her hand in marriage, as he should. Well, if that was what he needed to do, he thought, he could take care of that right now. He came to his feet and asked, "Is your pa inside?"

"He is."

"I'll be back."

She stopped him with a word. "Bill." He paused and looked at her. "It really is up to you, what you decide about the marshal's job. I have to admit, though, I can't really see you spending the rest of your life behind a store counter."

Bill felt relief go through him when she said that. He'd been worried that she would be adamantly opposed to the idea of him being a lawman. If she had been, he wasn't sure what he would have done.

Now all he had to do was convince her father.

He went into the house and found Perry Monroe sitting in the parlor, reading the most recent issue of the town's weekly newspaper, the Redemption *Star*. Monroe still tired easily these days, but other than that he seemed to be back to his old self. He glanced over the paper at Bill and said, "I hear Roy Fleming and Kermit Dunaway came to see you this afternoon."

Bill chuckled and shook his head. "One thing about a little town, everybody knows everybody else's business, don't they?"

"Oh, people still manage to keep a few secrets, I suppose. For instance, I don't know what those two wanted."

"They didn't come to buy supplies," said Bill.

Monroe lowered the paper. "Then why were they there?"

"With all due respect, Mr. Monroe, there's something I have to ask you first." Bill drew in a deep breath. His heart was pounding almost as hard as if he were facing a gunfight. "I plan to ask your daughter to marry me, sir, and I'd like your blessing."

Monroe stared stonily at him for a long moment that seemed even longer than it really was. Finally, he said, "Well, I can't say as I'm surprised. I can't say that I'm all that happy about it, either." He held up a hand to forestall any protest Bill might make. "You're a brave, decent young man, no doubt about that. You risked your life to help us, more than once. But you're still a Texan."

Bill kept a tight rein on the sudden surge of anger he felt, but it wasn't easy. "Yes, sir, I am," he said. "I always will be. But, Mr. Monroe . . . you're wrong about us. You can't judge all Texans, or even all cowboys, by a few troublemakers. Just like I wouldn't say every Kansan is like Frank Porter or Zach Norris."

Monroe rattled his newspaper in curt disgust. "You'd better not," he said. He glared at Bill a moment longer before he nodded. "I'll give you my blessing," he said with obvious reluctance. "I know it's what Eden wants, and Lord knows I've always tried to see to it that the girl's happy. But I'll be keeping an eye on you. If you don't treat her right, I don't care where you're from, you'll answer to me, by God."

"You don't have to worry about that," Bill assured him. He couldn't stop the grin that broke out on his face. "Thank you, Mr. Monroe. You won't be sorry about this."

"I hope not," said the old man with a sigh. "It's a hard thing for a man to give up his daughter to another man. I wish . . . I wish Eden's mother were here . . ."

He looked away, and Bill quickly left the parlor so Monroe could be alone with his emotions.

When he stepped onto the porch, Eden was standing at the railing, gazing out at the night. She turned toward him, her blond hair shining palely in the shadows. With a hint of her usual mischievousness in her voice, she said, "Now, was there something you wanted to ask me, Bill?"

"Yes, ma'am." He started to get down on one knee, the way fellas did in storybooks.

"Oh, don't do that," she said quickly. "You've got a bad leg. It isn't necessary."

"You're sure?"

"Of course."

"Well, then . . . Eden Monroe, you'd make me the happiest cowboy who ever rode out of Texas if you'd marry up with me. Will you do it? Will you be my wife?"

"Yes," she whispered. "Oh, yes."

And as she came into into his arms and he kissed her, Bill thought about how he had expected a lot of things to happen when he threw in with Hob and started on the long trail north to the railhead.

This wasn't one of them.

But at this moment he was happier than he had ever been before in his life, and he figured things were just going to get better from here on out.

After that he stopped thinking for a while and concentrated on kissing his future wife.

The future wife of the marshal of Redemption . . .

Chapter 24

Since he was a politician, Mayor Fleming wanted a public swearing-in ceremony, with a lot of hoopla and the town band playing and maybe some red, white, and blue bunting hung from the false fronts of the buildings on Main Street.

Bill didn't waste any time turning thumbs down on that suggestion.

"I'd just as soon not make a big show out of it," he told the mayor.

"But you want everybody to know that you're the new marshal," argued Fleming. "It'll be good for the town to know we have a lawman again."

"Word'll get around quick enough. I plan to make regular rounds, so it won't be long before most folks have seen me wearing the badge."

Fleming sighed and shook his head in obvious disappointment. Clearly, he couldn't comprehend the idea of anybody passing up an opportunity to make a speech.

Bill had gone to the bank to give the mayor his decision the morning after Fleming and Dunaway had come to the store to offer him the marshal's job. After they had settled the question of whether or not there would be a public swearing-in ceremony, he asked, "When do you want me to start?"

"Right away," said Fleming as he stood up from the desk in his office. He opened a drawer and took out a ring of keys that he handed to Bill. "Here are the keys to the marshal's office, as well as the cells in the jail. We'll go down there right now and pick up Kermit along the way. He can swear you in . . . if you're sure about the ceremony."

"I'm sure," Bill said with a nod.

The mayor put on his hat and led Bill out of the bank, calling out to the teller that he would be back shortly. A couple of customers were in the bank, and Bill saw them watching curiously as he and Fleming left. The gossip would be flying in a matter of minutes, he figured.

When they stopped at Kermit Dunaway's law office, the justice of the peace greeted them with a pleased grin. "The future Mrs. Harvey must have given her approval to our proposition," he said.

"Nobody said anything about a future Mrs. Harvey," Bill pointed out.

"You didn't have to, my boy, you didn't have to." Dunaway put one of his usual unlit cigars in his mouth. "When's the swearing-in ceremony?"

"There's not going to be a ceremony," Fleming said as if he still couldn't believe it.

Dunaway's bushy, reddish-gray eyebrows rose in surprise. "No speeches? No brass band?"

Bill reined in the impatience he felt. "Look, I just want to get started, all right? Is there anything wrong with that?"

Dunaway held up a hand, palm out, and shook his head as he said, "No, no, of course not. A very commendable attitude, I must say."

"Come with us, Kermit, and you can administer the oath of office," said Fleming.

"Let me get my hat."

When the three of them reached the marshal's office, Bill used one of the keys on the ring to unlock the door. As he swung it open, a musty odor drifted out. The office had been closed up for a couple of weeks.

"You'll want to air the place out," Fleming commented.

Bill nodded. "Yeah. I'll need to get rid of the smell of skunk."

Quite a few people had noticed the three men walking toward the marshal's office. As he and Fleming and Dunaway went inside, Bill glanced over his shoulder and saw a small crowd gathering in the street and talking in low voices. He closed the door until they got the official business taken care of.

He had asked Eden if she wanted to come along this morning, but she'd declined. This was his business, she had told him, and anyway, she needed to be at the store to help her father, now that Bill wasn't going to be around to lend a hand at the mercantile anymore.

The windows on either side of the door in the marshal's office didn't have curtains on them, so plenty of light made its way inside. Bill stood just inside the door and looked around.

The front room wasn't very big. A dust-covered desk and chair were to his left, in front of a gun rack on the rear wall. A couple of ladder-back chairs sat in front of the desk. That side of the room also had a filing cabinet in it.

To his immediate right as he stood near the door was an old, worn divan. A man could probably sleep on it if he wanted to, but he'd have to be careful of broken springs poking him. A potbellied, cast-iron stove sat in the right rear corner, cold now since there hadn't been a fire in it for a couple of weeks. On top of the stove was a coffeepot. A small table and a couple more chairs completed the furnishings in the office.

Directly in front of Bill, in the middle of the rear wall, was the door leading into the part of the building that housed the jail. The cell block door was thick and heavy and had a small, barred window set into it at eye level. Bill walked over to the door and slipped one of the remaining keys into the lock. It opened with the second key he tried.

He swung the door out and stepped into the cell block, which was more shadowy than the front room because the barred windows in it were smaller. There were two cells on each side of a short corridor that ended in a blank stone wall. The doors and dividing walls of the cells were formed of cross-hatched iron bars.

It looked like all the other jails Bill had seen, which admittedly weren't that many.

"Four cells has always been plenty," said Fleming. "Most of the time you won't have anybody locked up."

"We can hope so, anyway," added Dunaway.

Bill nodded. He reached and grasped the barred door on one of the nearer cells. He gave it a good shake and was pleased that it didn't budge.

"Seems solid enough," he said.

"Oh, it is," said Fleming. "The town fathers didn't skimp on building this jail. We always knew Redemption would have to have law and order if the town was going to grow and thrive."

Bill nodded and backed out of the cell block. He closed the door but didn't lock it.

A smaller door in the left rear corner of the office led into a narrow storeroom, and a back door opened from it onto the alley running behind the jail. Bill checked the lock on it and thought it might be a good idea to replace it with a stronger one. When he mentioned that, Fleming said, "I'll make a note of it. The town will take care of it."

"The sooner the better," Bill said. "A jail's only as strong as the easiest way into it."

"The boy's got a knack for this, Roy," said Dunaway.

"More like common sense," said Bill.

He continued looking around the place for a few minutes, opening the drawers in the desk and pawing through the wanted posters and assorted papers that filled them. He took a half-full bottle of whiskey from one of the drawers and handed it to Fleming.

"Won't be needing that."

"You don't drink?" asked the mayor.

"Not Frank Porter's whiskey," Bill said. "You can pour it out as far as I'm concerned."

He didn't find a spare marshal's badge in the desk, but there were several plain, unmarked tin stars in one of the drawers. Bill figured they were deputy badges. But he didn't have a deputy, so one of them would do for him.

As Bill started to pin it on, Dunaway spoke up, saying, "Wait a minute, you haven't been sworn in yet."

"Well, let's get it done, then." Bill had seen a Bible in one of the drawers. As he took it out, he thought about how ironic it was that a cold-blooded killer had the Word of God in his desk. Too bad Porter had the Devil in his heart, thought Bill.

He gave the Bible to Dunaway, who held it out and said, "Put your hand on it and repeat after me . . . I solemnly swear to fulfill the duties of the marshal of Redemption, Kansas, and faithfully uphold the laws of the United States of America, the state of Kansas, and the town of Redemption, so help me God."

"That's a mouthful. How about I just say I solemnly swear, so help me God, and let it go at that?"

Dunaway chuckled. "It'll do. You're now the marshal of Redemption, son. What's your first order of business?"

"I'll finish pinning on this badge, I reckon," Bill said.

After Fleming and Dunaway were gone, Bill sat behind the desk and took a deep breath. Hard as it was to believe, he was a lawman now. The star on his shirt said so.

He wouldn't get rich on the salary the mayor had promised him, but it was more than he would have earned as a cowboy. Steady work, too. It wouldn't be long before he and Eden could start thinking about setting a date for their wedding. Even though she had agreed to marry him, they hadn't discussed just when that would happen.

He sat there a few minutes, trying to come to grips with everything, then got to his feet. He couldn't just wait in the office for trouble to come to him. As a lawman, it was his job to get out and stop it from happening in the first place.

Some of the people who had gathered in the street in curi-
osity were still standing there when Bill stepped out onto the
porch. They appeared to be waiting for him. An excited buzz
of conversation came from them when they saw the badge
he wore.

"Is it true, Bill?" one of the men asked him. Bill recognized him as a customer who came into the Monroe mercantile. "Are you really the new marshal?"

Bill smiled. "That's what it looks like."

"Hot damn! After the way you stood up to those killers, I
feel better already."

"Hope you feel that way after I've worn this badge for a
while," Bill said.

He gave the citizens a friendly nod and started walking
down the street. Everyone he passed smiled at him and many
of them spoke, saying they were glad he had taken the job of
marshal, but he sensed a certain wariness in many of them,
as well.

You couldn't blame them for that, he thought. Porter and
Norris had probably seemed like friendly, competent, honest
lawmen at first. When they had taken care of the problem
with the trail herds and the Texas cowboys, they had been
hailed as heroes by the people who lived in Redemption.

It was only after more time had passed that folks began to
see Porter and Norris for what they really were. That made
some of them suspicious of Bill. Plus he had the disadvan-
tage, in their eyes, of being from Texas.

He didn't mind being patient. He would do the best job he
could, and he was confident he would win over the doubters.

He walked all the way up Main Street from the marshal's
office, then crossed the broad, dusty street and headed back
down the other side. When he came to the mercantile, he
thought about going on past it and continuing his rounds, but
he couldn't resist the temptation. He was just vain enough to
want to show off his new badge to Eden.

Quite a few customers were in the store, so she didn't notice him right away. He crossed his arms, lowered his head
so the brim of his hat shielded his face, and stood in line

at the counter, like somebody waiting his turn to buy something. After a few minutes, the people in front of him cleared out, and he was able to step up where Eden could see him. Her eyes widened in surprise.

"Oh, my goodness," she said. "It's real. You really are the marshal."

"Did you think I was making it up?" he asked with a grin.

She shook her head. "No, of course not. I knew the town council really offered you the job, and I knew you were going to accept. But seeing you standing there with that badge on your shirt . . . well, it's just going to take some getting used to, that's all."

"Maybe it won't take too long."

Perry Monroe came up, studied Bill from head to toe with pursed lips, and finally nodded. "I have to admit, you look like a lawman. Now if you can just do the job . . ."

"He'll be a vast improvement over what we had before," Eden pointed out.

"I'll do my best," said Bill. "You've got my word on that."

"Well, if it doesn't work out," said Monroe, "you can always clerk here in the store."

That wasn't going to happen, thought Bill. No way in hell. His clerking days were over. But not wanting to hurt his future father-in-law's feelings, he didn't say that.

He would have visited longer with them, but just then he heard some commotion in the street outside, loud talk mixed with hoofbeats and the creak of wagon wheels. He inclined his head toward the front door and said, "I'd better go see what that's about," even though he had a pretty good idea.

Sure enough, he saw when he stepped out onto the high porch of the store, a caravan of freight wagons was rolling into Redemption from the west, on their way back from Santa Fe. The bullwhackers were cursing and whipping their oxen. As Bill hooked his thumbs in his gun belt and looked at the wagons rolling past, he thought that the days of such caravans probably were numbered. With the way railroads were spreading all over the country now, it wouldn't be long before all the goods traveling from one place to another would be shipped by rail.

He was musing on that when he heard an angry voice say, "Well, I'll be a son of a bitch. It's *you*."

Bill looked down and saw one of the burly, bearded freighters glaring up at him. It took him a second before he recognized the man as the one called Blaisdell who had caused trouble in the mercantile weeks earlier. An ugly grin stretched across the man's whiskery face as he went on, "I been hopin' I'd meet up with you again, you gimp bastard."

Chapter 25

Bill reined in the surge of anger he felt. A lawman was going to be cursed and called names from time to time. It was inevitable. He had to be able to control his temper and stay coolheaded when somebody tried to provoke him.

"Howdy, Blaisdell," he drawled. "Maybe you better take a closer look. I'm not on crutches anymore, and there's a star pinned to my shirt."

Blaisdell's eyes narrowed. "So there is. What happened to that son of a bitch who threw down on me last time I was here?"

"He's dead."

"You killed him and took his job?" Blaisdell laughed. "That sounds pretty far-fetched to me, kid."

"I didn't say that's what happened. But I *am* the marshal of Redemption now, and I don't want any trouble while you're in town."

"Sort of jumpin' the gun, ain't you? We just got here. I haven't done a damned thing yet."

"I'm just letting know," said Bill. "As long as you and your friends act decent, there won't be any problems."

Blaisdell gave a contemptuous snort. He turned back to

his stream of oxen, popped his whip over their backs, and let loose with a stream of sulfurous profanity. The wagon creaked on down the street with the others, heading toward the piece of ground on the eastern edge of town where the caravans usually camped next to the small, cottonwood-lined stream meandering through there.

Bill watched them go. He knew from experience that the freighters sometimes caused trouble while they were in town, although never enough to make Redemption bar them the way it had with the Texas cowboys.

But that was all right, he told himself. Sure, this was his first day on the job, but there was nothing wrong with settling in quickly.

"That was Clint Blaisdell, wasn't it?" Eden asked from behind him.

He turned to see the worried frown on her face. "Yeah, but I warned him not to cause any trouble while he's in town this time."

"Do you really think that'll do any good?"

"It better," Bill said with a firm nod. "If it doesn't, he'll find himself locked up again and facing another fine."

Eden didn't look convinced. She said, "Be careful. I don't trust him."

"I don't, either," Bill said.

He gave Eden a quick kiss on the cheek and resumed making his rounds. He stopped at several other businesses to chat with folks he knew from their visits to the mercantile, including Josiah Hartnett at the livery stable and Phillip Ramsey, the editor and publisher of the Redemption *Star*. Ramsey wanted to interview him, but the idea of answering a bunch of questions about his life made Bill uncomfortable, so he promised to think about it, hoping Ramsey would move on to something else.

When he stopped at the café run by Gunnar and Helga Nilsson, the walrus-mustached Gunnar wiped his hand on the apron he wore, shook Bill's hand, and said, "You can eat as many meals here for free as you want, Marshal."

His wife, Helga, nodded, adding, "It'll be a pleasure to

feed a real lawman, after those two who were always in here wanting meals on the cuff . . . and more besides."

"I'm obliged," Bill said, "and I'll take you up on the offer. I'll try not to take advantage of it, though."

"We'll start by giving you lunch," said Gunnar. "I'll go fry up a steak right now."

Bill didn't protest. He'd heard that the Swedes put on a good feed, and he was eager to find out if it was true.

It certainly was, and he was pleasantly stuffed when he left the café a while later. After a meal like that, it felt good to walk around, so he made another circuit of the town. Redemption was busy, but everything was peaceable.

It remained that way through the afternoon. By the time Bill went down to the mercantile as Eden and her father were closing up, he figured his wages for the day were just about the easiest money he had ever earned.

Monroe went on ahead. Bill and Eden lingered behind so they could walk together and talk quietly. Bill said, "I was thinking I might fix up the sofa in the marshal's office so I can sleep there nights."

Eden sounded surprised as she asked, "What's wrong with our spare bedroom?"

"Well, now that we're engaged and all, it's not hardly proper for us to be living under the same roof until we're married."

"But it was proper *before* we were engaged?"

"Don't ask me to explain it," said Bill. "That's just the way it feels to me."

Eden laughed, and he liked the sound of it. "Some wild young cowboy you are," she said.

"Not anymore. I'm a lawman now. Sober as a judge. Upright as a preacher. Speaking of which, we haven't talked about which church we're gonna get married in."

"Father and I are Methodists."

Bill winced. "I was brought up Baptist, myself, but maybe I've backslid enough I can see my way clear to marrying a sprinkler."

"Well, I have to put up with a dunker, so I think I'm the one who's having to be tolerant."

"We'll sort it out," Bill said with a grin. "The Methodist church it is. But to get back to what I was saying . . . I think it's a good idea for me to stay at the office at night in case anybody comes looking for the marshal, too."

"There's that to consider, I suppose. You can't spend the nights there after we're married, though."

"Oh, no! I don't intend to." Bill made a face as he realized he'd probably answered a mite more vehemently than he'd intended to. "What I mean is, when that time comes, I'll probably ask the mayor and the town council to hire somebody to work as a night deputy."

"That's a good idea. And when is that time going to come?"

"When we get married, you mean? That's sort of up to you. You're the bride."

"And you're the groom. You've got a say in it."

Bill thought it over. "How about a month from now?" he suggested. "Is that long enough for you to get ready for a wedding?"

"That's more time than I need," said Eden. "I already have the dress. My mother's wedding gown."

"Well, then, how about two weeks?"

She thought about it and nodded. "Two weeks." She slipped her arm through his as they walked along. "I like that. In two weeks I'll be Mrs. William Harvey."

Bill swallowed hard. He wanted to marry Eden more than he'd ever wanted anything in his life . . . but even so, hearing it put into words like that was almost enough to spook a fella who had spent his whole life as a fiddle-footed cowboy.

He didn't have time to think about it, because at that moment rapid footsteps sounded behind them. Bill stopped and turned, freeing his arm from Eden's so he could move his hand closer to the butt of his gun. He saw a man hurrying toward them in the dusk.

"Hold it," Bill said. "You looking for me?"

"Marshal? Is that you?" The man sounded out of breath, and as he came to a stop, Bill recognized him as Benjy Cobb, the swamper from the saloon.

"Yeah, it's me. What's wrong, Mr. Cobb?"

"Fred sent me to see if I could find you. He said for me to tell you . . . He said for me to tell you he thinks there might be some trouble brewin' at the saloon. That bullwhacker Blaisdell's playin' cards with a tinhorn gambler who drifted into town a few days ago, and he don't like losin'."

"Who doesn't like losing? Blaisdell?"

"Yeah. That tinhorn's gonna clean him out, the rate he's goin'."

Bill didn't give a hoot in hell whether or not Clint Blaisdell lost every bit of his money. But if Blaisdell raised a ruckus about it and started wrecking the saloon, that was another matter entirely. It was his job to put a stop to that, or see to it that it didn't happen in the first place.

"Sorry, Eden," he said. "Reckon I'd better go with Mr. Cobb here and see if I can settle things down."

"Should I keep your supper warm for you?" she asked in a voice drawn tight with worry.

"Sure," he answered easily. "This won't amount to much. I won't be gone long."

He hoped that was true. But as he started walking back toward Main Street with Benjy Cobb, he thought about how the possibility existed that he might never come back. That potential for danger was something a lawman just had to live with . . . and so did a lawman's wife.

"I figured I might find you at the Monroe place, Marshal," Cobb said. He sounded nervous, and Bill thought he was probably talking just to give himself something to do. Bill had heard enough about Cobb to know that the swamper had spent a lot of years drinking and wasn't in very good health. The job at the saloon was all he could manage. His nerves and body were just about worn out. He went on, "Is it true what I heard, that you and Miss Eden are gettin' hitched?"

"It's true," Bill told him. "Two weeks from now."

"Well, ain't that mighty fine! Congratulations, Marshal. You won't find no sweeter gal than Miss Eden."

Bill grinned. "You're not telling me anything I don't already know, Mr. Cobb."

"Oh, you should call me Benjy, like ever'body else. Ol' rumpot like me don't deserve to be called mister."

"I wouldn't say that. I was raised to respect my elders. I reckon it'd be all right, though, if I called you Benjy because we're friends."

"Really?" The swamper looked over at him, beaming with surprise and pleasure.

"Sure. I suspect you know a lot about the folks who live here and what goes on in Redemption."

"Oh, I do," said Benjy. "I surely do."

"Since I'm new at this law business, I'm liable to need to ask you some questions every now and then."

"Anything you need to know, I'm your man," Benjy said proudly. "I'd be honored to give you a hand, Marshal."

"I appreciate that, and I'll keep it in mind."

They had reached the saloon. Even before they went inside, Bill knew the situation had worsened while Benjy was looking for him. He heard Blaisdell's loud, blustery voice raised in anger. Bill went in first, pushing the batwings aside with his left hand and stepping into the room.

As he did, his eyes took in the scene instantly. Fred Smoot sat at the far end of the bar in his wheelchair, his hands tightly gripping the chair's arms. The bartender, who had replaced the one killed by Zach Norris, was behind the hardwood near Smoot. Half a dozen customers were gathered at that end of the bar as well. They had cleared the area around a poker table topped with green felt where two men sat facing each other. The one with his back toward Bill was Clint Blaisdell. Bill knew that from the man's massive shoulders, tangled thatch of dark hair, and rumbling voice.

"—Been cheatin' me all night, you damn tinhorn, and I've had enough of it!" Blaisdell was saying as Bill came in.

The small, thin, goateed man sitting across from Blaisdell was dressed in dapper but somewhat threadbare fashion. His face held the pallor of a man who seldom saw the sun. His expression was eerily serene as he said, "I'm afraid you're going to have to back that up, my friend."

"Oh, I'm gonna!" Blaisdell bellowed as he shoved the

chair back and started to his feet. His shoulders bunched as his arm moved toward his waist.

"Blaisdell, no!" Bill shouted as he put his hand on the butt of his gun. He hoped the warning was in time to head off what was about to happen.

It wasn't. The gambler moved a lot faster than the lumbering bullwhacker. He came up out of his chair like an unleashed spring, his hand darting under his coat as he did so. When it came out, he held a small pistol that he thrust across the table and fired. The gun went off with a sharp crack.

Blaisdell grunted, took a step backward, and stopped pawing at his belt. Instead he pressed both hands to his chest. "You son of a bitch," he said in a voice tinged with awe. "You've killed me."

He half turned, so Bill could see the blood welling between his fingers. Then he fell onto his knees and from there slowly crumpled onto his side. Every detail was etched into Bill's brain. He saw how wide with pain and shock Blaisdell's eyes were and how beads of sweat had popped out on the freighter's forehead. A few tiny places on the front of Blaisdell's shirt smoldered where burning grains of powder from the pistol's muzzle had landed.

Bill heard the wheezing rasp as Blaisdell struggled to keep drawing breath in his body. He saw Blaisdell's mouth move, but no more loud, angry words came out, only a thin whine that ended in a sigh.

That was it. Blaisdell was dead.

The gambler placed his still-smoking gun on the felt-covered table in front of him. A frosty smile curved his lips as he said, "Self-defense, Marshal. You saw it yourself. That oaf reached for his gun first."

Bill's Colt was still in its holster. He should have drawn it before now, he thought. If he pulled iron after the shooting was over, he would just look foolish. So he took his hand off the gun butt and walked over to where Blaisdell lay. He looked down at the bullwhacker and asked, "What gun?"

The gambler frowned. "He reached for a gun. You must have seen it."

"He's not wearing a gun," Bill said with a shake of his head. "Look for yourself."

The gambler didn't come out from behind the table, but he leaned forward to get a better look. Using the toe of his boot, Bill rolled the corpse flat on its back. Blaisdell's coat fell back, revealing the bullwhip wrapped around his thick waist.

"That's what he was reaching for," said Bill. "His whip."

The gambler's eyes narrowed. His gaze darted toward the pistol on the table in front of him, and for a second Bill thought the man was going to grab the gun and try to shoot his way out of the saloon.

He could probably do it, too, Bill realized. He had seen how fast the gambler moved. There was no way he could haul his Colt out and get off a shot before the tinhorn cut him down.

But then the gambler said, "It doesn't matter. You've seen what those freighters can do with a bullwhip. In the hands of a man like him it's just as dangerous as a gun. He would have cut me to ribbons."

Bill knew the gambler was right. If Blaisdell had been trying to shoot the man or stab him with a knife, the law wouldn't have recognized any difference between those two threats. It was the same with the bullwhip. The gambler couldn't have known Blaisdell wasn't carrying a gun, and even if he had, it was still self-defense.

It wasn't Bill's job to determine that, though. He said, "There'll have to be an inquest. Until then, you're under arrest." He stepped closer to the table and put his hand on the Colt again. "I'll take that gun."

The gambler's eyes flicked toward the pistol again. Bill's pulse thundered, but he forced himself to remain outwardly calm. After a second, the gambler shrugged his narrow shoulders and relaxed.

"Why not?" he asked with a smile. "The bunks in your jail had better be comfortable, though, Marshal."

Chapter 26

Bill didn't relax until the cell door clanged shut behind the gambler, whose name was Amos Dailey, and the man's pistol was safely locked up in one of the desk drawers. Then he sat down behind the desk, dropped his hat on top of it, dragged in a deep breath, and let it out in a sigh.

The office door opened and Eden hurried in. "Bill, are you all right?" she asked.

He got to his feet and smiled. "I'm fine," he told her. "Blaisdell's the one who got shot." He shook his head. "There I was, worrying that I might have trouble with him, and he's the one who winds up down at the undertaker's before he's in town more than a few hours."

"Well, thank God it was him and not you. That old drunk from the saloon said you almost got in a gunfight with the man who shot Blaisdell."

Bill had asked Benjy Cobb to go down to the Monroe house and let them know he wouldn't be there for supper and wouldn't be spending the night in their spare room. He had already talked about that with Eden, of course, but now he would definitely stay at the marshal's office tonight, since he had a prisoner locked up in one of the cells.

"It wasn't that bad. The fella came along peaceable-like."

"He thought about trying to kill you, though, didn't he?"

"Lots of people think things," said Bill. "It's what they do that counts."

She came over to him, put her arms around him, and leaned her head against his chest. "This is going to take some getting used to," she said in a half whisper.

"Yeah, for me, too," he agreed. "Maybe you want to change your mind about marrying me."

He was half joking, but only half. He wouldn't hold her to what she said when he proposed if she had decided she couldn't be married to a lawman.

But she lifted her head, smiled up at him, and said, "Not a chance, cowboy." She put a hand on his chest, pushed him toward the chair, and went on, "Sit down. You haven't had your supper yet. I'll bring you a tray."

"I hate to put you to that much bother."

"It's no bother. And it won't be the first time I've brought you your supper, now will it?"

He had to admit it wouldn't be. And he was grateful for it, too.

Almost as grateful as he was that Eden still wanted to marry him.

The inquest was at ten o'clock the next morning, with Justice of the Peace Kermit Dunaway presiding. Bill testified as to what he had seen in the saloon the night before, as did Fred Smoot and several of the customers. That was enough for the hastily sworn-in six-man jury to return a speedy verdict of self-defense.

Blaisdell's boss from the freight caravan was there in the town hall where the proceedings were held, and he frowned as the verdict was announced. Bill wondered if the man was going to cause trouble about it, but after Judge Dunaway dismissed the jury, told Dailey he was free to go, and adjourned the court, the freighter came up to Bill and said, "This is twice in a row we've had trouble in Redemption,

Marshal. I don't reckon we'll be stopping here next time through."

"That's your decision to make," Bill told him. "For what it's worth, though, the jury was right. It was self-defense."

The wagon boss waved a hand. "Oh, hell, I know that. Blaisdell was always spoilin' for trouble. He was gonna come to a bad end sooner or later. But still, my men won't like it."

"As long as they don't cause any trouble before you leave . . ."

"They won't." The man clapped his hat on his head. "We'll be rolling in ten minutes. We've already wasted enough time here."

He turned and stomped out.

The shabbily elegant gambler walked up to Bill next and said, "I'll have my gun back, Marshal."

Bill nodded. "You sure will. And you'll take it and get out of Redemption."

Dailey looked surprised. "What do you mean by that? I didn't break any laws. You don't have any call to run me out of town."

"You killed a man. I don't want you here. That's call enough for me."

The gambler shook his head stubbornly. "That's not legal. You can't do it."

"Then you can stay, and I'll arrest you for disturbing the peace every time you win a hand of cards."

"Winning at poker is my job. It's not disturbing the peace."

"That's not the way I see it," said Bill. "You won when you played Blaisdell, and a man wound up bleeding on the floor. Seems likely it might happen again, so it's my job to prevent it."

"You're a brave man, Marshal." Dailey's voice was low and soft but tinged with menace.

"Not hardly. Next time I hear there's trouble in the saloon, I'll bring a shotgun with me. And I'm liable to spread some buckshot around first and then sort things out."

The two men traded stares for a long moment. Dailey was the one who looked away first. "All right," he muttered. "Hell, there are plenty of towns where the pickings are a lot richer than they are in Redemption."

"That's right," Bill said, "and if you leave right now, maybe you can be in one of them by nightfall."

After all the trouble that had cropped up on his first day as the marshal of Redemption, Bill worried that every day was going to be like that.

It wasn't, though, and a week passed without anything else happening . . . except that his wedding to Eden was a week closer.

Since he was from South Texas, with its heavily Spanish culture, he was accustomed to folks sort of taking it easy for a while every afternoon following their lunch. Here in Kansas, people didn't take siestas, but things did slow down a mite during the heat of the afternoon.

During those times, when it seemed most likely his services as a lawman wouldn't be needed, he went to Hartnett's stable, saddled his horse, and rode out of town to the west. He could tell Josiah Hartnett was as curious as all get-out about where he was going, but Bill didn't offer any explanations.

A couple of miles west of town, out of earshot but before he reached the sand hills, Bill reined to a halt at the mouth of a draw. He swung down from the saddle and led the horse into the arroyo. Water ran through it during cloudbursts, but the ground was baked hard and dry as rock at the moment.

Bill tied the reins to a scrubby bush and walked on up the draw a short distance. He stopped and faced the western bank from a distance of about twenty feet. He pulled in a couple of deep breaths and blew them out.

Then he drew his gun as fast as he could and fired at the eight-foot-tall earthen bank.

Echoes of the shot rolled across the prairie. Bill lowered the Colt and studied the spot where his bullet had hit. It was a little more than four feet off the ground. Chest-high on a man.

He holstered the revolver, set himself, drew, and fired again. The second shot smacked into the hard-packed dirt only a few inches from where the first one had hit. Bill repeated the process three more times, emptying the Colt.

As he reloaded, he looked with approval at the cluster of bullet marks on the bank. A chuckle came from him. "You're damn deadly when it comes to shootin' dirt, old son," he said aloud.

He was pleased with the improvement he was showing, though. This was the sixth day he had ridden out here to practice getting his gun out faster and still being able to hit what he shot at. The first day, the one after the inquest into Clint Blaisdell's death, he had been able to draw fairly quickly, but his shots went high, low, and every which way. Slowly but surely as he worked on it, they had moved in, centering themselves where a man's chest would be if Bill was facing him in a gunfight.

He knew he would never be a famous pistoleer, but he was young and strong and had good reflexes. There was no reason he couldn't get better at handling a gun.

One thing was certain in his mind: if he'd had to fight the gambler Dailey, he would have died. Just as he would have died in a straight-up showdown with Porter or Norris. No man had a guarantee he would see the sunset that evening when he woke up every morning, but it was just common sense to give himself as good a chance as possible.

So he came out here every day and practiced. He didn't want anybody to know about it, especially Eden. He didn't want her to see the doubts that plagued him. He wanted her to respect him and believe in him and love him. If he ever lost that, he didn't know what he'd do.

He slid the Colt back in the holster and started all over again.

He was reloading for the third time when the thudding clatter of hoofbeats drifted to his ears. Sounded like several horses, he decided. A wagon team, maybe, or a handful of riders. He hoped whoever it was would just go on past the draw. They must have heard the shots, but maybe they wouldn't be curious enough to investigate. Most folks on the frontier minded their own business.

Not this hombre, though. As Bill looked toward the mouth of the draw, he saw a wagon come to a stop there.

The white-bearded figure who climbed down slowly and painfully from the wagon seat was familiar. Perry Monroe came toward him and called, "Bill? Bill, is that you?"

"What are you doing here, Mr. Monroe?" Bill asked as the storekeeper came up to him.

Monroe frowned at him. "The question is, what are *you* doing here? From the sound of all the shooting, I thought there was a war going on."

Feeling uncomfortable about it, Bill waved toward the bullet-pocked bank. "I've been practicing. I want to have a better chance if I come up against a fast gun again."

Monroe studied the dirt wall. "Looks like your aim is pretty good. How's your speed?"

Bill shrugged. "Getting better, I think."

"Let's see."

Bill wasn't fond of the idea, but he didn't think he could very well refuse. He had already pouched his iron. He motioned for Monroe to step back. He would try something a little different this time, he decided.

He palmed out the Colt and thumbed off all five rounds as fast as he could.

The shots rolled out like thunder, coming so close together they sounded like one long roar. Bill fought down the recoil each time, and when he lowered the revolver, he was pleased to see that while the new bullet marks were a little more scattered than the earlier ones, they were still fairly close together. At least three of the five would have hit an opponent.

Of course, he thought, it would all be different if somebody was shooting back at him.

"Pretty impressive," said Monroe with a nod. "I'm glad to see this is what you're doing, son."

"What made you follow me out here, anyway?" asked Bill.

"Josiah spoke to me, told me you were riding somewhere out of town every afternoon." Monroe held up a hand to forestall the angry response that came to Bill's lips. "Now, don't get mad at him. He and I are old friends, and he thought he was doing the right thing. You know, looking out for Eden's best interests."

"What in blazes did Hartnett think I was doing?"

"Well . . . when a man starts acting mysterious-like and sneaking around . . . there's usually a woman involved."

Bill stared at the old man, flabbergasted.

"I didn't figure there was really any good place out here for you to be meeting a woman," Monroe went on, "and I was damned if I could figure out who you might be carrying on with, if you were. There aren't all that many young, single women in Redemption except the ones who work for Fred Smoot and Miss Alvera, but there are a few. I decided I had to be sure, for Eden's sake."

The anger seeped out of Bill. He couldn't blame Monroe for wanting to protect his daughter.

"I wouldn't do that," he said as he started thumbing fresh cartridges into the Colt's cylinder. "Not ever. I give you my word, Mr. Monroe."

"I believe you, I believe you. It's still a relief to know I don't have to worry about you cheating on my little girl." Monroe paused. "It's plenty to have to worry about her marrying up with a man who's liable to get shot by some gunslinger or outlaw."

"I worry about that, too," said Bill as he holstered the gun and turned toward the earthen wall of the draw.

A heartbeat later, gun thunder rolled across the prairie once more.

Chapter 27

Benjy Cobb never thought about the past. He had learned through painful, bitter experience not to. Memories just tortured a man. So he pushed them away, and when he wasn't strong enough to do that anymore, whiskey blotted them out. Fred Smoot wasn't exactly a friend, but he felt sorry for Benjy, gave him a job, gave him the booze he needed to banish the past. It wasn't a good life, by any stretch of the imagination, but it was the best Benjy could manage.

His grip on the broom kept him from falling down as he swept the porch in front of the saloon. The hour was late, and only a few customers were still inside. Fred and the new bartender would be closing up soon. Benjy couldn't remember the new bartender's name just yet. He'd get it, sooner or later, but things like that usually took him a while these days. He wasn't quite as sharp as he'd once been.

A couple of the customers pushed the batwings aside and stepped out onto the porch, talking and laughing softly. Benjy shuffled toward them, still sweeping. He kept his head down and his eyes on the planks. Folks generally didn't like it when he looked straight at them. He had learned that the hard way, too. He'd been slapped around a few times because of it.

"—Tomorrow, Doc," Benjy heard one of the men say to the other.

That made Benjy curious enough to glance up. Redemption didn't have a doctor. Maybe one of the fellas was a sawbones and was planning to move here. That would be good. A town needed a doctor.

Neither of these hombres really looked like a medical man, though. They both wore range clothes, and the one addressed as Doc had long, fair hair under his hat and a beard that jutted out from his jaw. He muttered something in reply to his companion. Benjy caught the word "wedding."

Why, they were talking about Bill and Eden's wedding, Benjy realized. No surprise there. A lot of folks in town were talking about it. Everybody liked Eden and her pa, and even though Bill Harvey hadn't been in town all that long, most people liked him, too, and thought he was doing a good job as marshal. The Methodist Church would be packed tomorrow afternoon at two o'clock when the two of them got hitched. Benjy even intended to be there himself, although he would just slip in the back after the ceremony got started and try to see to it that nobody noticed him. He didn't want to embarrass his friend Bill.

"—Whole bunch," said the first man, and Benjy wondered, *A whole bunch of what?*

And then the fella who might be a sawbones but didn't look like one laughed and said something else, and Benjy would have sworn he heard a familiar name.

Norris.

Benjy jerked the broom as a memory bulled its way into his mind. He didn't want to remember how Zach Norris had tormented him, but he couldn't help it. The deputy had always picked at him, jabbing him with cruel insults about how he was a worthless old drunk who ought to be taken out and shot.

"You're wastin' perfectly good air somebody else could be breathin', Benjy," Norris had said, and laughed at his own wit. He had called Benjy all sorts of ugly names, and late one night, while Benjy was out back of the saloon emptying the spittoons, Norris had come out of the shadows and grabbed him and started hitting him. Benjy had begged him to stop, but Norris wouldn't listen. Benjy fell down and Norris kicked him, again and again, and then the deputy had dumped one of the spittoons on him. It was what a pathetic old bum like him deserved, Norris had said.

Benjy thought maybe somewhere in the middle of all that, Norris had called him "Pa," like Norris had mistaken him for his pa or was at least taking out his hatred for his pa on him, but Benjy couldn't be sure about that. His memory wasn't what it once was.

But he remembered how bad he'd hurt after that beating, and the thought made him flinch and jerk the broom, and the man called Doc suddenly swung toward him, grabbed the front of his shirt, and hauled him up on his toes.

"You tryin' to sweep dirt on my boots, you sorry ol' son of a bitch?" the long-haired man demanded.

Benjy didn't think a real doctor would talk like that.

"No, I—I'm sorry," he stammered. "I swear, I'm sorry, mister. I didn't m-mean to."

"Aw, leave the drunk alone, Doc," said the other man, and there was no doubt about the name now. Benjy heard it loud and clear, but it still didn't make any sense, because the man didn't look like any doctor he'd ever seen. The other man went on, "He don't even know what he's doin'."

"No, I guess not," growled Doc. He pulled Benjy closer and glared down into his face. "Your brain's so pickled in booze you don't know a damned thing, do you, old man?"

"Nothin', not a damned thing, I don't know a damned thing," Benjy babbled as he tried to control his terror. He struggled not to piss himself.

Doc gave him a hard shove that sent him staggering against the wall. Benjy dropped the broom, and the handle of it got tangled up with his feet. He fell, sprawling on the saloon's porch.

Both men laughed. "Come on," Doc said. He and his

companion stepped down and went to the hitch rail where
their horses were tied. Before swinging up into the saddle,
Doc paused and said, "Hey. Rumpot."

Benjy lifted his head and looked up at the man, afraid not
to. His rheumy eyes blinked rapidly.

"If I see you again tomorrow, you better run the other
way," Doc said as he pointed a finger at Benjy. "Because the
next time I lay eyes on you, I'm gonna kill you. You understand what I'm sayin'?"

Benjy gulped and managed to move his head up and down
in a shaky nod.

Doc laughed. "Oh, hell, you won't remember. You're too
whiskey-soaked to remember anything. So I guess I'll just
have to shoot you."

He mounted up, and still laughing, the two men loped
their horses out of town, heading west. Benjy gaped after
them.

There was something important about what he'd heard,
he told himself. Something in what the men had said . . . He
felt like if he could just remember all of it and put it together
in the proper order, along with other things he knew, ought
to know, it would all make sense and it was important somehow . . . He lay there, blinking furiously as he struggled to
pull his thoughts together.

"Hell, Benjy, you fall down again?"

Benjy turned his head and looked up. One of the customers from the saloon had stepped out and seen him lying there
on the porch. The man leaned over, took hold of his arm, and
helped him to his feet. He picked up the broom and handed
it to him.

"There you go. You better be more careful. You're liable
to hurt yourself if you don't watch what you're doin'."

"Yeah," Benjy said. "I got to be more careful."

"Well, good night." The man walked away, leaving Benjy
standing there leaning on the broom.

He had been trying to think of something a moment earlier. At least, that was the way it seemed to him now. But

danged if he could remember what it was. His brain was like that. Sometimes things dropped through it like it was a sieve.

He started sweeping again, whistling a tuneless little melody through his teeth.

Bill had gone to sleep the night before thinking about the wedding, and he woke up the next morning thinking about the wedding.

He was getting married today, doggone it. Really and truly. Married.

He looked at himself in the mirror he had nailed up in the storeroom at the jail and blew out his breath. "Married," he said. "Hitched. Holy matrimony. If that don't beat all."

He wondered if anybody would come after him if he went down to the stable, saddled his horse, and lit a shuck for Texas.

Probably not, he decided. The citizens of Redemption would probably just say good riddance. After all, they had known all along he was nothing but a damned fiddle-footed Texan.

Eden would say good riddance, too, and declare how happy she was she'd gotten shed of him so easily.

"No, she wouldn't," Bill said to himself in the mirror. "She'd likely cry her eyes out."

And he could never do that to her.

Bill knew what Hob would say if he was here: *Cold feet, boy, that's all. Ain't nothin' unusual about that. Every fella has doubts 'fore he gets hitched. But if it's the right woman, he can just put 'em aside. You can do that, son.*

"I can do that," said Bill as he nodded at his reflection. "I'm getting married today."

He cleaned up and went over to the Nilssons' café for breakfast. The wedding wasn't until two o'clock. Until then, he was still the marshal of Redemption, not a bridegroom.

"This is the big day, eh, Marshal?" Helga asked as she poured coffee for him.

Bill nodded. "Yep. I guess so."

"Eden is a wonderful young woman. You will love being married to her."

"Yes, ma'am, I expect I will."

She glanced over her shoulder through the window over the back counter that opened into the kitchen and said quietly, "Don't you tell this to that big Swedish oaf back there, but the day I married him was the best day of my life. I wish you all the happiness we've had."

"I appreciate that, Miz Nilsson. I surely do."

The congratulations and well wishes came fast and furious as Bill made his rounds that morning, along with handshakes and slaps on the back. Everybody in town seemed to be looking forward to the wedding.

It was funny, mused Bill, but he had never felt this much respect and camaraderie from the folks in Victoria and Hallettsville, down there in Texas. To them he was just a ragtag orphan boy who'd grown up to be a shiftless cowboy. Maybe eventually he would have amounted to something if he had stayed there, but there was an even better chance he wouldn't.

But here in Redemption he was already somebody. Folks accepted him, respected him, liked him.

Funny how he'd had to ride hundreds of miles, all the way to Kansas, and get his leg torn half off by an ornery old brindle steer, just to find himself a home.

The mercantile was closed today, he noted as he walked past it. Eden and her father were home, getting ready for the wedding. He hadn't seen Eden for the past couple of days—Perry Monroe had explained that she thought it would be bad luck—and Bill missed her. He wouldn't see her until he turned to look down the aisle of the church and watch her walking toward him in her mother's wedding gown.

Josiah Hartnett had agreed to stand up with him. One of Eden's friends from town was doing the same for her. From everything Bill had heard, there was going to be a big crowd on hand for the ceremony. That made him a little nervous.

He hoped he wouldn't mess up somehow and make a fool of himself.

When he got back to the marshal's office, he was surprised to find Perry Monroe waiting for him. "What's wrong?" Bill asked.

"Wrong? Why should anything be wrong?" Monroe clapped a hand on his shoulder. "I brought your suit. The best we have in the store."

He gestured toward the clothes lying on the sofa. "A suit," Bill said. "You know, I hadn't even thought about that."

"You didn't think I was going to let you marry my daughter dressed like a cowboy, did you?" Monroe held up a hand. "Not that I have anything against cowboys. You taught me and everybody else in town that they're not all alike."

"I'm much obliged for the suit, Mr. Monroe."

"You're going to have to start calling me Perry sometime, you know."

Bill smiled. "Yeah, but I'm not married to your daughter just yet."

Monroe laughed and said, "I'll see you at the church."

"I'll be there," Bill said with a nod.

"And leave that here," added Monroe as he gestured toward the Colt on Bill's hip. "You won't need it."

Bill frowned. He didn't expect to need the revolver, either, but it seemed to him that a lawman always ought to have a gun handy, even at his own wedding. Especially a lawman who didn't have any deputies. It would be different if there were two or three fellas he could depend on to handle any trouble, but there weren't.

He skipped lunch. Just couldn't come up with any appetite. He wasn't sick or anything, just not hungry. He wound up sitting at the desk and watching the clock on the wall of the marshal's office. The hands on it moved inexorably toward two o'clock.

When he thought it was time, he got dressed in the white shirt and dark suit Monroe had brought him. There was a string tie with it, too, and Bill struggled to get it tied properly around his neck. He had never worn a fancy getup like this. He squinted at himself in the mirror and finally was satisfied that it looked all right.

He came out of the storeroom and paused beside the desk. He had coiled his shell belt and placed it and the holstered gun on the desk. He looked at the Colt now, trying to figure out what he should do. After a long moment, he slipped the revolver from its holster and tucked it behind his belt. When the coat was buttoned, it would cover up the gun.

He had just finished doing that when the office door opened and Josiah Hartnett came in. He was dressed in his Sunday best, as well, since he'd be standing up in front of everybody at the church just like Bill.

"Ready to go?" he asked with a grin.

Bill nodded. "Ready as I'll ever be."

That brought a laugh from Hartnett. "Don't worry about it," he said. "I never knew a man who didn't feel like that when he was about to give up his freedom. But let me tell you, it's worth it."

"I hope so," muttered Bill. He reached for his hat.

Main Street was crowded with people converging on the Methodist Church at the eastern end of town. Bill frowned at them and said, "It's like a holiday . . . or a hanging."

"Yeah, people show up for anything out of the ordinary. Just about everybody in town will be there. The farmers from hereabouts drove in with their families, and some of the ranch crews from the spreads to the southwest are here as well. There won't be an empty pew."

"You're not making me feel any better, you know, Mr. Hartnett."

"It'll be fine. You'll see."

The throng of people going into the church parted before them when Hartnett called boisterously, "Here's the groom!" Cheers went up. Hands reached out to slap Bill on the back as he and Hartnett made their way into the church.

The young pastor, Jeffrey McKenna, was waiting at the front of the church. He shook hands with Bill and Hartnett. "Are you ready?" he asked Bill.

Hartnett chortled. "As he'll ever be!" he answered for Bill. That brought a knowing grin from McKenna.

"Don't worry," said the preacher. "It may not seem like it now, but you'll survive, I promise you. I've never lost a groom yet."

Bill fought down the urge to tug at the tight collar around his neck. "Thanks, Reverend. I guess."

Once all the guests had made their way into the church and packed the pews, McKenna slipped a turnip watch from his vest pocket, flipped it open, checked the time, and closed it with a snap as he looked up and nodded to someone in the rear of the church. He motioned for Bill and Hartnett to take their places. A woman began playing the piano over in the corner. Bill swallowed hard as he recognized the familiar notes of that song they always played at weddings, whatever it was called.

Everybody stood up and turned toward the back of the church. Bill looked that direction, too, and saw two figures appear in the open doorway, silhouetted against the bright afternoon sunlight. Eden and her father walked slowly into the church. Even if Bill hadn't already been having trouble catching his breath, the sight of Eden would have stolen it from him. She was that beautiful, and suddenly Bill knew all his worries had been for nothing. Everything was going to be all right. Behind Eden and Monroe, one of the townsmen moved to close the church doors . . .

Only to be knocked back a step as somebody burst through the doors, practically on the heels of Eden and Perry Monroe. Bill stiffened as he recognized the shabby figure of Benjy Cobb, the swamper from the saloon.

"Outlaws!" howled the swamper. "There's a whole gang of outlaws headed for town—*right now!*"

Chapter 28

About a mile west of town, Dock Rakestraw reined his horse to a stop and looked over at Zach Norris, who had halted as well.

"You ready, Zach?" Rakestraw asked with an ugly grin.

Norris nodded. "More than ready." His thin, pale face and his sunken eyes testified to the ordeal he had endured as he recuperated from the wounds he'd received at the hands of that damned Texan. He hadn't completely recovered yet, but he wasn't willing to wait any longer for his vengeance. Norris went on, "Remember, Harvey's mine." His features twisted in a grimace. "I can't believe those bastards actually made him the marshal."

"Yeah, all folks in town can talk about is what a fine young fella he is, and what a nice couple him and the Monroe girl will make." Rakestraw checked his pocket watch. "The ceremony ought to be gettin' under way right about now. Nearly the whole town will be there, so it'll be easy to ride in and pin everybody down. We'll loot the whole place, then set fire to the church."

"After Harvey comes out so I can kill him," said Norris.

"Yeah, sure, Zach. That's what I meant."

Truth be told, though, Rakestraw didn't give a damn one way or the other about Bill Harvey. He wanted Eden Monroe if he could lay his hands on her, but even she wasn't all that important in the big scheme of things. More than anything else, Rakestraw wanted the pile of loot they were going to take out of Redemption. The bank probably had quite a bit of cash in its safe, and there would be money in the various businesses, too. It would all add up to a nice haul, more than enough to take the gang to the gold fields of Colorado.

For the past week, one or two members of the gang had been riding into Redemption at night to have a drink in the saloon and get the lay of the land. Last night, Rakestraw and Andy Singer had been there, and when they'd heard all the talk about the wedding, Rakestraw knew today was the right time to strike. It would be easy.

He turned in the saddle to look at the fifteen hard-bitten men behind him. He had picked out half a dozen of them and given them their orders: surround the Methodist Church and kill anybody who tried to get out. The rest of the gang would spread out through the town, collecting the loot and killing anybody who wasn't at the wedding.

"Ready, boys?" he asked. He got several curt nods and mutters of agreement from the other outlaws.

Rakestraw faced toward Redemption again, which was visible across the mile of open prairie. "Let's go clean us out a town!" he whooped. He jabbed his spurs into his horse's flanks and sent the animal thundering toward the settlement at a gallop.

"Somebody get that crazy old drunk out of here!" Josiah Hartnett ordered as everyone in the church stared in shock at Benjy Cobb, including Eden and her father, who turned around in the aisle to see what the source of the disturbance was.

Cobb tried to rush past the two of them, but Monroe grabbed his arm and stopped him. "What's the meaning of this?" he demanded. "How dare you interrupt my daughter's wedding?"

"You gotta listen to me!" said Benjy. "They're gonna attack the town, the whole bunch of 'em! Dock Rakestraw and his men! I heard 'em!" The swamper's stricken face peered past Monroe's shoulder at Bill. "You gotta believe me! I'm tellin' the truth!"

Hartnett said, "That old saloon rat wouldn't know the truth if it bit him." He started past Bill. "Don't worry, I'll throw him out—"

Bill stopped the liveryman with a firm hand on his arm. "Wait," he said. He strode up the aisle. "Sorry, Eden," he murmured as he passed her. He hoped she would forgive him, but every instinct in his body told him he needed to at least talk to Benjy and see what the man was babbling about.

Monroe let go of Benjy's arm. The swamper clawed at the sleeve of Bill's suit coat with both hands. "You gotta believe me, Bill," he said. "I saw him. Dock Rakestraw! It took me a long time to remember, but I know it was him. I saw him one time at a tavern over in Missouri, and the folks there said he was a bad outlaw."

"I believe you, Benjy," said Bill. "But what's some outlaw in Missouri got to do with Redemption?"

Benjy gulped. "He was here last night! In Fred's saloon with another owlhoot. He said he was bringin' his whole bunch to town today while you were gettin' married."

Monroe snorted. "This outlaw told you he was going to attack the town today?"

"N-no . . ." Benjy shook his head. "I heard him and the other fella talkin' as they were leavin' the saloon. I was sweepin' the porch when they come out. I heard the other fella call him Dock, but I thought he was a doctor. I didn't remember until . . . until a little while ago where I seen him before." Benjy scratched his beard-stubbled jaw and looked apologetic. "My memory ain't so good no more."

Hartnett had come up beside Bill. He waved a hand at Benjy and said, "You can't go by anything this old rummy says, Bill. It's just some drunken dream he had."

"No, it ain't!" insisted Benjy. "Rakestraw said he was bringin' his whole bunch to town today . . . and he's got Zach Norris with him!"

Bill stiffened. So did Eden. "Norris!" she said. "But he's bound to be dead."

Bill glanced over at her and shook his head. "We don't know that. All we know for sure is that he was wounded when he rode out of here. That was weeks ago. He could've recovered from what happened to him that night, just like your father and I did."

One of the townsmen spoke up, saying, "I've heard rumors it was Rakestraw's gang that's been rustling cattle from the trail herds as they come through here."

"Anybody know what he looks like?" asked Bill.

Benjy's hand tightened on his arm. "I do! I saw him last night. He's got long hair, down over his shoulders like a woman, and a beard that sticks out a mite."

Bill drew in a deep breath. The memory of the man he had seen on the night of the stampede, the man who had shot at him, was still vivid in his mind. Benjy didn't have any way of knowing that, though. For the description of the man he was talking about to match so closely, there had to be something to what the swamper was saying.

An idea occurred to Bill. He said, "There's an easy way to find out if Benjy's right. If Rakestraw is going to raid the town with a whole gang, their horses are bound to be kicking up quite a bit of dust. Let's go have a look."

"You don't really believe him—" Hartnett began.

"It won't take but a minute to have a look," said Bill. He smiled at Eden. "I'll be right back."

She managed to smile as she nodded.

Bill walked out of the church with Benjy hurrying along beside him, still babbling. "Should'a figured it out sooner, I just forgot, I just forgot, my brain don't always work so good no more, I knew I'd seen him somewhere before—"

"Don't worry about it, Benjy," said Bill.

"But I ruined your weddin'!"

"No, we'll get back to the wedding in a little bit." Bill

stopped in the middle of the street and peered east and west, shading his eyes from the midafternoon sun with his hand. He didn't see anything unusual when he looked to the east.

But there was a cloud of dust boiling up west of town, about half a mile away.

Perry Monroe, Josiah Hartnett, and several other men had followed Bill out of the church. Monroe looked at the dust and muttered, "My God! Do you really think—"

Tension suddenly filled Bill. "Get everybody out of the church," he snapped at Monroe and Hartnett. "Tell everybody to go home, fast! The men need to get their guns and get ready to fight."

"But . . . but you're the marshal," one of the men said.

"And this is your town," said Bill. "Don't you think it's time you stood up and defended it?"

"Bill's right," said Monroe. "We let him take on Porter and Norris when we should've done it ourselves. For God's sake, he can't fight a whole gang of outlaws by himself!"

Hartnett said, "I'll get my shotgun as soon as we've started the people clearing out of the church."

"Get moving," Bill ordered. "We don't have much time."

Shouts of warning rang out as the men hurried back into the church. More commotion arose as people began piling out of the building.

The outlaws would be here in a matter of minutes. Bill didn't know how many of the citizens would stand with him against them, but he hoped enough would take up arms to make a difference.

"Find cover!" he called to the men who ran past him. "Rakestraw and his men won't be expecting a fight! We can take them by surprise! Let 'em come into town and then open fire! Pass the word!"

He was about to start toward the marshal's office to grab a rifle when suddenly Eden was beside him, clutching his arm. She had thrown the wedding veil back so he could see her face as she looked up tensely at him.

"I'm coming with you," she said.

"No, you go with your pa—"

"Damn it, Bill! I haven't even married you yet. I'm not going to let you get killed. I can shoot a gun—"

He pulled her toward him, brought his mouth down on hers in a hard, swift kiss. "I appreciate that," he told her as he stepped back, "but you go with your pa."

Before she could argue, he pushed her into Perry Monroe's arms. Monroe started leading her away. Eden struggled and looked back over her shoulder at Bill, but she couldn't get away from her father.

He ran toward the marshal's office, casting a glance toward the western end of Main Street as he did so. The street had cleared amazingly fast as people scurried for cover. The dust cloud that marked the location of the approaching riders was only a few hundred yards away from town now.

Panting from the effort of keeping up, Benjy Cobb ran along with Bill. "Gimme a gun," he begged. "I can shoot."

"You're gonna watch the jail for me, Benjy," Bill said as they reached the marshal's office. "If those outlaws get past me, you'll have to protect the place."

"Really?"

"You bet. I'm counting on you."

Benjy nodded. "I won't let you down, Bill. I swear."

Bill yanked one of the Winchesters out of the rack on the wall behind the desk, pulled a box of cartridges from a drawer, and started thumbing bullets into the rifle. When it was full, he crammed more rounds into the pockets of his coat. As he stepped to the door, he looked back at Benjy and said, "You did good by coming to the church and warning us. You may have saved the town."

"Me?"

Bill flashed him a grin. "You."

Then he opened the door and walked outside, striding purposefully to the middle of the street. He could see the riders galloping into the far end of town and knew they could see him, too. For a brief second, he thought, *What if they aren't* outlaws?

Then the raiders opened fire and there was no longer any doubt. Bill flung the Winchester to his shoulder and started working the rifle's lever and throwing lead at the outlaws as he ran back toward the office. They charged him recklessly, just as he had hoped they would. As far as they could tell, only one man was defending Redemption.

Then a huge volley of gunfire roared out from the buildings on both sides of Main Street as all hell broke loose.

Chapter 29

Bill felt the wind-rip of bullets around his head as he dived back through the open door of the marshal's office. He rolled, twisted around, and knelt in the doorway to return the fire. Several of the gang's horses were down already, kicking and screaming from the wounds they had received, and a couple of the outlaws lay motionless in the street as well.

But most of the men were still mounted and fighting back now against the unexpected resistance. Windows shattered as slugs punched through them, and Bill knew some of the defenders would be wounded, probably even killed, before this fight was over.

The people of Redemption were fighting, though, fighting as they never had before. Maybe his lone stand in the face of the charging desperadoes had inspired them, or maybe they had just found the true strength that had been inside them all along. Either way, for today, at least, they weren't going to allow evil to run roughshod over them as they had with Frank Porter and Zach Norris.

Bill's ears searched the chaos in the street for Norris but couldn't find him. Dust and powder smoke clogged the air, increasing the confusion. Bill aimed at several of the outlaws and cranked off three rounds, but he couldn't tell if any of his shots had found their target.

One of the mounted men suddenly loomed out of the swirling dust and smoke right in front of the marshal's office. The gun in his hand spouted flame as he fired at Bill. The slugs chewed splinters from the doorframe that stung Bill's face as he lunged aside. He got a good look at the long hair flying around the man's head and the beard jutting from his chin, and then those features dissolved in a crimson spray as Bill shot him twice in the face with the Winchester. The man went backward out of the saddle as if he'd been slapped by a giant hand.

Dock Rakestraw, if that was his name, would never stampede another herd of cattle.

Another man galloped past the marshal's office. Bill caught just a glimpse of him, but that was enough for him to recognize Zach Norris. Benjy had been right about that, too, thought Bill as he snapped a shot at Norris. The former deputy's horse didn't break stride as it vanished around a corner.

Somehow, Bill knew where Norris was going. The Monroe house lay in that direction. Bill surged to his feet and ran after him. Shooting continued behind him, but not at such a fast and furious pace now. The defenders had the advantages of both numbers and shelter. Bill was confident the citizens of Redemption would emerge from this battle triumphant, now that they had found their courage.

The slight limp in his bad leg slowed him down a little. His heart hammered wildly in his chest as he thought about what might happen if Norris reached the Monroe house too far ahead of him. Thankfully, it wasn't far, only a few blocks. But even so, as he ran toward the house as fast as he could, he saw Norris's horse standing in front of the gate with an empty saddle.

The front door of the house was wide open, too.

As Bill started up the walk, Norris suddenly appeared in the doorway with Eden held in front of him in the white wedding dress. His left arm was brutally tight around her neck.

His right hand pressed the barrel of a Colt into her side. Bill skidded to a halt at the terrible sight.

"Eden . . . ?" he said.

"She's fine, you son of a bitch," said Norris, "but she won't be if you don't drop that rifle."

Bill hesitated. He didn't have a good enough shot at Norris to risk it. With no other option, he tossed the Winchester to the ground in front of him.

Norris looked like he'd been sick, and as a wracking cough suddenly came from him, Bill realized he still was. Norris might have recovered from his wounds, but he would never be the same man as he'd been before. That gave Bill a tiny sliver of hope.

"What are you gonna do now?" he asked. "Shoot me down without even giving me a chance?"

"A chance to what? Draw against me?"

"I've been practicing," said Bill. "I think I can take you, Norris."

That brought a harsh laugh from Norris and a tiny shake of the head from Eden. Bill could tell she was pleading silently with him not to do this, but it seemed to him like the best chance to get her out of the line of fire.

"No damn Texan was ever born that could beat me to the draw," said Norris. "Sure as hell not some cowboy."

"Only one way to find out," said Bill.

Norris's mouth twisted in a snarl. With a curse, he gave Eden a hard, abrupt shove that sent her plunging off the porch and down the steps. She cried out as she fell, but she was able to catch herself as she sprawled on the ground between Bill and Norris.

Bill would have reached for his gun then, but in a flash of movement too fast for his eye to follow, Norris already had him covered. The Colt was leveled and pointed right at him. Norris might be sick, but his hand was steady as a rock.

He grinned as he lowered the gun and slid it back in the holster. "All right, Tex," he began, "we'll just see—"

Bill didn't wait. He grabbed the Colt behind his belt and dragged it out with all the speed he could muster.

He was faster than he'd ever been, but not fast enough to get off the first shot. His gun roared just a hair behind Norris's weapon, though. Something slammed into his side, knocked him back a step.

On the porch, Norris took a staggering step. Blood welled onto the chest of his shirt where Bill's bullet had driven deep into his body. He stayed on his feet, grimacing as he tried to lift his gun and line up a second shot.

Bill felt a great weakness washing through him. He knew he had only instants before his strength was gone. He pointed his Colt at Norris, but before he could pull the trigger, a rifle cracked sharply. Norris doubled over as a slug ripped through his guts.

Bill fired again, putting a bullet through Norris's brain. The man finally fell, already dead when he thudded against the porch planks.

Bill looked down, saw Eden on her knees with the Winchester in her hands. She had grabbed up the rifle and fired that shot. She threw it down now and scrambled to her feet, turning to Bill and reaching out for him.

"Took us both," he croaked, feeling the warm trickle of blood on his side, "but we . . . got the varmint."

Her arms went around him, steadying him. Their faces were only inches apart. As he looked into her blue eyes, trying to make her see how much he loved her even though he couldn't talk anymore, she said, "Don't you die on me, cowboy. Don't you dare die on me."

When Bill woke up, he found himself naked between clean sheets in the bedroom he'd been using at the Monroe house. This was getting to be a habit, he thought before a feeling of amazement that he was still alive went through him.

He lifted the sheet. Yep, naked, he thought, except for the bandages wrapped tightly around his midsection. Every time he took a breath, he felt a little twinge of pain in his side. He winced.

"You've got a cracked rib," said Perry Monroe. "Norris's

bullet glanced off it. But that saved your life, so it's a pretty small price to pay, I suppose."

Bill turned his head and saw the storekeeper sitting in a rocking chair. Monroe's left arm was bandaged and in a sling, but other than that he seemed to be all right.

"Eden . . . ?" Bill asked.

"She's fine. Upset that she got grass stains on her mother's wedding gown, not to mention a considerable amount of your blood, but she'll be all right." Monroe's voice softened. "All she really cares about is you, son."

"Where is she?"

"Helping out in town." Monroe's face and voice grew solemn. "You and I weren't the only ones hurt in that fight, you know."

"How bad is it?"

"Two men were killed, and a dozen more wounded, some of them pretty bad. But we came out of it in a lot better shape than those outlaws. They were wiped out to the last man."

Bill closed his eyes for a moment. Monroe was right. He was sorry for the losses the people of Redemption had suffered, but it could have been much worse. It would have been, if they hadn't found the courage to fight at last.

When he opened his eyes again, Bill said, "I reckon Norris must've winged you."

"Yeah. He hit me bad enough to put me out of the fight, but Eden patched me up. I'll have to hire somebody to help out at the store, but it was high time I did that, anyway. Benjy Cobb, maybe. He could use a job where he's not around liquor all the time."

Bill nodded. "That sounds like a good idea." He paused. "I sure hope Eden isn't too mad at me."

"Why in the world would she be?"

"Well, the wedding is ruined now."

Monroe shook his head. "Postponed, not ruined. Eden says you'll be up and around in a few days." He smiled. "I suspect that as soon as you're able to stand, we'll all be down there at the church again. She wants to marry you before anything else has a chance to happen!"

"That sounds good to me—" Bill began, but before he could finish he heard the front door of the house open and close. Light footsteps hurried down the hall.

"I got back as soon as I could," said Eden as she appeared in the doorway. "Is Bill—"

Then she saw he was awake, and with a happy cry she rushed to the bed and threw her arms around him.

With a chuckle, Monroe got to his feet while Eden pressed kisses to Bill's face. "I reckon you two are close enough to married to leave you alone for a while," he said. He patted his daughter's shoulder and left the room.

Eden wound up lying on the bed next to Bill with her head pillowed on his shoulder. She still wore the grass- and bloodstained wedding gown. With his arms around her, he said, "This isn't quite the way I pictured things."

She laughed softly. "They'll be better soon enough."

"Not soon enough to suit me."

"Well, you cowboys always were impatient . . ." She lifted her head and held something out in her hand. "I brought this from the office for you."

Bill looked down at the tin star she held. He took it from her, rubbed his thumb over its slightly dented surface.

"You're still the marshal of Redemption," she said.

"After everything that's happened . . ."

"There might not be a town anymore if not for you. You're the reason people fought those outlaws."

Bill closed his hand around the badge and tightened his embrace as Eden snuggled against him. He had no idea what the future might bring, but right now, in this moment, he had everything he needed. He was a long way from Texas.

But he was home.